Ladies of
INTRIGUE

3 Tales of 19th-Century Romance with a Dash of Mystery

INTRIGUE

MICHELLE GRIEP

BARBOUR BOOKS
An Imprint of Barbour Publishing, Inc.

The Gentleman Smuggler's Lady ©2017 by Michelle Griep
The Doctor's Woman ©2016 by Michelle Griep
A House of Secrets ©2017 by Michelle Griep

Print ISBN 978-1-68322-826-4

eBook Editions:
Adobe Digital Edition (.epub) 978-1-64352-119-0
Kindle and MobiPocket Edition (.prc) 978-64352-120-6

Cover Photography: Lee Avison / Trevillion Images

Published by Barbour Books, an imprint of Barbour Publishing,
Inc., 1810 Barbour Drive, Uhrichsville, Ohio 44683,
www.barbourbooks.com

*Our mission is to inspire the world with the life-changing message of the
Bible.*

Member of the
Evangelical Christian
Publishers Association

Printed in the United States of America.

Contents

The Gentleman Smuggler's Lady 7
The Doctor's Woman 113
A House of Secrets 195

The Gentleman Smuggler's Lady

Dedication

To the One I lean on when there is no one else,
and to all the Poldark fans out there who love
a great gallop along the Cornish cliffs.

Acknowledgments

Julie Klassen: Brainstormer Extraordinaire

Kelly Klepfer: Male POV Guru

Shannon McNear: Horse Aficionado

Ane Mulligan: Fierce First Reader

MaryLu Tyndall: Editor Supreme

Chawna Schroeder: Plausibility Princess

Chapter One

1815
Port village of Treporth, Cornwall, England

Pretend I am courageous.
Pretend my heart still beats.
Pretend all manner of blissful things. . .
and that I shall find him alive.

Recreasing a worn scrap of foolscap, Helen Fletcher tucked the paper into her valise, then snapped shut the clasp, wishing most of all she'd never received such horrid news. No one had ever warned her about the dangers of parchment.

Pretend the world is right and well. . . For it would be—or she would die trying to make it so.

She rose from her sleeping berth and paced the few steps to the small mirror on the wall. Grey-blue light, the last from the end of a melancholic day, leaked through the porthole into her tiny accommodations. The vessel *Nancarrow* had never been meant to haul passengers, but the captain had made an exception because of her plight, thank God. Removing her hat from a hook, she did her best to pin up her dark hair beneath the brim, then tied the ribbon securely. Now that they were docked, she'd not be sorry to leave this tucked-away compartment.

"Of course Father will be fine," she whispered to her reflection, taking courage in the voicing of such a hope. She lifted her chin, staring into her own eyes. "And you will be too."

Whirling about, she retrieved her valise and left her sanctuary of the past fortnight. The corridor was a maze and a dim one at that. Very few vigil lanterns lit the way. She edged past stacks of crates secured against one wall, then turned sideways to squeeze through a narrow throat of a space next to a post. Though she ought be used to it by now, the tight quarters smelled of brine and dampness and overworked ship hands—an odor she wouldn't miss.

At last she made it to the stairs leading to fresh air and England. She'd never been to Cornwall, Bath having been her home before leaving for Ireland as a governess. But as long as she was with Father, it would no doubt feel like home.

She gripped the railing with one gloved hand and ascended the wooden rungs. Her other hand held tightly to all she owned in this life, which was precious little. No matter. God would provide. He always did. Was not the very fact she'd been sent passage to attend her ailing father proof enough of God's surprising provision?

The closer she climbed toward the top deck, the louder shouts echoed and boots thudded. Strange. When they'd set sail from Ireland's green coast, the crew had sung ditties of brisk winds and prows cutting through the ocean blue. Ought not the ballads of mooring at a friendly port be jolly as well? She frowned. No, those rumbles and curses were decidedly not merry at all.

She cleared the last step. Three paces later, she froze. The crew stood against one rail, hands behind their heads. Two masked brigands aimed guns their way. In the center of the deck, the trapdoor of the hold flung wide with more masked scofflaws descending into it like an unholy swarm. Not far from her, the largest man of them all trained a pistol on the captain's chest. A nightmare on the wrong side of slumber.

Captain Ogden's gaze darted her way, the slight tip of his head urging her to retreat back below.

Too late.

Before she could consider the possibility, the scoundrel threatening the captain slipped her a sideways glance. Though brief, she'd never forget the intensity in those brown eyes, commanding her without words to stay put.

"Blast!" the man roared at the crew. "I thought you said you cleared the cabins."

One of the men, the first in a chain of thieves leading from the hold to the gangplank, grunted as he passed a crate on to the next man. "Aye, sir. I did."

"Apparently, you missed one." The cloth tied over the bottom half of the big man's face riffled with a growl. "You, my lady, over here, if you please."

Though her heart beat hard against her rib cage, she got the distinct impression he meant her no harm—but that didn't mean she'd comply. Biting her lower lip, she studied the distance between her and the side of the ship. Could she jump from railing to wharf? How big the gap? How great the fall?

And why was no one stopping these thieves? Though it was dusk, surely not all from the village could be abed. Perhaps if she merely screamed for help, there'd be no need to risk a twisted ankle. . .or worse.

She opened her mouth—and a glove pressed against her lips. A strong arm pulled her against the side of the man dressed in black. How had he moved so quickly?

"Hush, lady. I'll have none of that. Do you understand?"

His free hand yet aimed the gun at the captain, but his terrible gaze stared into her soul.

Pretend that I am brave. Pretend that fear is strength.

For her father's sake, she had to get off this ship. Now. She blinked up at him and nodded.

His hold on her slackened.

Then she twisted and jerked up her knee, driving home a solid blow he'd remember for a very long time.

❧

"Oof!"

Wind rushed out of Isaac Seaton's lungs. Sharp, sickening pain rose up his throat.

Thunder and turf! The little spitfire. Scarcely able to breathe, he released the woman. It was either that or drop the gun, which could be deadly.

But so could the snippet of skirt who even now lurched toward the side of the boat. Blast! Sucking in salty air, he barely snagged her arm before she was out of reach. She was fast. He'd give her that.

"Join the captain," he strained out, then he shoved her toward the man. Stunning, this fiend he'd become—all because of Brannigan. Thank God this was his last raid.

She stumbled forward, still clutching her valise. When she joined the captain's side, she turned and glowered, the fury in her gaze calling down the wrath of God upon Isaac's head.

He stifled a smile. A worthy opponent. But no time now to dally with such thoughts. Glancing past the woman and the captain, he checked on progress. Wooden crates passed from man to man, slowly filling the wagon on the wharf. Too slow. The free flow of ale at the Pickled Parrot was paid for until the last of light, at which point some very drunk dockhands could pour out the door and discover this little escapade.

"Make haste, men!" he barked.

"God sees your evil deed." The captain's eyes burned like embers, his glower condemning him to the pits of Sheol.

"Yes, God sees. But evil deed?" Beneath his kerchief, Isaac's mouth curled into a half smile, one that tasted bitter. "That's debatable."

The lady gasped. "Thievery is wrong."

Indeed. A principle he knew as intimately as a lover—one no honest man should ever have to bed. He narrowed his eyes, considering the slip of a woman who accused him. What kind of lady would speak her mind so freely while at the wrong end of a loaded pistol? She stood barely the height of his shoulder, and that with a bonnet atop her head. Brown eyes, not as dark as his own, stared back at him. She was fine of bone, almost birdlike. So slight, should a good wind come along, she might fly off.

But there was nothing fragile about the way she denounced him. Her indictment crawled beneath his skin. "One man's theft is another man's restitution." His voice came out harsher than intended, and he cleared his throat. "Tell me, is it wrong to reclaim what was yours in the first place?"

The captain snorted. "This shipment belongs to Brannigan, unless you wear the Brannigan crest on your finger."

"You are mistaken. Part of this shipment belongs to me." The sight of a barrel—not a crate—slipped by, just past the captain's shoulder. Isaac's free hand curled into a fist. "Blast it! Put those spirits back."

"Aww, but one barrel ain't gonna—"

"Do it." He growled.

Young Graham Ambler, easily distinguishable by the gimp in his step, wheeled about and disappeared into the hold.

Isaac turned back to the captain. "Leastwise the blasting powder is mine. I assure you nothing more will be taken." He fumbled with a pouch tied to his belt and tossed the leather sack to the captain. "For your trouble."

The man caught it, a mighty frown tugging the corners of his mouth. "This does not atone for your behavior."

The captain's words struck him as brutally as the pain left over from the woman's knee. "I don't expect it to, sir."

A sharp thwack rent the evening as the cover on the hold slammed shut. The last of the crates hefted from man to man, until finally the men themselves emptied down the gangplank.

He whistled for Rook and Hawker to withdraw from guarding the *Nancarrow*'s crew, then lowered his pistol. "For future reference, Captain, I suggest you comply more agreeably should smugglers or pirates ever board one of your vessels. Others will not be as forgiving as I."

A curse flew from the captain's mouth, tingeing the lady's cheeks with a fine shade of scarlet.

The wagon rolled down the wharf—just as bawdy drinking songs belched out of the Pickled Parrot, farther up the shore. Clearly if Captain Ogden could not control Isaac's band of well-intentioned smugglers, he'd not be able to contend with besotted dockhands should any decide to ramble this far.

Isaac glanced at the lady, her outline smudging into the darkness nearly upon them. It was neither safe for her to remain here nor to venture into town past those men. He huffed out a sigh at both alternatives, feeling the weight of responsibility.

Bending slightly, he hooked her into his arm and up over his shoulder, like a sack of grain.

"Put me down!" She whapped his back with her satchel, a far cry easier to bear than her former attack.

The captain bellowed for his men to pursue—and the chase was on.

Isaac sprinted down the gangplank then swung the lady and himself onto Duchess, his dappled grey waiting where he'd left her. By the time Captain Ogden's crew cleared the deck, Duchess was already crushing gravel beneath her hooves and tearing up toward the village proper.

The lady wriggled in his grasp. "Put me down!"

"In due time." He flexed his arms into bands of steel as she flailed. Clearly, she hadn't the horse sense to know she'd probably be killed if she fell from a galloping mount.

Ahh, yet he could not help but admire such pluck. A slow smile stretched across his face. He might almost enjoy this were he not posing as a felon.

He reined Duchess to a stop in front of the Candlelight Inn. Swinging his leg over, he dismounted and pulled the woman down along with him. She squirmed, and in the scuffle, his kerchief fell to his neck.

His hand shot up, about to tug the cloth into place, but as she glowered at him, he froze. Locks of raven-coloured hair had loosened, lending her a wild appearance—yet altogether lovely. The flush of fear and wind pinked her skin to a most becoming shade. Beneath the fabric of her sleeve, frailty and strength contradicted one another.

Without thinking, he pulled her close and breathed in her sweet rosewater scent—and lost any reason whatsoever. "It is customary, lady, to reward a good deed with a kiss."

"Good deed! You've taken me from the sanctity of a ship to God knows where—"

"The Candlelight Inn," he interrupted.

Her eyes narrowed. "For what purpose I can only imagine."

"For the purpose of saving you from a drunken band of longshoremen and delivering you to a coaching inn that will provide you with the means of getting to wherever it is you're going." He retreated a step and flourished a bow. "Now, about that kiss?"

"After delaying me from my father's sickbed? You, sir, are a miscreant." She sidestepped him and darted toward the safety of the inn.

He watched until the hem of her skirt disappeared through the inn's front door. Then he hoisted himself back into the saddle. Of course, he'd never see her again.

But that didn't mean he wouldn't like to.

Chapter Two

Helen nudged open the door to her father's chamber, her hands full with a morning tea tray and her heart filled with a fresh hope—for Father's smile, albeit weak, greeted her from across the room. She'd been hard-pressed to decide which had frightened her more these past two days: her disturbing encounter with smugglers or the deadly state of her father's health. But perhaps today would be the day he turned the corner toward healing.

Pretend it will be so.

"Good day." Her father's words wavered on a wheezing breath, ravaged by age and dropsy.

"It is a good day, for you are awake." She set the tray on a bedside stand and pulled over the only chair in the small room. "I am glad of it."

"And I am glad for another day, Daughter."

"So should we all be, hmm? Now, let's prop you up." Sliding her hand behind his shoulders, she lifted him and his pillow, choosing to ignore the swelling in his neck and fluttering breath.

Once settled, she retrieved the mug of tea and bottle of chamomile syrup, stirring a spoonful of the tincture into his drink. "Here you are."

Some of the mixture leaked from the sides of his mouth, and she snatched a coarse cloth from the tray, the cheap fabric a bit rough for his frail skin. She frowned. "Would that I had been a son, and a prosperous one at that."

"Pish!" His bare head, long removed of the dark hair she remembered, shook against the cushion. "I couldn't have hoped for a better daughter. Nor a better patron."

"Forgive me, Father. I did not mean to sound ungrateful. I *am* thankful for the Seatons' generosity, and I shall let them know how much as soon as you are on the mend."

He reached for her hand, his fingers swollen to the size of sausages. "There will be no mending. Not this time. My breaths are numbered, and the sum is small."

"Do not speak so. You must live, for me, for your congregation."

"We are all mortal, Daughter."

She patted his hand, unwilling to acknowledge the grotesque changes destroying his body. "It benefits no one to accept defeat, even death, and so I shall endeavor to fight against it—for both of us, if need be."

"This is not your fight."

She squeezed his hand, then let go of his hold and his words. "I will not concede. You are all I have left."

"No, child. There is *always* God."

"Yes, of course, but. . ." She sighed. Why could doubts not be as easily exhaled?

"But what?"

"Well, I know in my head God is always present, but in my heart? I cannot credit it."

A sliver of morning light angled through the single window, washing her father's face in a pool of yellow light. "You keep your heart too well guarded, I fear."

Of course she did—and always would. There was no better protection against hurt. "In the homes where I've served, I've seen what men do to women's hearts."

"You can't judge all men by the actions of a few. Did you ever stop to think that by shutting off your heart from man, you've closed the door to God's love as well? Those who leave everything in God's hand will eventually see God's hand in everything. . .even in man."

A rap at the front door jarred her as much as her father's words, and she patted his shoulder. "I shall return."

Exiting his chamber, she crossed the small main room and opened the door. An angel of light appeared—or so it seemed.

Sunshine haloed a woman slightly taller than herself, but judging by the smoothness of her skin and brilliance of eye, she was roughly the same age as Helen. The visitor was dressed in an emerald pelisse devoid of any decoration or embellishments. Blue skirts peeked out beneath, their former brilliance subdued by several years of wear. But whatever elegance the lady's clothing lacked, her lovely smile more than made up for it. Portrait artists would pay dearly to capture a beauty such as this.

"Good day," she said. "Are you Helen Fletcher?"

"Yes." Helen nodded at the wicker basket clutched in the woman's grasp. "And you must be the good fairy who's left food at our door the past two days."

"I am Esther Seaton, but I adore the alias *Good Fairy*." She angled her face, and a true pixie could not have looked more mischievous. "Mind if I borrow it sometime?"

"Not at all. Come in." Helen stepped aside, allowing the lady to pass and setting her offering upon the table at the center of the room.

"Welcome to Treporth, Miss Fletcher. I trust you are settling in well." The lady swept out her hand, encompassing the interior of the small cottage. Then slowly her fingers dropped, as did her smile. "I heard of the scuffle at your arrival, and for that, I apologize. Truly, the folk around here are not a bad sort, and I am sorry for the impression you must have."

"It was harrowing, but I will not allow one bad experience to taint my opinion of all."

Miss Seaton's grin returned in full, and she crossed the room to gather Helen's hands in her own. "I have the feeling we shall be the best of friends."

A cough rattled out from Father's chamber, and Esther's gaze drifted toward it. "How is your father today?"

Shame tightened Helen's throat. Had she not moments earlier begrudged the roughness of a cloth, given along with a roof overhead and food for their bellies? She squeezed the lady's fingers then pulled back. "He is rallied this morn. I am hoping he shall be on his feet in no time."

"Really? I'd been led to believe otherwise." The lady's brow knit together but unraveled as quickly. "Still, I am glad of your report."

"And I am glad for your provisions. You have been more than generous."

A delicate shrug lifted Miss Seaton's shoulders. "Do not

thank me. I merely deliver. It is my brother who provides."

"Then I hope to meet him someday and thank him in person."

Miss Seaton arched a brow. "Would you?"

"Of course."

"Then come to dinner this evening at Seaton Hall. There's a government official recently arrived, and the conversation will no doubt turn tedious. Politics is not my topic of choice." She leaned closer. "I am sure you and I can find much to divert ourselves. Do say you'll come."

Helen bit her lip. Should she spend an entire evening away from Father? Somehow, it did not seem right, for he was the sole purpose she'd come here. "I am grateful for your invitation, Miss Seaton, but—"

"Esther, please."

She couldn't help but smile at the warmth in the woman's voice. "Very well, Esther, I should like to go, but—"

"Your father wishes you to go, child." The words traveled out the open door of her father's chamber.

"There you have it." Esther grinned. "Will you?"

Helen studied the worn floorboards, as if an answer might be found on the swept wood. She hadn't left Ireland for socializing, but this would be a prime opportunity to thank their benefactor. What was the right thing to do?

Slowly, she lifted her head. "My answer is yes."

❧

Yes! Yes, yes, yes!

Isaac set the pen in the holder and leaned back in his chair. Two years of hard work had finally elevated the negative numbers to zero. A blessing, that. As was the improved state of his tenants. Perhaps his Robin Hood days were truly behind him.

But. . .

Sighing, he scrubbed a hand along his jaw. The relief was strange—like a rotted tooth pulled from his mouth, one that had festered far too long. It was good to have the thing removed, but hard not to continue probing the gap left behind. If he gathered his crew for just one more shipment, positive numbers could seed the new venture he'd been planning, and then some. Yet would that not be dangerous with a revenue man sniffing about?

Or as greedy as Brannigan?

He laced his fingers behind his head and stared up at the ceiling. *Well God. . .what would You have me do?*

The clock ticked overloud on the mantel. Windowpanes rattled from a gust of wind. In the hearth, flames licked lumps of coal, the low crackling the only other sound in the room.

Isaac grimaced. *Just as I thought. No answer. Again.*

"Here you are." His sister flounced through the door, a sweet pout painted on her lips. "I sent Roberts half an hour ago to retrieve you. Can you not be finished with your paperwork? Our guests are arrived."

"Guests?" Sitting upright, he closed the ledger and frowned at her. "I thought only Mr. Farris would be joining us."

"Oh! I forgot to tell you." Lamplight sparkled in his sister's amber gaze. "I invited the parson's daughter, Miss Helen Fletcher."

"She's arrived, then?" He shoved back his chair and stood, doubt rising along for the ride. How many other matters had he let slide these past months? "I didn't realize she'd be here so soon."

"I daresay you'd not notice should the world stop spinning."

"Such saltiness from you, Esther?" He rounded his desk, trying in vain to keep a sheepish grin from twitching his lips. "I suppose I deserve it."

She returned his smile. "That and more."

Isaac's heart warmed. This sister of his would make a fine wife for some deserving man—yet another thing he'd put off pursuing. But no more. Now that his financial pre-occupation was at an end, he'd have more time to escort her to dinners and dances where she could meet some eligible bachelors.

Crooking his arm, he offered her a wink along with it. "Shall we?"

She rested her fingers atop his sleeve, and they left behind the confines of his study.

"I think you shall like Miss Fletcher." The way his sister tipped her chin, a cat with a saucer of milk couldn't have looked more pleased.

"And why is that?"

"Besides her beauty, she seems quite amiable, especially given the circumstances of her arrival."

"Indeed." He blew out a low breath. Taking in Parson Fletcher despite his poor health had been a gamble—a wager all would be sorry to lose. "How is the parson faring? I own I've neglected him of late, but I intend to rectify that."

"Despite what Miss Fletcher says, I fear he's not long for this earth."

He patted her hand, a worthless consolation, but what else could he do?

The hallway emptied into the foyer, and he steered his

sister to the farthest door on the right. Allowing her to pass before him, he trailed her skirts.

"Brother, may I introduce Mr. Farris and Miss Fletcher?" She beamed at their guests then swept her hand toward him. "And here, at last, is my wayward sibling, Mr. Isaac Seaton."

Before he could get a good look at the parson's daughter, a curly haired man, red of lips and cheeks, dashed up to him and reached for his hand, pumping his arm as he might a well handle. His clothes were surprisingly tailored in the latest fashion, odd for a government official whose job could sometimes turn violent. Whose nephew or cousin was this? For surely the fellow had not landed the position by merit alone.

"Delighted to meet you, Mr. Seaton." The man's voice was as overeager as his grip. Even more irritating, the fellow's gaze never left Esther. "I am thrilled to have met your fine sister. I know we shall get on quite merrily."

Isaac cleared his throat, shoving down a remark every bit as salty as his sister's. "I trust your business here will not take very long, Mr. Farris."

Hopefully. For besides the fact that Farris was a revenue man on the prowl for smugglers, Isaac could not stomach the man's obvious interest in his sister, in spite of his wishing to see her married. Something was wrong about Farris.

"I shall do my best to remain in the area as long as possible." Farris finally let go and swooped over to Esther.

Which gave Isaac full view of Miss Fletcher.

Her gown flowed along delicate curves, so slight her bearing, so small her frame. The woman floated toward him, almost like. . .a bird.

His gaze shot to her face, where brown eyes flashed recognition. Her lips parted.

His breath caught.

One wrong word, and a noose would bite into his neck.

Chapter Three

What did one say to an abductor? A smuggler? A thief? So many accusations clogged Helen's throat that none got out. What manner of man was this Isaac Seaton, to so brashly pillage a ship at dock, dare to take her by force on a wild ride, yet now stand here calmly in the guise of a gentleman?

A very polished one, apparently. He captured her hand in his and bowed over her glove, pressing his lips to her fingers. Straightening, he arched a brow, his gaze tethering her to him in a way that quickened her pulse. "I am enchanted to meet you, Miss Fletcher."

She snatched back her hand, denying the urge to rub where his breath had heated her skin. Perhaps such charm would silence other women, but not her. She opened her mouth—

But before she could speak, he continued. "I am happy you are arrived safely from Ireland. No doubt your previous charges shall miss their governess, yet your father must be exceedingly grateful for your presence here."

She clamped her lips, trapping angry indictments behind her teeth. So, that was his game. Remind her of Father's debt before she snapped at the hand that fed. An audacious move, yet not surprising, for had he not shown such boldness aboard the *Nancarrow*?

Esther swooped over and linked arms with her. "Let us take this conversation into the dining room, shall we? I, for one, am famished."

Grateful for Esther's rescue, Helen kept step with her hostess, leaving Mr. Farris and the smuggler to follow.

Esther dipped her head toward her as they traversed a hall, their steps echoing on a floor absent of carpeting. "I am glad you are here." Her voice lowered for Helen's ears alone. "I'm not certain I trust that Mr. Farris. He seems an awfully forward fellow."

La! She could say the same of the lady's brother. Helen's step hitched, and she begged off Esther's arm. Did this lady know of her brother's smuggling escapades?

They entered a dining room surprisingly devoid of finery. Plain paneled walls surrounded them. Drapery, striped with too many years spent in the sun, hung on the windows. The table was set with plain white ironstone on linen a step above sailcloth. Ought not a thief have more riches than this?

Confused, Helen sank into a chair.

And the smuggling gentleman sat next to her.

Directly across the table, Mr. Farris leaned forward, nearly colliding with a bowl of soup being placed in front of him by a servant. "Tell me, Miss Fletcher, as Mr. Seaton intimated you are recently arrived from Ireland, did you by chance happen to hear of the fate of the ship *Nancarrow*?"

She sipped a spoonful of beef bouillon, savoring the saltiness along with the thought that she might be the one to bring criminals to justice. "As a matter of fact, sir, I was aboard that very ship. Furthermore—"

Isaac Seaton's spoon clanked against the edge of his bowl. "Excuse me, but how does your father fare, Miss Fletcher?"

Drat the man! Well did he know her father would've expired long ago had he not intervened with medical care. She lifted her face to the bully. "He is weak, yet lives."

He flashed a smile, the gleam in his eye far too knowing. "I am glad of it."

Mr. Farris shoved his bowl aside, ignoring the broth. "Were you on board for long after it harbored, Miss Fletcher?"

"Indeed." She glanced sideways at the big man next to her. "I was there when the brigands attacked."

"Were you? Splendid!"

Mr. Seaton's gaze shot to hers. Was that slight dip of his head a request or a threat?

Esther motioned to a servant for the first remove. "I fail to see how such a frightening experience could be splendid, Mr. Farris."

"Nor I." Isaac Seaton's deep voice filled the room. "This is hardly a conversation fit for dinner. Tell us of your own travels—"

"I shall." Mr. Farris waved off a refill of his wineglass. "But first I must know, Miss Fletcher, what you saw, or more importantly *who* you saw. Would you be able to recognize any of the men should I apprehend them?"

The smuggler at her side ran his palms along his trousers, a movement only she could witness. Clearly, he waited to see if she'd hand him over as easily as the footman passed a platter to Esther.

Should she? There was no debating Isaac Seaton had broken the law and therefore ought to be held accountable. But by implicating him, was she sentencing her ailing father to destitution? Was it right to repay her benefactor with such a harsh retribution? She'd not even thanked him yet for his provision. How had something so straightforward tangled into such a snarl?

She set down her fork and nodded for her plate to be removed. "It all happened very quickly, Mr. Farris, and it was near to dark."

"Justice might hinge upon your word, so please, consider. This is a serious matter, for the shipment taken belonged to the Brannigans. They do not take loss lightly."

She studied Mr. Farris's fleshy face for a hint of what that might mean, but he merely blinked. "What exactly would justice imply?" she asked.

The man's thick lips parted in a smile. "Why, the noose, of course."

Isaac Seaton tossed back the contents of his entire drink.

Esther placed her hand on Mr. Farris's arm. "My brother is correct. This conversation is not fit for dinner."

Mr. Farris looked from Esther's hand to her face. "Forgive my manners, Miss Seaton. I would do anything to please you." Then his gaze shot back to Helen. "But I must ask, Miss Fletcher, is there any hope of you identifying the lawbreakers?"

"If you please, sir!" Isaac Seaton's fist rattled the tableware. "I believe my sister and I have made it quite clear this conversation is ended."

Mr. Farris's lower lip quivered, like a tot who'd been scolded.

And the sight kindled the first ember of compassion Helen had felt for the man all evening. She offered him a weak smile. "I am sorry to disappoint, Mr. Farris, but every one of the brigands wore a mask. I am afraid I wouldn't be much help to you, and so there truly is nothing more to say."

"I am sorry to hear it." His quivering ceased, and his voice hardened to a sharp edge. "Such thievery has got to stop, and so it shall, for I will not leave Treporth until the criminals are caught."

Every bite of dinner stuck in Isaac's throat like a fish bone—and fish was not on the menu. Mr. Farris alternated between fawning over Esther and Miss Fletcher, though Esther tallied the lion's share of the man's compliments. At least the fellow had dropped the topic of smuggling, for now.

Esther dabbed her mouth with her napkin then pushed back her seat. "Shall we retire into the drawing room? Unless you men would prefer to take port beforehand?"

He stifled a smirk. No doubt Farris would jump at the chance to drink with the leader of those he sought.

"I think not, Sister, for I trust Mr. Farris would agree that your company, ladies, is more desirable."

"Well said, sir. Shall we?" Farris shot up from his chair and immediately offered his arm to Esther.

She slipped Isaac a withering glance, then ever the gracious hostess, allowed the man to lead her toward the door.

Miss Fletcher followed—until Isaac stopped her with a touch to her sleeve before she could escape. "A word, Miss Fletcher."

The fabric between her shoulder blades drew taut as a sail in the wind, but she turned with a quirk to her brow. "Yes. I should like a word with you, sir."

As master of Seaton Hall, he'd met women from all stations

of society—but none so curious as this petite governess. "You are quite the contradiction."

She tipped her pert little chin. "What do you mean?"

"You wish to speak with a. . . What was it you called me when we last met?" In his mind he traveled back to that darkened night in front of the Candlelight Inn, with those big brown eyes assessing him and a severe retort on her lips. "Ahh, yes. You called me a miscreant. By your own word, you disdain who I am, so why not reveal me to Mr. Farris?"

"I came here to thank you, sir, not indict you. You paid my passage, you provide for my father, and for that I acknowledge your generosity." Her gaze hardened. "But for keeping my silence, I consider that debt now paid in full."

"I required no repayment. It was a gift, free and clear."

She retreated a step, angling her face to study him. "You are wrong, Mr. Seaton. It is you who are the contradiction."

He sucked in a breath. The same rosewater scent she'd worn the night he'd abducted her hung in the air, a fragrance as delightful as her intriguing mind. "I?"

"You play the part, no"—she swept out her hand—"you embody the essence of a gentleman. Upright. Noble, even." Her eyes narrowed. "Yet it is an undeniable fact that you led a mob to rob a ship and threaten the lives of the crew."

A chuckle rumbled in his chest. "I'd hardly call eight men a mob, nor were any of the crew's lives in danger. I merely removed what was mine in the first place."

"Mr. Farris said that shipment belonged to Brannigan."

The name curled his hands into fists, a base reaction, yet entirely unstoppable. "You have no idea who that is. Or what the Brannigans are capable of."

"What I know, sir, is that smuggling is wrong. Stealing for any reason shows a lack of trust in God's provision. And deception is as equally abhorrent. You are guilty of both."

Deception? Yes. But smuggling? Not if he ended his ventures now that he'd broken even from his losses—his *stolen* losses. He stared at the small woman, so unwavering in her beliefs that she didn't flinch beneath his assessment. Was this petite beauty God's answer to his earlier prayer for guidance? A smile lifted the corner of his mouth. If so, a very pretty reply.

"I do not deny your charge of deception, madam, and for that I freely repent. But I am no smuggler."

Her nostrils flared. "I saw you!"

Ahh, but his fingers itched to smooth that angry furrow on her brow. How soft the skin? How warm and—

He clasped his hands behind his back, lest they touch her without permission. "Sometimes what we see, Miss Fletcher, and what is truth are two different things. The world is not as black and white as you seem to believe. More often it is grey."

"Then you are no God-fearing man, Mr. Seaton."

"On the contrary, I acknowledge God as the Creator of all colours."

A small snort blew from her lips. "You play with words as easily as you disregard the law."

"Come with me and my sister tomorrow, and I will show you grey." He pressed his mouth shut. What was it about this woman that made him issue such an invitation? He ought keep his distance from this parson's daughter, for her convictions did strange things to his conscience.

She shook her head. "I cannot leave my father for long periods. In truth, I should stay here no longer tonight."

"Then I will provide a maid to sit with him."

Her brow creased, not much, but enough to hint she considered his offer. "Have you an answer for everything?" she asked.

"Usually."

But not for her. She neither feared nor revered him. What kind of woman was Miss Helen Fletcher?

Chapter Four

Sunshine dappled light through a canopy of elms. Helen grasped the side of the pony cart and angled her face upward, closing her eyes. Esther was a competent driver, and the steady plod of Mr. Seaton's horse ahead of theirs set an easy pace. Yet the pattern of dark and light against her lids was as splotchy as her thoughts.

Each of the families they'd called on this morning had widened the crack in her heart, until she feared visiting any more would bleed out the last dregs of emotion. And then what? Was it possible to sympathize so thoroughly that no feelings would remain? These people were in dire need—and there was nothing she could do about it.

Could she?

"Nearly there." Esther's voice ended the debate.

Helen opened her eyes to a small cottage built into a rise of grassy earth. Mr. Seaton dismounted and offered her his hand as Esther set the cart's brake.

He leaned toward Helen as he helped her to the ground. "Are you starting to understand the plight of these people, Miss Fletcher?"

"I believe that I am, yet I fail to understand what any of this has to do with your..." She glanced to where Esther retrieved a basket from the cart, then lowered her voice. "Other diversion, shall I call it?"

"No, not a diversion. A necessity." He flashed a roguish grin. "One I will no longer pursue, thanks to you."

Her brows shot skyward. "Me? Why?"

"Master Isaac!" The screech of his name upset a swoop of martins from the neighboring elms.

The three of them turned toward the cottage door.

Out flew a grey-haired lady, mobcap askew and apron strings flapping like an extra pair of legs. If she could move this spritely now, what kind of whirlwind had this woman been in former years? She plowed into Mr. Seaton. "How I've missed ye, lad."

He wrapped his arms around her and chuckled. "Good to see you also, Mrs. Garren."

Esther set the basket down by the lady's door, beaming at the sight.

Helen pursed her lips. The man was a paradox: one day brandishing a pistol at a captain and another embracing an elder half his size.

Isaac set the lady from him then bent on one knee. Taking her hand into his, he kissed her fingers. "My deepest apologies for my absence, madam. Forgive me?"

"Posh!" She swatted him on the head. "Who can stay angry with you, lad? Now then, who is it ye've brought?"

The lady's gaze landed on Helen. Her eyes were like two tiny coals, deep and dark, and entirely warm and cozy. Hopefully this woman had many grandbabes to dandle on her knee, for such was the love in her scrutiny.

"Annah, I present to you the parson's daughter, Miss Helen Fletcher." Esther joined Helen's side. "Helen, this is Mrs. Annah Garren."

Helen dipped a bow. "Pleased to meet you, Mrs. Garren."

"Oh posh! Only Master Isaac gets away with such formalities. Call me Annah." Her right eye winked—or was it a tic? "Come in, come in! Take a cup o' nettle tea."

Esther placed a hand on the lady's shawl. "I am sorry, Annah, but we must be off."

"So soon?"

"I've yet to see to the village children. And Miss Fletcher's father is very ill. We shouldn't keep her from him for too long."

Without so much as a goodbye, the old lady pivoted and darted into her house. Mr. Seaton swung back into his saddle, and Esther crossed to the pony cart. Was that it? Helen frowned. Not a very fond farewell after such an intimate welcome.

Annah reappeared before Helen could climb back up on the cart. She dashed toward them, her speed once again belying her age. Drawing close, the old lady pressed a stained piece of fabric into her hands. "For your father, child."

"Thank you for. . ." She turned the small piece over in her fingers. It was too small to be a kerchief, though clearly the scrap was a gift of some kind. She smiled at the old lady. "Thank you."

"Posh!" Annah waved her off then lifted her face to Mr. Seaton. "Hie yerself back here more often, Master Isaac. Take care of our lad, Esther."

Then Annah vanished back into her cottage.

Helen climbed up on the cart and sat next to Esther,

puzzling over the odd encounter. "That was. . .interesting. What is this?" She held out the scrap for inspection.

Esther glanced at it and urged the pony to walk on. "Except for the shawl from her shoulders, I suspect it's all Annah had to give you. Since her husband died, my brother has provided as best he can for her and all the tenants you've seen today. Isaac is a generous soul—overmuch at times. Often he goes without sleep or meals to come up with a way to continue providing."

Continue providing? The cart juddered over a rock in the road, and Helen grabbed hold of the side while also trying to grasp Esther's information. Thinking back on the sparse decor at Seaton Hall, it all started to make sense. "So, I take it finances are an issue, then?"

"Well. . .Mr. Farris did mention the Brannigans last evening, so I don't suppose Isaac would mind me telling you." Though her brother rode ahead of them, well out of earshot, she dipped her head closer to Helen. "My father owned a successful enterprise, shipping over the finest Irish blasting powder for the copper and tin mines hereabouts. When he died, the business went to Isaac."

Helen's gaze shot to Mr. Seaton. The fabric of his suit coat stretched across his shoulders like a mantle of power. "He seems well suited for such a venture."

"Indeed—were it not for Richard Brannigan. There's bad blood between the two. When Richard heard of my father's death, it's rumoured he put into play a smuggling scheme to relieve all incoming ships of Isaac's cargo."

"But wouldn't whoever had insured those loads pay your brother for his losses?"

Esther sighed. "Not if the insurance company is so heavily

burdened by payouts that they are driven out of business. Such was the case."

"Why not simply employ a different company?"

"Brannigan's *is* the only remaining insurance provider in these parts." She jutted her chin toward her brother. "And he can't bear the name, so please, hold in confidence what I've told you."

"Of course."

Esther fell into a silence, and while she drove on, Helen tried to reconcile the ill-treated gentleman trotting in front of them against the bold thief who'd accosted her only days before. She tapped a faint pattern against the square of cloth on her knee as they rattled along, yet could not solve the mystery of the fellow even by the time they slowed near the outskirts of Treporth.

A salty breeze welcomed them. They stopped in front of a collection of row houses, leaning against one another like sailors after a night of ale. Mr. Seaton had barely assisted her and Esther down before a mob of children burst out the doors, one after the other, like a tumbling chain of dominoes falling all over themselves. Eventually they huddled around Esther.

Helen peeked up at Mr. Seaton. "What's this about?"

He grinned. "Not a day goes by Esther doesn't come to tell Bible stories to the children. As you can see, they love her for it."

She looked from one Seaton to the other. In all the fine homes she'd served, all the gentlefolk she'd encountered, none compared to the heart she'd witnessed in these two.

Behind them, horse hooves thundered. Esther ushered the children forward, while Helen and Mr. Seaton turned toward the sound.

The rider reined his mount to a stop in front of them. "Mr. Seaton, sir." The man tugged the brim of his hat in respect. "I'm looking for a Miss Fletcher. I was told you'd know her whereabouts."

Mr. Seaton looked from the rider to her. "You have found her."

"This be for you, miss." Bending, the man handed over a folded slip of paper.

Her heart thumped hard as she opened the note.

Pretend it is good news.

But as she scanned the words, her world tipped sideways.

Isaac studied Miss Fletcher's face as her gaze dropped to the note. The more she read, the more her lips flattened, until eventually her whole countenance deflated. He stood at the ready should she hit the ground.

"What is it?" he asked.

"My father." Big brown eyes peered into his. "He's taken a turn for the worse."

"Then we must leave. Now."

After a word with Esther to explain their haste, he left his sister in care of the children and retrieved Duchess. Miss Fletcher allowed him to lift her, and he waited a moment for her to straighten her skirts as she sat sidesaddle. He swung up behind her, feeling like a beast stationed behind such a small woman.

"What of your sister?" she asked.

"She'll return shortly." He jabbed his heels, and Duchess took off, though he held her to a canter. The set of the woman's shoulders in front of him, the quietness of her small frame caused an ache in his belly. Would that he could protect her from the inevitable end of her father.

"Thank you for your kindness, Mr. Seaton."

He'd been thanked before, and often, but coming from this lady, the gratitude sank low, filling him like the pleasantness of a fine meal. He leaned closer, breathing in her sweet scent, then immediately drew back. What the deuce was he thinking? The woman rode toward a father who might be dying and here he was, playing the lovesick schoolboy.

He cleared his throat. "Tell me, what did you think of the people you met today?"

She turned toward him, a small smile curving her lips. "I understand your affection for them—and theirs for you."

"Really? A miscreant such as myself?"

"Well. . ." Her smile spread. "I suppose I was a bit harsh in my first assessment."

"So, you've grown to appreciate my charms, hmm?"

Her grin twisted into a smirk. "I wouldn't go that far."

The road forked, and he urged Duchess eastward, onto Seaton lands, though he needn't have. The mare could travel this route with a hood on her head.

Miss Fletcher faced him once again, yet she said nothing. What went on behind those brown eyes?

"Go on," he encouraged. "I see by the quirk of your brow you have more to say."

"I am wondering. . .what did you mean when you said you had me to thank for your decision to stop smuggling?"

"Just that. You voiced aloud concerns I've often thought. If one cannot trust in God's provision, then perhaps one has no business professing a faith at all."

"Then why did you not stop sooner?"

Her question struck harder than a well-aimed right hook. How did one explain the loss a man feels when income, inheritance, even justice were ripped from his grasp? "It's. . . complicated."

"I suppose you have a point, somewhat. Stealing *is* wrong—but so are the miserable lives of your tenants. Why is it that good things do not always happen to good people?"

"You have no idea how often I've wrestled with that very question."

She angled her head, like a sparrow considering a worm to be devoured. "And the outcome?"

"My only conclusion is that we are not in control, and we never were." He reined Duchess to a halt in front of the parsonage and leapt down, then reached up to aid Miss Fletcher.

"I don't know whether to thank or condemn you for such frank conversation." Her breath warmed his cheek as he lowered her to the ground.

"Neither. The gratitude is all mine."

For a moment their gazes locked, and the space between them rippled, like the charge in the air just before lightning struck earth. Was he addled—or did she feel it too?

Without a word, she pulled from his hands and dashed into the cottage.

He hesitated long after she disappeared. For the first time in a long time, he dared hope that God not only would answer his prayers—but in fact, already had.

Chapter Five

The loamy scent of earth washed fresh by rain would make a fine cologne. Helen breathed deeply as she tread the road into town, pondering such a fragrance. She'd label it *hope* and purchase a bottle to keep in her pocket. The past several days at her father's bedside had drained her reserves.

Rounding a bend, she stepped to the side of the thoroughfare, happy to see Esther's pony cart drawing near—and happier still to see her new friend smiling back at her.

"Good afternoon, Helen." Esther halted her horse. "What an exotic sight you are, my dear. Your blue skirts are so vibrant against a backdrop of dampened wildwood. You are a picture."

Helen laughed. "Someone's been reading novels, hmm?"

"I wish it, but no time." Her smile faded. "Is your father faring any better since his attack?"

For three days now, her father had mumbled nothing but gibberish—but at least he still breathed. She straightened her shoulders. *Pretend that you are strong.* "As of yet, he's unable to move the left side of his body, but with effort, he manages to smile, albeit crookedly. I thank you for the care you and your brother have provided—oh, and especially for Gwen. I hope by lending her to us, you are not short staffed at the hall."

"It's the least we can do. Isaac and I are both truly sorry. Your father is a fine man." Leftover drops from the earlier rain dripped like tears from the canopy of trees, adding a gloomy encore to Esther's lament.

Helen forced lightness into her tone. "I trust he will recover with sufficient rest. Even now, I am on my way to the apothecary for a sleeping draught."

"I could use the opposite." Esther glanced at the bundles heaped atop the seat next to her and at her feet.

Helen peered at the piles of fabric. "What is all this?"

"A boon *and* a load of work. Old Mrs. Turner headed up a charity drive for the poor of the parish."

"What has that to do with you?"

Esther sighed, the force of which distracted her pony—who stamped a hoof, eager to be off. "I offered to mend and reissue any garments she collected. I had no idea she'd meet with such success. With this much sewing, I'm afraid I'll have to cut short my story time with the children." For a moment, a shadow darkened her lovely face, like the flash of a spring storm, then surprisingly cleared away. "But on the bright side, it's a ready excuse should Mr. Farris come to call. Which he does. Far too much for my liking."

If nothing else, the man was persistent, for Helen had seen his mount passing by her own cottage several times on his way to Seaton Hall. Thankfully, he'd been too focused on Esther to pay her any mind.

"I have plenty of time to sew while sitting with my father. If you wouldn't mind stopping by the cottage, you may drop off some of your load." Helen stepped closer and smiled. "Not so much as to take away your excuse, though."

"You are a dear—and so I've told my brother on many occasions."

Her cheeks heated. But such warmth ought be blamed on the ray of sun breaking through the branches, not on the mention of Esther's brother.

Esther's brow rose, her brown eyes twinkling almost golden. "Good day, Helen. Godspeed."

"Good day." Grasping her skirts to keep clear of mud, she whirled about and hastened her step. Though Gwen sat with her father, it wouldn't do to dawdle.

The road to Treporth truly was a lovely walk, from flatlands higher inland down to the more wooded stretch just before town. Despite the chore of keeping her hem from the dirty road, she relished the break from sitting indoors.

Closer to town, pounding hooves rumbled, and a horse appeared, the rider dressed in the official coat of a revenue officer. Once again, Helen stepped to the side of the thoroughfare.

Mr. Farris reined in his horse and tipped his hat. "Miss Fletcher. Delighted."

"Mr. Farris." She dipped a bow. "On the hunt for more smugglers?"

"Actually, I'm on my way to see Miss Seaton."

Helen stifled a frown. If he caught up to Esther on the road, her friend would have a hard time avoiding the man. "I am afraid you will not find her at home."

"Oh?" His lips folded into a pout. "Do you know when she will return?"

"I do not. She is a very busy young lady. Good day, sir." She strode away before he could needle her with further questions.

It would be wrong to lie—but just as devious to reveal Esther's whereabouts.

The rhythmic stomping of the horse caught up to her side. "Where are you off to this fine afternoon, Miss Fletcher?"

She peered up at him yet did not alter her stride. "Not that it signifies, but I go to the apothecary for my father."

"Then you must allow me to give you a ride."

"Do not trouble yourself. It's not that much farther."

"No trouble at all, since my errand seems remiss at this point." Bending toward her, Mr. Farris held out his hand. "Come along."

This time a frown would not be stopped. Should she? Despite the man's odious company, riding would be faster, shaving at least a quarter hour—maybe more—from her task, and she'd be back to her father's side that much sooner.

Grabbing hold of his hand, she raised her foot to use his boot as a step, then allowed him to hoist her up in front of him. She sat sideways, as she had on Mr. Seaton's horse, but Mr. Farris sidled against her far closer than Mr. Seaton ever had.

She faced forward, straining away from him. *Pretend this wasn't a mistake.*

"It is dangerous for a lady to roam alone in this wild countryside."

Indeed, for she'd run into him. The retort died an anguished death on her tongue, so dearly did she wish to speak it.

"It's a good thing I came along to rescue you." He scooted nearer.

The pride of the man! She scowled. "I was hardly in danger, sir."

"Still, one never knows with smugglers about. You would

do well to think on finding a husband." His arm reached out, pulling her against him.

She plucked his sleeve aside, refusing so much as a glance over her shoulder. "You are very forward, sir."

"I find I must be in my line of work." His words warmed her ear, for he bent near, almost cheek to cheek.

She stiffened. "Put me down. I shall walk the rest of the way."

"No, no. I won't hear of it. We are nearly there."

No wonder Esther clung to an excuse to stay away from this determined rake. Helen leaned so far forward, the horse's mane tickled her nose. Thank God the road opened onto the outskirts of Treporth. With witnesses, surely he'd stop his advances.

Wrong.

He grasped the reins with both hands, closing his arms against her—a hold only an intimate couple might dare in public. "With Miss Seaton so occupied, perhaps I should call on you instead."

She squirmed. The crazed ride she'd endured with a masked smuggler had been far more desirable than this. "Mr. Farris, if you've finished with your job here in Cornwall, I suggest you go back to wherever it is you came from. Now put me down."

"London, Miss Fletcher. I hail from London. And there are many ladies in that fine town who are hoping for my return as a bachelor." His lips brushed against her ear. "But I wonder if you will be the crusher of their dreams?"

"No!" She wriggled and wrenched—but his grasp was relentless. "Put. Me. Down!"

"You heard the lady." A deadly still voice rumbled like a coming storm. "Let her go."

Vile words sat on Isaac's tongue, spiky and bitter. He bit down until the salty taste of blood kept them from spilling. Seeing Miss Fletcher struggling in this man's embrace left a putrid aftertaste.

"Mr. Seaton." Farris smiled down at him, entirely fake. More like the mask of a boy who'd been caught dipping snuff and scrambled for a reason to deny it. He loosened his hold of Miss Fletcher—but did not release her. "Good afternoon."

Isaac glowered. "It will be good once you let the lady go as she asked."

Dropping his arms, Farris gazed at Miss Fletcher. "Allow me to revise that. It's a *beautiful* afternoon, actually."

Isaac shot out his hand for Helen to grab hold of, better that than yanking the scoundrel off his horse and pounding him a good one. Wait a minute. . .

Helen?

A charge raced through him. The last time he'd thought of a woman by her Christian name, things did not end well.

She reached for his hand, allowing him to lower her to the ground. Her face was dangerously close to his as she whispered, "Thank you, Mr. Seaton."

Her gratitude—or dare he hope, admiration—stoked the fury in his gut for Farris's bold moves. He glared up at the man. "Is your business in Treporth not yet finished?"

"No." His eyes followed Helen's step. "There is much here to keep my attention."

"Then I suggest you see to your work and leave off the ladies."

A leer slashed across Farris's face. "All work and no play makes one very dull."

Isaac's hands curled into fists. If he listened to any more of this, he'd be charged with assault. He wheeled about and caught up to Helen. "Are you all right?"

"Yes, but good thing you came along when you did." She slid her gaze to him, a pert lift to her brow. "Or I would have been forced to hurt him."

He snorted, remembering their first encounter—or rather his meeting with her very strong knee. "No doubt. Shall I accompany you to. . . Where are you going?"

"The apothecary's, and yes, you may."

He matched his step to hers, fighting the urge to speed her along. If he were late to his meeting for such a reason as this, well, then may his punctual reputation be hanged.

"If you don't mind me asking," he glanced over his shoulder to make sure the revenue man was gone, "why did you agree to ride with Mr. Farris in the first place?"

"I was on my way to town when he came along. I thought it would be faster."

"Hmm. I suppose I shall have to remedy that."

Her brown eyes studied his for a moment, curiosity adding a lovely sparkle to their depths, yet she said nothing more— nor did he, all the way to Krick's Powders and Pills.

Stepping from her side, he bowed, flourishing his hat in one hand. "I bid you good afternoon, my lady."

"Thank you, Mr. Seaton." She dipped her head. "I am in your debt once again."

He watched as her skirts slipped through the door, then turned on his heel and yanked out his pocket watch. Blast!

He darted past pedestrians and a few street hawkers selling their wares, running all the way to Mr. Henry Green's, esquire and banker extraordinaire. He slipped through the man's office door, out of breath and cravat askew.

Green looked up from a stack of paperwork. "What's this? Isaac Seaton late?"

"Sorry. Had to save a damsel in distress."

Green chuckled. "Ever the hero, eh lad?"

He advanced, pulling out a packet of banknotes from a leather wallet and slapping them on the desk.

"What's this?"

"The rest of what I owe." He sank into one of the leather high-backs.

"So. . ." A smile spread across Green's face, erasing years from his weathered skin. "Ready to get back in business then?"

"No." He sniffed, the scent of spent cheroots and sweaty men striking trade deals thick on the air. "I'm ready to own the business."

"Really?" Green reared back, staring down his nose. "And what would that venture be?"

Isaac planted his hands on his thighs and leaned forward. "An old friend of my father's recently stopped in for a visit, mourning the decline of the Anglesey mines. Opencast mining was never the way to go, in my opinion, and so I wasn't surprised. But our discussion sparked an idea that's since burned out of control."

He paused, the concept so stunning yet so organic in its conception, he was almost afraid to voice it aloud, lest it disappear.

"Yes?" Green prompted.

"As you know, the Tregonning mines are putting out ore like never before. Why it never occurred to Father or to me is. . . Well, I suppose we were too focused on supplying mines rather than running one. But Seaton lands touch Tregonning Hill!"

"Are you saying you want to open a mine?"

He jumped up, spreading his hands. "Is that not a brilliantly simple idea?"

Green folded his arms, and they rode the crest of several large breaths before he answered. "Perhaps. But the scope of opening a new mine is immensely expensive."

"I know."

Green narrowed his eyes. "So why are you grinning at me like a lovesick bridegroom on his wedding night?"

"You, my friend," he grinned in full, "are just the man to find some investors. Sir Francis Bassett, George Hunt—"

Green's hand shot up. "Stop right there. Your reputation will precede you, Isaac. Bassett, Hunt, and everyone else knows you'll throw caution to the wind in order to thwart Richard Brannigan. I'd have to be able to assure them you will not continue your vendetta against the man. Your focus would have to be solely your new mining venture. Can you agree to that?"

He paced the length of Green's office. A fair question, but one he wasn't sure he could answer. He and Esther had suffered two years of barely getting by with meager fare and threadbare clothing. Even worse, he'd been unable to buy seed for his tenants—and farming was hard enough on this rugged patch of land even with prime seed. The deprivation, the worry of debtor's prison, near starvation and disease, all this was Brannigan's fault.

Isaac stopped at the hearth and stared into the coals. Was it right to let a thieving bully like Richard Brannigan escape justice?

Chapter Six

Outside the cottage, the lonely cry of a collared dove hovered on the air, so bittersweet, Helen couldn't decide if she should weep or sing along with the beauty of the sound. But neither would do. Not when there was sewing aplenty and her father to tend. She drained her tea and pushed away from the table.

The bird suddenly silenced, and Helen cocked her head. Horses' hooves pounded closer. She crossed to the window and peered through the curtain, then stood there, mesmerized. Coming up the drive were two horses. One occupied, the other tethered to Mr. Seaton's mount. But it was the man that captivated.

He swung his long leg over the saddle and dismounted, landing on the ground like a reigning king. Morning light warmed his face to a burnished, almost golden hue. La! Everything about the man was royal. From the confidence in his stride to the broad shoulders that could carry the weight of the world he lived in—or she did. What might it feel like to have such a man care for her?

She jerked back from the glass. What was she thinking? The only safe love was God's, not man's.

Pretend that you are happy. Pretend you are fulfilled.

A sharp rap rattled the quiet inside the parsonage. She opened the door to Isaac Seaton's smile flashing brighter than the April morn.

"Good morning, Miss Fletcher."

"Good morning." Her voice was breathy. A miracle, really, that it worked at all. How was one to speak—let alone think—with such a direct gaze consuming hers?

"I . . ." She cleared her throat, willing the traitorous thing to allow words to pass. *Pah!* What was wrong with her? Surely he wasn't here to see her. She greeted him with a smile as melancholy as the bird's cry. "I am happy you called, yet sorry to refuse you. My father still isn't well enough to receive visitors."

"Though I wish your father well, in truth, I did not come to check on him." He bent, face-to-face, a rogue tilt to his chin. "I came to call on you."

"Me?" Her hand flew to her chest.

He straightened, his grin growing. "I've brought you something." But instead of handing over whatever it was, he pivoted about and strode away.

Pursing her lips, she hesitated. Was this real? Or was she pretending again?

She followed to where he untethered a beautiful Irish hunter. Rich brown in colour, surprising flashes of a red undertone gleamed where the sun painted with a broader brush.

Helen stroked the mare's nose. "My, but she's lovely."

Isaac's gaze slid to her, a curious sparkle in his eyes—one that did strange things to her stomach.

"Yes. I quite agree." The words were husky, as if, perhaps, he may be speaking of more than the horse.

Of course he spoke of the horse! Regardless, heat crawled up her neck and flushed her cheeks. She turned to the mare. "What's her name?"

"Red Jenny. Jenny for short." He patted the mount's strong neck. "And she's yours."

"Mine?" She snapped her face toward his. "But I cannot accept such a gift."

"You can. . .unless you prefer riding into town with Mr. Farris?"

The question constricted as tightly as Mr. Farris's embrace of the previous day. No, that was not an experience she wished to repeat. She ran an absent finger along the mare's muzzle, thinking aloud. "Even so, this is too much. How would I keep her?"

"There's a shed around back. I'll send Sam over to clean it out, lay fresh straw, and deliver some hay and oats."

Did the man have an answer for everything? She shook her head. "No, this is well beyond my means, not to mention highly improper, and—"

"Miss Fletcher." He planted himself firmly in front of her. "Think of this as a gift for your father, if you please. A means to get him pills and powders when needed. Now, are you going to spout more excuses as to why you should not have ready transportation into town, or shall we take a jaunt around so you get the feel of her?"

"No—yes—I mean. . ." She retreated a step from the horse—and the man. "I hardly know what to say."

"How about that you'll go grab your hat and gloves and join me?"

Should she? Riding the countryside with a handsome gentleman was not at all what she ought to be doing. Her brow pinched. Then again, nothing about this trip had happened as she'd planned. And he was right. Getting to and from town would be a lot easier. Well. . .for Father, then.

Whirling, she strode back inside and peeked into her father's room. By all appearances, he slept peacefully.

Gwen, the serving girl sitting at his bedside, lifted green eyes toward her. "Everything a'right, mistress?"

She nodded. "Think you can manage if I'm gone for half an hour?"

"Aye, he's resting well."

With one last glance at her father, Helen withdrew to the main room of the cottage. Gathering her spencer, bonnet, and gloves, she donned each, mind wandering. Was this the right thing to do? It seemed decadent to ride away a spring morning while her father lay abed.

But she revised that opinion when she paced back outside and caught sight of Mr. Seaton's fine profile, all muscle and strength.

Pretend this isn't wanton.

He turned at her approach, holding out a riding crop. "Ready?"

Was she?

She grasped the thin rod in her hand. "Ready."

Crouching, Mr. Seaton laced his fingers together, allowing a hold for her foot. As she climbed, she caught a whiff of his clary sage aftershave—a fine addition to a glorious morning. She grabbed hold of the pommel and, once seated on the sidesaddle, settled her skirts while he mounted Duchess.

Jenny took an impatient step sideways, and though horsemanship wasn't Helen's mainstay, she knew enough to rein the animal under control before they took off.

Mr. Seaton led them on a merry ride, past Seaton Hall and through the woods sheltering the manor. Eventually the land opened up onto a grassy flat with a sliver of grey sea beyond. He continued to skirt the edge of the trees, but slowed, allowing her to catch up.

"How is she?" he asked.

What a question. The mare was perfect in every way—just like the man. "Wonderful."

He said nothing, yet didn't pull his gaze from hers.

"I, uh. . ." Where were her words this morning? She wetted her lips and tried again. "I feel as if I shall never stop thanking you or your sister."

"No need. It's entirely my pleasure. Besides. . ." He faced forward then, and the loss was as tangible as the clouds suddenly hiding the sun. "It is I who should be thanking you."

"For what?"

"Helping Esther. Not many governesses would so willingly take on the menial task of repairing worn garments for the sake of poor fisherfolk."

"Nor many gentlewomen, so perhaps you ought to be thanking your sister. But such a trait runs strong in your family, does it not?"

He reined Duchess around to face her. "What trait?"

"Doing the unexpected."

"Me?" His brows rose.

She quirked her lips into a saucy grin. "You are a gentleman smuggler, are you not?"

With a tap of the crop to Jenny's side, she urged the horse ahead before he could reply—but then the flash of a brown wing flapped up from the tall grass at the wood's edge, startling Jenny. The horse broke into a gallop.

Helen grabbed the pommel. Tight.

Stay on. Just stay on.

Wind caught her hat, flinging it behind her. The ribbon cut into her neck. Tears stung her eyes, and the world blurred.

She bent nearly double.

Stay on!

In her mind, she screamed for the horse to stop—but screaming was impossible. So was breathing.

Her legs ached. Her hands. Her back. How much pain would a body feel before all went black? If she fell now, there was only one of two outcomes.

Either her skirt would catch, and she'd be dragged.

Or she'd break her neck.

"Helen!"

Was that primal shout really his? Had to be, for Isaac's throat burned.

He spurred Duchess headlong after the nightmare. Helen's horse stretched full-out, racing toward the cliffs. Racing toward death.

God, no!

Leaning into his mount, Isaac became one with the horse. An animal. Ferocious in speed and bent on his quarry.

He drove Duchess on, urging her to pass the runaway mare. Helen's hat and hair streamed behind her, but she held. Thank God, she held.

Sound receded. No more thundering hooves. No sea or wind. Just a rush of breath. In. Out. Focus. *Focus!*

The instant Duchess gained enough lead on Jenny, he jerked his mount close to Helen's. Reaching. Stretching. His fingers spread to grab hold of Jenny's rein, which slapped like a crazed lash, scaring the horse further.

He strained a little more and. . .

Contact.

He veered right, commanding both animals into a circle. Wild spree thus interrupted, Red Jenny eventually submitted, though not without a few fierce jerks of her head. After several circles, both horses trotted, until he could halt them and jump down.

He dashed around to Helen's side, where she yet clung to the mare's neck, breathing hard.

"Helen!" He reached for her, pulling her down into his arms. "Are you all right?" He leaned back for a better view. "Are you hurt?"

A wide-eyed stare met his. Face mostly pale, except for the unnatural redness of her cheeks. Dark hair, loosened and long, curled past her shoulders. She was a savage picture, untamed and fierce. Yet a pampered London lady could not have looked more ravishing.

"I am shaken." Her voice caught on a little hiccup. "I might have. . .I could have—"

She broke then, trembling so violently, tears cut loose.

He drew her close, wrapping his arms around her. "Shh. All's well now." He spoke as much to himself as to her. Indeed. He very well could have lost this precious woman. They shuddered in unison. With effort, he forced his thoughts from what could have been and instead focused on meeting her need for the here and now.

How long they stood there, he couldn't say. An eternity wouldn't have been long enough, so right, almost holy, did the moment feel.

But eventually she pulled away, her big, brown eyes gazing up into his. Her lips parted.

And he immediately put his finger against them. "Do not thank me again."

Beneath his touch, her mouth curved into a smile. If only he weren't wearing gloves and could feel the softness of those lips. If only it wasn't his finger pressed against such temptation, but his mouth. Desire stoked a long-banked fire in his gut.

He retreated, unwilling to look at those lips a minute more. Any longer and he'd act on the impulse. Duchess stood nearest, so he strode to collect Jenny first. Once both horses were gathered, he handed the reins of the Irish hunter to Helen.

She accepted them, but a fine flare of her nostrils revealed remnants of terror.

"How about we lead them a bit before riding?" he asked.

The admiration shining in her gaze was a pleasure so intense, he nearly moaned with the pain of it. He strode ahead.

She caught up to his side. "You are very thoughtful."

"So now I am a thoughtful gentleman smuggler, eh?" He smiled at her.

She swatted his arm.

What kind of a woman went from terror to brokenness to playful, all in a manner of minutes? He blew out a long breath. One that he wanted, that's what.

"Why did you never marry?" The question flew out before he thought. Would she even answer? Not that he'd blame her if she didn't. He'd taken a slap for questions less delicate.

She merely shrugged, never missing a step. "A governess doesn't have much opportunity. And you?"

Her response hit him broadside. The woman parried with more speed than an expert swordsman. He hadn't spoken of Catherine in over a year. Should he now? Was that hurt not long buried?

But unbidden, words tumbled out of his mouth. "I almost did, once."

"What happened?"

Memories crashed against him like the dull roar of the sea just past the cliffs. A bitter taste filled his mouth. He'd sworn off women, yet here he stood, walking side by side with one. "Perhaps you can tell me." He gazed down at her as they plowed through the grass. "How is it a woman can pledge undying love for a man—until his business fails and wealth is no longer part of the equation?"

With one hand, she pulled hair from her eyes and gathered the thickness of the loosened bulk at the back of her neck. "Shortsightedness, I suppose."

His brows shot up. "In what respect?"

"Clearly the woman in question did not take into consideration the determination and probability of said man to eventually conquer the world."

Unbelievable. Helen Fletcher was a jewel with so many facets, he longed to see which side of her would shine next. A slow smile stretched his mouth. "I own that reason never once came to mind. . .but I like it."

And her.

A blush deepened on her cheeks, a healthy colour, not the fearful scarlet of before. They walked in silence for a ways, the breeze cooling their mounts so that riding again would not be a concern.

"Might we get a view of the sea before we head back?" Helen pointed to a worn path leading downward.

He frowned. Tremawgan's trail. One he knew well. Too well. And had vowed to never know again.

"No." The refusal sounded abrupt even to his own ears.

She peered at him. The sting of his harshness weighted her brow, like a young girl showing her father a treasure and having it slapped from her hand.

He softened his tone and his frown. "It's a risk not worth taking. That trail is treacherous even for the best of riders. Stay away. Your horse is too skittish."

She tipped her chin to a saucy angle. "*And* I might run into smugglers?"

"Would you not say, lady," he stepped closer, "that you already have?"

Chapter Seven

The following day, Helen stood inside Seaton Hall's receiving room, waiting upon Esther. Drawn toward the only ornament gracing the chamber, she crossed to the mantel and traced her finger over a carved box. Somewhat rough-hewn, this was as common a cheroot case as she'd ever seen. Nothing hinted at pomp or pretense, so like the master of the house. Her pulse quickened. Had Isaac's hands also touched the wood this very morning?

For a moment she gave in and closed her eyes, reliving the way he'd held her. The feel of his strong arms sheltering her against his chest. The heat of him. His scent. If she breathed deeply now, would she catch a leftover remnant of clary sage?

"Helen! What a surprise, yet lovely to see you."

Helen jumped at Esther's voice. Good thing the woman could not see into her mind. She sucked in a breath, shoving down the shameless thoughts of the woman's brother. "Good day, Esther. I was hoping to catch you at home."

"Oh dear." The curls framing Esther's face trembled as she crossed the room and reached for Helen's hands. "I hope you're not here because of your father."

"No, thankfully, though I am sad to say there has been no

improvement." She squeezed Esther's fingers then let go. "I came because I've finished that load of mending you dropped off and wondered if you might send someone by to pick it up."

"So soon? You are more proficient with a needle than I, for I've barely made it halfway through my pile."

"Would you like me to take on more?"

"Don't even think of it, but it is sweet of you to offer." Esther swept over to the settee and patted the cushion beside her. "I daresay Isaac thinks you sweet as well."

Pretend her words are true. Pretend he cares for you.

Shirking off the notion, she settled her skirts next to Esther. Of course he wouldn't think of her in that way. He was kind to everyone. Romance was for storybooks and naive girls, not a governess tending to a sick father.

She lifted her face to Esther. "His opinion of me may have lowered since yesterday after the way I lost control of my horse."

Esther shook her head, light catching copper strands in her hair, so like Isaac's. "Any time my brother gets to play the champion is a boost for his confidence, which believe it or not, is sorely needed. The past few years have been hard on him." She went silent. Though Esther still sat on the settee, clearly memories crowded behind her eyes, so faraway her gaze.

Helen patted her arm. "I am sorry to hear it."

"Hmm?" Esther jolted at the touch, but a smile soon curved her lips. "All that's changed since you arrived. My brother is happier now. Lighter of spirit. You are good for him."

"Don't be silly. It can't be because of me."

"No, you're wrong. I really think he—"

"Pardon me, miss." A black skirt entered the room, ushering

in a red-faced housekeeper and the waft of linseed oil. She dipped a bow to Esther. "There's a Mr. Farris here to see Master Seaton. I told him the master weren't home, so he insists on speaking with you instead."

Esther shot a gaze to Helen. A trapped fox couldn't have looked more desperate.

Helen leaned near and whispered, "I will stay until he leaves."

A flicker of gratitude lit Esther's eyes, then she flattened her lips and faced the housekeeper. "Very well, send him in."

They stood as the revenue man entered.

He wilted into a sloppy bow, hat in hand. "What's this? Two beautiful women when I anticipated only one? It is my lucky day, is it not?"

To her credit, Esther dipped a polite nod. "Perhaps not, Mr. Farris, for my brother is gone to town, and it's my understanding you were calling on him."

"Pish!" He fluttered his fingers. "Only a slight inconvenience, and besides. . ." In three strides, he closed in on them. Taking each of their hands, he pressed a kiss to their skin simultaneously. "I'd much rather call on pretty ladies."

Helen yanked her hand away. Did the man think of nothing else? No wonder he failed at the task for which he'd been sent. Taking Esther's arm, she guided her friend back to the settee and made sure to spread out her gown so that the fellow couldn't barge in between them.

Planting his feet wide, he frowned at her maneuver.

She smiled up at him. "Mr. Farris, have you any news of the smugglers you were after?"

"None about the scoundrels who raided the *Nancarrow*."

A squall raged on his creased brow, the jaunty curls of his hair unwinding a bit. Then he snapped his fingers and perked up. "But not to worry. I have a plan afoot to entrap those thieves. Actually, that's what I was hoping Mr. Seaton might help me with."

"Oh?" Alarm lifted gooseflesh on her arms. "I hope it's not dangerous."

The man's chest filled out, straining the buttons on his waistcoat. "I thrive on danger, Miss Fletcher, but don't fret. I shall keep Mr. Seaton perfectly safe. I merely need an extra pair of eyes."

Next to her, Esther stiffened. "Are you expecting trouble, sir?"

"What I am expecting, ladies, is a ship to arrive in three days. The perfect bait for those who cannot keep themselves from pilfering others' goods."

Helen leaned forward. "And if none do?"

"Hadn't thought of that." He rubbed his jaw, the rasp of poorly shaven whiskers overly loud in the room.

A slow smile slashed across his face, entirely too suggestive. "You have a quick mind, Miss Fletcher, one I should like to know better."

She stood. Enough was far more than enough. "Allow me to be plain, Mr. Farris. Your attentions toward me are not only a waste of your time but are unwelcome. I am not now, nor ever will be, inclined to foster your acquaintance."

Deep red spread up his neck like a wound.

Good. She stepped closer. "Furthermore, sir, since Mr. Seaton is clearly not at home, I suggest you go and find him, for there can be no more for you to say to us."

Behind her, Esther gasped.

Mr. Farris jammed his hat back atop his head. "Well," he blustered. "Good day, then, ladies."

He stalked from the room, steps stilted and neck stiff. The picture of a reprimanded schoolboy.

Laughter begged to run free past her lips, but she slapped her hand to her mouth. Oh, what must Esther think of her to so rudely upbraid a guest in her home? She spun, horrified, and held her breath.

Esther stood, wide-eyed. "Did you see his face?"

"I did."

Slowly, Esther's lips curved, higher and higher, until she burst into laughter so merry that Helen couldn't help but join in. They giggled like girls, and finally Esther had to dab at the moisture in her eyes.

"Oh Esther, please forgive my breach of manners, but the man was simply not to be borne."

"No apology required." Esther flew to the window and parted the curtain, then winked back at Helen. "There he goes. I wouldn't have known how to shoo him off so efficiently, but I am a quick study. I shall endeavor to be as forthright as you in the future."

She gained her friend's side and stared out at the retreating backside of Mr. Farris's horse. "In the case of Mr. Farris, pride is his Achilles' heel. Strike that, and he'll leave you be."

Her smile faded as the man galloped off. She'd steered him away from herself and Esther for now, but hopefully she'd not shoved him more forcefully into seeking out and arresting the area smugglers.

Namely Isaac.

Patting the signed document in his pocket, Isaac stepped out of Mr. Green's office. The man was a miracle worker. Only one more investor—*one*—and the mine wouldn't be merely an idea, but a money-making reality for him and his tenants.

He strolled down High Street with a lift to his step. Out of debt. A lovely woman living in the parsonage. A new business venture to pursue. He tugged his hat with a smile and a hearty "Good day" as he passed old Marnie Winkler, selling last year's apples. Then on second thought, he doubled back and flipped her a coin, just for the joy of it.

She dipped her head. "God bless ye, Master Seaton."

"Indeed, He has, Mistress Winkler."

He continued on, but as he crossed over to Fore Street, his step hitched. He paused, listening hard.

Cack. Cack.

There it was again. The raspy cry of a corn crake—a bird more inclined to a hayfield than a village.

And one that sang only at night.

Slowly, he slid his gaze across the street, to a thin gap between two buildings. The black outline of a bony man emerged, but even as daylight engulfed the fellow, he was little more than a dirt-coloured smudge. Stained breeches. Soiled dress coat. Even the man's shirt had yellowed into the dull drab of hopelessness. His dark gaze met Isaac's, then he slipped back into the shadows.

Billy Hawker. A growl rumbled in Isaac's throat. Glancing up and down the street, he waited for a dray to lumber past, then took off at a run. The gap between buildings was barely wide enough for Billy, let alone Isaac's shoulders. Sideways, he scraped on as best he could, until the passage opened into a narrow alley, hidden from the street on one side by a stack of crates. The other end curved slightly, blocking pedestrian views.

Isaac grabbed the man by the collar and shoved him up against a brick wall. "Blast it! I told you we were finished."

Hawker's eyes bulged. "But there's something you should know."

"Not in public! Never in public." Isaac ground his teeth. If anyone saw him with a known free trader, the gossip could not only tarnish his reputation but raise Farris's suspicions. Isaac's fingers clenched tighter, cutting off Hawker's air supply. The man wriggled beneath his grasp.

"Bah!" He let go.

Any damage was already done.

Hawker slumped over, gasping. "I din't. . .din't know how else. . .to reach ye."

Isaac sighed, flexing out the leftover rage still tingling in his hands. "What is it?"

After a few more gulps of air, the man straightened. "I were slinging back a pint at the Pickled Parrot last eve when in walks Grimlox."

Folding his arms, Isaac leaned against the opposite building. "Jack Grimlox?"

"Aye."

The leader of a rival gang of smugglers? He frowned. "What's he doing showing his face around here?"

"That's what me and the boys thought." Hawker's thin shoulders raised like tent posts holding up a worn canvas. "Din't much care, though, after he bought a few rounds o' drinks."

"That doesn't make any sense." Isaac shook his head. "What's he after?"

"Silence."

"What?" He stepped away from the wall, studying Hawker's face. Was this some kind of ruse?

Hawker retreated, until his backbone smacked against the bricks. "I can explain. Seems there's a shipment on the move, three days hence. Grimlox and his gang aim to relieve her and want us to lay low."

"So, he bribed you."

"Aye."

"Well, well." Isaac chewed on that morsel of information, the fat of which satisfied. "I'd say that round of drinks was Grimlox's loss, for we aren't in the smuggling business anymore. But"—he narrowed his eyes—"why was it so important to tell me this?"

Hawker dragged his sleeve beneath his nose, leaving a darkened smear on the cuff. "I never saw Grimlox looking better. He were all cleaned up, he were. Dandy clothes. A jingle in his pocket, e'en after he paid for our night o' ale."

The man advanced a step, glanced both ways, then leaned in close to Isaac.

"And he were wearin' a seal ring."

Isaac's muscles clenched. If Hawker took the risk to single him out on a public street, then the ring must be of deadly importance. "Whose?" he asked.

"Brannigan's."

"Blast!" He reeled about and smashed his fist into the wall, wishing to heavens it was Richard's face. "I knew the two were connected. I knew it!"

"I say if you really want to take a jab at ol' Brannigan, then we lift the goods before Grimlox and his gang can get to it. Brandy, tea, rum, tobacco. . .it's a mite fair load. Bring a fancy price."

Breathing hard, he lowered his hand, ignoring the pain and the warmth of blood dripping down his fingers. Hawker's words were a temptation, a strong, flaming temptation. The chance to lash out at Richard Brannigan pounded louder with each beat of his heart.

Until the quiet voice of a small woman murmured in his mind.

"Thievery is wrong."

His shoulders slumped. This wasn't a shipment to recoup blasting powder that'd been taken from him. This time it truly would be thievery.

He turned back to Hawker, the weight of the document swinging his coat hem against his thigh. Had he not just minutes ago promised Mr. Green to leave his vengeance against Richard to God?

"Well?" asked Hawker. "What say you?"

"I say no. You and the boys will not plunder this shipment. It's too dangerous with that revenue man sniffing about."

"Danger don't mean nothin' when I've a wife and five littles at home. We be fine now, but winter comes the same time every year. I won't be list'nin' to their cryin', not when I've a chance to set something by."

Reaching out, Isaac rested a hand on the man's shoulder, the bone of which cut into his heart. "I understand, Billy. Truly. Just be patient. I'm near to striking a deal that will benefit us all—for years to come."

"I'm glad for it. I am. But the thought o' Grimlox and his lot gettin' the whole load. . ." He shook his head. "Don't seem right."

"I'm coming to believe neither was it right for us to engage in the same dubious activities as Grimlox in the first place." He let go of the fellow. "We must put our trust in God alone, not in our own feeble attempts to enact justice. Let them have it, Hawker. All of it."

For a moment, the man stood there, his grey eyes agleam with a strange light. Then slowly it faded to a hollowness seen usually in the gazes of fisherfolk after a bad pilchard season. Hawker sniffed, and after a last swipe of his nose, stalked away.

Yanking out a handkerchief, Isaac pressed the cloth against his knuckles. Would Billy Hawker do as he said? Lord knew. And Isaac wouldn't blame him if he didn't. Only a month ago, he'd have done the same.

Balling up the cloth, he shoved it back into his pocket. Funny how a small governess could change his whole world.

Chapter Eight

Three sleepless nights. Three never-ending days. Helen lived and died in jerky starts and stops, and it seemed Father did too. He rarely opened his eyes anymore, let alone consumed any food or drink. On the chair next to his bedside, she planted her elbows on her thighs and her chin in her hands. Fatigue barged in like an unwelcome guest, and this time, she opened the door. Closing her eyes, she matched her prayers to Father's breaths, which wheezed in then slowly bled away.

Oh God, please. Heal this man. The world needs him. I need him. You can do this, for nothing is too hard for You.

"Helen."

She tensed. Her name was little more than a sigh in the afternoon quiet. Or was it a vain imagining? Not that she didn't believe God could answer in an audible voice, but here? Now?

Yes, Lord. I am listening.

"Helen."

Her eyelids flew open, and she lurched upright. "Father?"

Cloudy brown eyes stared at her—or did they? Father gazed as if he looked right through her. She shivered, recalling

Saint Stephen peering into heaven itself, moments before he died.

She shifted from her chair to his bed, reaching out to press her palm against his cheek. Cool skin met her touch, parchment thin and far too fragile. "You're awake. I am glad of it."

His lips worked, the left side lagging behind the right, but nevertheless working. "Let," he said.

Let? What on earth did he need her permission for? She bent, leaning close. "Let what?"

His face moved almost imperceptibly beneath her hand, but this time his voice was a sail catching wind, stronger and with more force. "Letter."

She couldn't help but smile. "Oh, a letter. You want to write a letter?"

"Nay, already written. For you."

Her throat tightened. "You've written a letter to me?"

"No. God did." His gaze strayed to his Bible on the bed stand. "His Word is a letter to you."

Reaching for it, she retrieved the book, running her hand over the cracked leather cover. How many messages had he prepared from this text? How many words of wisdom gleaned? She shook her head. "Oh Father, I cannot take this. You are getting better. You shall need it."

"It is yours now." His withered hand crept atop the counterpane, inching toward her own. "This isn't..." His fingers met hers, resting like the last leaf of autumn fallen to the ground. His Adam's apple bobbed, and he sucked in a breath. "This isn't the day I would have chosen to die, but it is not of my choosing."

She shook her head, over and over, as if the movement could prevent his words from reaching her ears. Hugging the Bible to her chest, she drew what strength she could from the feel of it then laid it back where it belonged. "This is the most you've spoken in a fortnight. You are on the mend."

"I love you, child."

"Oh Father… I love you too." She pressed her lips shut, lest sorrow suddenly break loose.

"Now." She stood. "How about some broth? Gwen made a pot of stock before she left at noontide. She even made biscuits to hold us over until her return on the morrow. Would you like some?"

The clouds billowed back over his gaze, thick and milky. Nevertheless, he nodded, and while only once, the movement was sure and strong.

She darted out to the main room. A bit of broth and watered ale, both would surely feed this sudden strength he'd shown. She dipped some soup into a bowl, letting it cool as she gathered a mug—but then a rap on the door pulled her from filling it.

Isaac's broad shoulders crowded the doorframe, his presence a brilliant light in the grey afternoon. He doffed his hat, and his dark hair glistened at the edges where mist had snuck beneath. "Good day, Miss Fletcher."

"Good day, Mr. Seaton." She swept out her hand. "Will you come in?"

"No, I was merely on my way home and thought I'd check on your father." His gaze held her in place. "And on you."

Despite the chill moisture seeping in the open door,

warmth spread from her tummy to her chest. "My father seems to be rallying. I think he is finally and truly on the mend."

"I hope it, for his sake and yours." He cocked his head, his eyes narrowing as he searched her face. He reached, slowly, as if she might skitter away, and his thumb traced the curve beneath her eyes. "You look weary. How are you faring?"

She bit her lip. Besides her father, was there ever a more thoughtful soul?

"Bearing up," she murmured.

"You're a brave one." His hand dropped, and he grinned. "You know, I think you'd make a fine smuggler."

"An offer I heartily refuse, sir. . . Oh, but that does remind me, has Mr. Farris caught up with you yet?"

"No." His smile faded. "Why?"

She tensed. Would it be spreading gossip, since clearly the man hadn't tried very hard to find Isaac? "Well, perhaps Mr. Farris has changed his mind, but he did mention to me and Esther that there's some shipment coming in he intends to use as a lure for smugglers."

Isaac grunted. "What has that to do with me?"

"Nothing—I hope?" Holding her breath, she studied his eyes, first one then the other, fearing yet needing to read the truth.

His gaze bored into hers, steady and sure. "I give you my word, I am well and truly finished with such a trade."

She blew out her relief. "I am glad of it."

"Yet. . ." His voice lowered to a gentle command. "There is something I should like your word on as well."

It took everything within her not to gape. What could he

possibly want from her? "Such as?"

"While your independent spirit does you credit, when the time comes for your father to. . ." Sorrow creased his brow. That he cared so deeply was a testament to the compassion of this man.

He stepped closer. "I would not see you grieving alone. Know that I am always available for you, no matter the time of day. Promise that you will lean on me for support."

Her pulse quickened. Surely he meant that not in a literal sense, yet she couldn't help but remember when he'd held her the week before, so strong, so compassionate. She swallowed the lump in her throat. "You are very kind."

"I am glad your opinion of me has altered since we first met."

"And I am glad your occupation has changed."

"Touché, Miss Fletcher." He donned his hat, his rogue grin returning. "Good day to you."

"Good day." She watched him stride away then slowly pressed the door shut behind him. How wicked was it to wish her father well, yet not so well that she would have to leave Seaton lands? With a sigh, she filled her father's mug, collected the broth bowl, and returned to his chamber.

As soon as she crossed the threshold, she stopped. The bowl hit the floorboards, soup splattering against her hem. The cup cracked like a broken bone. Father stared at her wide-eyed.

And dead.

❧

Isaac hunched his shoulders against the unrelenting mist, clicking his tongue to urge Duchess onward. The coming evening would not be kind to man or beast caught unawares.

Thankfully he'd be pulling off his boots in front of a warm hearth and drinking a glass of Madeira by the time a thick fog rolled in with the tide. Leaning forward, he patted his mount's neck. "And you'll be glad of a warm stall, eh girl?"

Despite the threat of poor weather, he whistled an old folk tune as he rode from the parsonage to Seaton Hall. Life hadn't been this good since Father's death. His shoulder bag bounced against his back, containing the signed contract for a new mine. The sweet smile of Helen lingered in his thoughts. Life was very good.

He turned onto the gravel road leading to home. Ahead, just in front of the manor, a blur of red poked a hole in the grey afternoon. His blood ran cold.

Redcoats. Four of them. Mounted and at the ready.

Oh God. Was this it? Had his past sins come to haunt in a way that would choke the breath from him at the end of a noose? What would happen to Esther? What of Helen?

The four men said nothing as he rode by, their stoic faces impossible to read—even when he tipped his hat to them. But they let him pass without hindrance, so surely that meant something. It *had* to mean something.

God, please.

He dismounted in front of the stairs, fully aware of the men at his back, just as a scarlet-faced Mr. Farris erupted out the manor's door, hat in hand.

Farris took the steps two at a time. "About time you show your face, Seaton!"

Isaac grabbed onto Duchess's headstall, calming the animal from the revenue man's advance. "Were you looking for me, Mr. Farris?"

Farris spit out a curse. "I've been looking for you these past three days, sir!"

"And so you've found me. But surely I am not the cause for your friends here"—he hitched his thumb over his shoulder—"or for your hasty departure from Seaton Hall."

"No. I have your sister to thank for that."

He frowned. What was he to make of that? Men generally ran toward Esther, not away from her.

"My sister?" he asked.

Ruddy splotches bloomed on Farris's face. "I suggest you spend more time at home, Mr. Seaton, schooling her in the proper arts of decorum and etiquette. I've never been so insulted."

"What's she done?"

"She cast me out, sir!" Tiny flecks of spittle flew from the man's mouth. "A finer catch she couldn't have found, nor will she. Her loss, though, not to mention yours."

An enraged child couldn't have looked more petulant. Tempted to laugh at the man, Isaac settled for clearing his throat instead. "I'm sorry, but did you say you were looking for me, not my sister?"

"Indeed." Farris yanked on his hat, his heaving chest slowly coming to rest. "I need your assistance in navigating the coastline hereabouts. You'd know it better than any since it's your land."

"What are you looking. . ."

Beyond Farris, a dark shape peeked out from around the corner of the manor, then immediately jerked back. Had Isaac not recognized that thin collection of bones, he'd have tallied it up to imagination. Blast it! Why would Billy Hawker show up here? Now? The redcoats at Isaac's back would need no encouragement to string Hawker up if they caught sight of him.

Farris narrowed his eyes at Isaac's sudden silence.

Immediately Isaac forced a cough, pulling out his handkerchief for extra measure. "Sorry. Been fighting a raw throat the better part of the day. Now then, what is it exactly that you're looking for?"

"You'd know if you weren't so deuced hard to track down." Farris stomped over to where his horse was tethered to a post, mercifully opposite where Hawker hid. "There was a ship to arrive this morn, yet it's now nearing dark. I suspect it was waylaid by smugglers last night, or worse, wreckers. I need you to mount up and help us find them." Farris swung into his saddle.

Isaac planted his feet. "Smugglers there may be, but you'll find no wreckers in Treporth. The people here are not that kind of folk."

"So. . ." Farris's eyelids tightened to slits. "You admit to smugglers, eh?"

Isaac shook his head. "I admit to nothing."

"Then mount your horse and let's be off."

"In this weather?" He threw out his hands. "It's a fool's errand. That ship is likely hunkered down in Galwyn Bay, not sailing through in a fog sure to come."

"Are you refusing to do your duty, Mr. Seaton?" The man's voice was a growl. One of the redcoat's horses stamped the gravel. Both indicted in a way that augured violence.

"Consider the possibilities." Isaac spread his words out slow, like a soothing balm. "If you make any headway, you won't get very far before you'll have to turn back. The tide rises in a few hours, and along with it a fog so thick, you'll be hard-pressed to find your way home."

"Then we'll move from shore to higher ground—as the smugglers must." Farris flipped aside the hem of his coat, revealing the handle of a pistol tucked into his belt. "Now, mount up."

A sigh emptied the last of his fight. There'd be no reasoning with this madman. "Very well, but my horse is done for. I've ridden her hard to Truro and back. Be on your way while I see to her and gear up a fresh mount."

Mist gathered like a shroud on Farris's shoulders, nature proclaiming this fool was on a death ride. Nevertheless, the man lifted his arrogant nose. "Do I have your word, sir?"

He'd have to give it or Farris would never leave. "You do," he said simply.

The pack of men heeled their horses about and rode down the road. Isaac waited until the last hint of red blended into grey.

Leaving Duchess where she stood, he took off at a sprint and rounded the corner of the manor. "Hawker! What the devil are you doing here?"

A sack of dark clothing rose from the shrubbery like a ghoul. Dark eyes drilled into his. "There's been a rockslide. Tegwyn and Rook are trapped."

"Blast!" Though the redcoats were long gone, he lowered his tone. "Where?"

"Blackpool Cove."

"The cove?" Growling, he yanked off his hat and slapped it against his thigh. It was either that or pummel the man in front of him. "You boarded that ship and pulled off goods, did you not?"

Hawker's thin shoulders shrugged. "She were fair picked over by the time we reached her."

"No doubt by Grimlox and his gang." He blew out a breath, long and low, and crammed his hat back atop his head. "You'll be the ones to hang if Farris finds you with the goods—and you know that's where he's headed."

Fear darkened the man's face like a thundercloud. "Then we must hurry."

Isaac's gut clenched. This was wrong. A trap. Certain death. But did he even have a choice?

Chapter Nine

Death was no stranger to Helen Fletcher. As a young girl, she'd held hands with the black specter while weeping at her mother's bedside. But here in a Cornwall parsonage as she knelt beside her father, tears spent, grief already unpacked and settled into the cavern of her heart, she knew instinctively this was different. She was alone in the world now. An unmoored ghost. Deserted. The fear she'd tried to ignore all her life suddenly rushed at her, stealing the breath from her lungs. Pretending wouldn't work this time.

And never would again.

She closed her eyes. *Oh God, how am I to bear this?*

Prickles tingled in her feet from her cramped position, heaping pain upon pain. It was all too much. She rose and fled from her father's chamber. Wild to be among the living, she grabbed her spencer and buttoned it haphazardly, then tied on her bonnet. Shoving her hands into her gloves, she escaped out the door into a world seeping with tears.

The mist followed her to the shed where Jenny stood, and though it took her several tries, she managed to saddle the horse. She dragged over an upturned bucket and mounted. Hopefully Isaac had meant his offer of support.

She straightened her skirts then urged the horse out into the monochrome afternoon. Fitting, really, that colour should die the same day as her father. She gave Jenny free rein, prepared for speed and heedless of the danger should she fall. So be it.

Fine rain needled her cheeks. The world smeared by. In no time, she rounded the bend to Seaton Hall—only to see a black horse taking off across a nearby field, heading toward the woods. Slowing, she squinted in the fuzzy light. The horse was definitely not Duchess, but the man astride? Wide shoulders. As animal as his mount. A silhouette of strength. It had to be Isaac.

She frowned. As the gap widened between her and the master of Seaton Hall, panic welled until something inside her broke. Something only he could fix. She needed his arms around her more than anything.

"Isaac!" she shouted, as stunned by the passion in her voice as by the use of his Christian name.

But he was too far ahead to hear. And once he entered the copse, she'd lose sight of him as well. Should she let him go? Turn back and seek some measure of comfort from Esther's company? She glanced over her shoulder at the manor as she rode. Small comfort was not the same as leaning on someone, and she'd promised to lean on Isaac.

With a crack of the crop, she plunged after him. The field was easy enough to cross, but once she entered the trees, she was forced to slow. She had to settle for simply keeping him in sight, and even that was a stretch, for he rode with far more experience. By the time she navigated to the end of the woods, her skirt hem was ripped, her bonnet dangled by the ribbons at her neck, and Isaac had already crossed the grassy ridge leading to the coastal cliffs.

Cupping her hand to her mouth, she yelled his name again.

But the misty air blunted the sound as effectively as a damp blanket dulls the roar of a fire. Defeat tasted bitter in her mouth.

She swallowed it back and pressed on, desperate. An insane chase were she of a right mind, yet nothing was right about this day—nor ever would be again, now that her father was gone. She drove Jenny across the ridge and reined her to a halt at the rocky trail disappearing over the cliff, the one Isaac had warned her about. She leaned as far as she dared without tumbling from the saddle, trying to catch a glimpse of the man. He was right. The path was narrow, jagged, and altogether foreboding. But down a ways, it flattened out before it hooked into a switchback. She'd go that far, and no farther, whether she glimpsed him or not.

Clicking her tongue, she gripped the reins until her fingers ached. Jenny's nose jerked up and her ears twitched, but she moved on. Leaning back for balance, Helen held her breath as the horse picked her way along the thin route and didn't release it until Jenny made it to the rocky landing.

This time Helen didn't dare to peek, so treacherously did the ground give way beside her. *Don't look. Don't look!* She forced her focus along the snaking trail. As Isaac had said, it plummeted at an alarming slope, nearly down to the rocky beach, then turned and disappeared into the mist. If Isaac had come this way, he was out of sight.

She frowned. He'd never admitted this was a smuggler's

trail, yet she couldn't help but wonder. What was left of her heart sank to her stomach. Surely Isaac was a man of his word. He said he'd given up such thievery. But why disappear down to the coast on a foul day such as this? La! What was *she* doing out here? She'd heard of the grieving committing strange acts, but she never expected to yield to such behaviour.

Nor would she. She'd wait for him at Seaton Hall. Pulling on the left rein, she attempted to turn the horse. "Let's go, Jenny."

But Jenny's rear hoof slipped. The horse panicked.

And Helen plunged.

She hit the ground at the same time Jenny's hoof smashed into her ankle. The horse galloped down the trail. Helen groaned, reaching for her foot.

But the rocks of the path gave way.

Helen bounced down the side of the cliff like a rag doll tossed from a coach window. Sky and ground blended together. Rocks cut. Scraping, scratching, ripping fabric and skin.

Then the world stopped.

How long she lay there, God only knew. Long enough to hate the pain, the drizzle, the hopelessness throbbing with as much agony as her bruised body. Most of all, she hated herself. What a reckless thing to have done.

Weary to the bone, she rolled over and pushed up. But when she tried to put weight on her ankle, a cry tore out her throat, and she dropped to her knees. Walking was out of the question.

Lifting her head, she scanned the immediate area. Nearby,

a gaping hollow opened onto the beach—not a cave, really, but shelter enough to get her out of the spitting rain.

Crawling in a wet skirt sapped the small store of strength she had left. Once inside, she stretched out her legs and leaned back against the rocks, weary beyond measure. Oh, to quit breathing, just like Father, but her body wouldn't oblige.

"God," she whispered, "what am I to do?"

Only the crash of wave against rock answered.

She lifted her voice, hurtling her words as viciously as the sea. "I cannot bear this. I cannot!"

Rage, sorrow, torment, all tore out her throat in a ragged cry. Was this how Jesus felt before He died, broken by a grief so great that He committed His spirit to God?

Committed His spirit to God.

The words played over and over in her head, cresting with each swell of the sea until suddenly it made sense.

Her head dropped, and she closed her eyes. For the first time in her life, she surrendered instead of pretending.

"Your will, God," she murmured. "Your will."

⁂

Isaac vaulted off his horse, his heels barely digging into the sand before he took off at a lope. To his right, a wall of fog crept closer with the tide. On his left, a cliff, pitted and gouged from the rockslide. And ahead. . .

Oh God.

It wasn't much of a prayer, but it was the best he could muster while speeding past one wagon and sliding to a stop at the back of another. Hawker squatted next to Rook, who propped himself up on his elbows, one of his legs trapped. A pace past Rook, Tegwyn lay insensible, the left side of his body hidden by the same boulder crushing Rook's leg.

Isaac crouched next to Hawker. "Hang on, Rook. Hawker and I will have you and Tegwyn out of here in no time."

"Aye, Master Seaton. No doubt ye will." Rook's brave words traveled on a groan, the pain distinguishable even above the crashing waves.

Rising, Isaac yanked Hawker up along with him and pulled him aside. "Where's the rest of the crew?"

"Davey musta run off when I come get you, the blackguard. He were gone by the time I got back." Hawker swiped his nose then averted his gaze. "No one else come."

"Do you mean to tell me you attempted this with only four men? Of all the incompetent, foolhardy—" He clamped his jaw shut. Hard. No sense berating Hawker. The man could hardly count to ten. Tegwyn must've been the brains behind this scheme—and now suffered the consequences of it.

Isaac sighed. "Come on."

Leaping over several scattered crates yet to be loaded, he dashed to where the rowboat was grounded. The bow was secure, hauled up on slippery green rocks, but the stern floated higher than when it had landed. Much longer and the sea would take it.

Leaning over the gunwale, Isaac grabbed the two oars and tossed one to Hawker. Not much daylight remained, and even that a poor gruel. Still, he strained to examine the top of the ridge for any flash of redcoats. Farris was out here, somewhere.

He sped back to the injured men.

"We'll have to wedge this boulder upward. We won't be able to move it much, but a little may be all we need." He crouched, searching for the best angle to drive in the oars, then shouted up at Hawker. "Cram an oar, paddle end down, in here."

Leaving Hawker behind, Isaac searched for the right size rock to use as a hammer. Big enough for powerful strokes, but not so big that he couldn't hold it, and—there. He scooped up a great, craggy chunk and ran back.

He nodded at Hawker. "You hold the oar, I'll pound it in."

Hefting the rock, Isaac whaled on the wood. Each strike juddered up his arms. Slowly, the oar sank, wedging the boulder up by hairline increments until—crack! The oar tip broke.

Hawker swore.

Isaac merely dropped his rock and grabbed the broken wood. A small space had opened where the paddle had sunk deep, and he crammed the shortened piece of oar into it.

Hawker frowned as he grabbed onto it, and Isaac didn't blame him. Now that the oar was shortened, if Isaac were to miss his aim, he'd snap the man's arm in two.

Praying for a good eye, Isaac threw all he had left into driving the rock against the oar. Sweat stung his eyes. His muscles screamed. But the wood inched earthward. When there was nothing left to pound, he met Hawker's gaze and nodded. They yanked Tegwyn free first. He didn't wake, but at least his crushed arm was still attached.

Rook screamed when they pulled him out. His boot stuck but his leg pulled free, a bloody pulp at the end of his smashed foot, leastwise what was left of it. He'd need that foot attended to immediately or risk losing it. Even then, there were no guarantees.

With Hawker's help, they hefted Rook up and heaved him into the back of the wagon. With his elbows, Rook scuttled over and propped himself against a crate.

They raced back to Tegwyn. Isaac grabbed the man's feet, Hawker his shoulders, and together they hoisted the fellow up next to Rook, then closed the wagon's back gate.

Isaac turned to Hawker. "Get these men out of here."

The mist ran rivulets down Hawker's face. "But the rest o' the load!"

"These men need help. Now!"

Ignoring him, Hawker stared at the goods, eyes transfixed as if nothing else in the world existed.

A growl rumbled in Isaac's chest. The dull-witted fellow was so focused on the goods that he couldn't see the need of his friends. If Isaac drove the injured men himself and left Hawker on his own, the scrawny man would no doubt struggle long to load the big crates and likely end up being drowned by the rising tide or caught by the redcoats.

"Blast!" he shouted at Hawker, the tide, the sky—and the frustration of the whole situation. "I'll see to the last crates and meet up with you. Go!"

It was all he could think of to get Hawker to move. But was it enough? Did the man even hear him?

Thankfully, it worked. Hawker rounded the side of the wagon and hiked his bones up into the driver's seat. With a snap of the reins, he got the two horses going—though truly it wouldn't have taken even that, so eager were the animals to escape the water lapping closer and closer.

Soaked by sweat, sea spray, and anger, Isaac loaded the last four crates into the second wagon. All the while, he scanned from an ever-narrowing beach up to the top of the cliff, keen to spy any hint of scarlet. By the time he finished, white foam licked his heels. He retrieved his own mount, for the horse had shied off to higher ground, then he tethered the beast to the back of the wagon. Crawling up to the driver's seat, he barely grabbed the reins before the workhorses set off.

He drove the length of the beach to where the sand cut away between an archway of rock. Passing beneath, he tensed. This road would likely be where he'd run into Farris—if indeed the man haunted this stretch of coast. It ascended to Isaac's left, fresh ruts ground in the earth by Hawker's wagon. To the right, the treacherous trail leading to Isaac's own lands, wide enough for only one horse—the horse bolting toward him. A flash of reddish-brown mane flew past him.

Isaac yanked the reins of the workhorses, heart dropping to his boots. Jenny. That was Red Jenny. Sidesaddle attached.

And riderless.

He jumped to his feet and stared as far as he could see along the narrow path.

"Helen!" he shouted.

No movement. Just mist and mud, rock and fear. Why would her horse be out here, unless she'd—?

Blast!

A rising tide. A missing woman. And a revenue man only God knew where with Hawker and two injured men hauling a load of contraband. Isaac roared along with the crashing waves and jumped down from the wagon.

There was only one thing to be done.

Chapter Ten

Jerking upright, Helen startled awake. Or was she? Darkness surrounded her. Her bones ached, her ankle throbbed, and dampness soaked her backside. But none of that mattered as much as the swell of cold water lapping at her feet. The rising tide. Soon it would reach in and drag her out to sea.

And she couldn't swim.

Fear unhinged her jaw, and she screamed, then held her breath, listening. Were this a dream, there'd be no echo—but the remnants of her cry hung in the darkness like a living thing. Indeed, this nightmare was very real.

"Helen!"

Her name was a lifeline, but did she only imagine Isaac's voice? Was the call of a loved one the last thing one heard before death?

"Helen!"

Did it matter?

"Isaac!" She crawled to the edge of the rocky recess, hands and legs submerged. "I'm here!"

Booming surf drowned her voice. She waited, listening for the break between waves, then invested everything into her next bellow. "Isaac!"

The silhouette of a man on a horse, black against the night, splashed close and stopped in front of her. Isaac sprang from his mount and swept her into his arms.

"Thank God." His breath warmed her brow.

"Oh Isaac! I was so—"

"There's no time."

He hefted her up into the saddle, and she sat sideways, allowing him to swing up behind her.

"Hold on, tightly," he directed.

Wheeling the horse about, he spurred the animal on. The rain had stopped and the sky had cleared, but sea spray broke over them with shocking force as they tore along the beach, drenching her already damp clothes. Knee-deep water hampered the horse's pace.

Isaac took a hard right, steering them onto a steep incline. Instinctively, Helen leaned forward against the horse's neck. Isaac's chest pressed against her back as he did the same. Hooves scrambled for purchase of earth, the horse frantic for a foothold. Were it not for Isaac's strong arms cocooning her, she'd surely fall.

Another turn, and the slope lessened. The narrow track widened and eventually changed into a road. The slap of waves shushed the higher they climbed. Finally, the track evened out, and Isaac stopped the crazed pace, slowing the horse to a walk. Hard to tell where they were, for shadows painted the landscape with an inky brush. But once they passed beneath the bower of a great brambly hedge, the ground flattened onto an open sward. Her eyes adjusted, and she could now see a road bathed in starlight. She had no idea where it went, but apparently Isaac did, for he clicked his tongue and swung the horse to the left.

He crooked his head close to hers. "Are you well?"

The question was too big to consider. Of course she wasn't well, not when Father lay cold in a bed. But the words were too awful to say, so she settled for a lesser pain. "I'm afraid I hurt my ankle. Jenny threw me."

"Then we shall get that attended to as soon as we reach Seaton Hall. What were you doing on Jenny in the first place? Why are you out here?"

"I. . ." Her tongue lay fallow in her mouth. Too many emotions wrestled for first place, and to her shame, the strongest one was to turn her face and rest her cheek against his. Shoving down the desire, she blurted out, "My father is gone."

He reined the horse to a stop, and before she drew another breath, he cradled her in his arms and pressed his lips against the top of her head. "Oh, my sweet Helen, I am so sorry for your loss. Would that I could take your pain."

Her throat closed, the compassion in his words breaking and mending at the same time. She leaned against him, allowing his strength to shore her up. "This is why I sought you," she murmured.

He pulled back, the horse shifting beneath his sudden move. "But how did you know I was out here?"

"I saw you riding off, and I didn't think. I simply followed." She peered up at his dark shadow of a face, his eyes unreadable beneath the brim of his hat. "What *are* you doing out here?"

Wide brown eyes stared into Isaac's soul, searching for truth. Though he wore layers of soggy garments, he felt as exposed as the day he'd graced the world with his first cry. "I'll answer you as we ride. You've got to get out of that wet gown, and I have yet one more engagement to attend to."

With pressure from his heels, he prodded the horse on toward Seaton Hall, where he'd deposit Helen with his sister for the night. Sleeping alone in a cottage with her deceased father was beyond a grievous act.

She faced forward, her loosened hair brushing against his chin as she turned. "Thank you, but all the same, I should like that answer now."

A grin stretched his lips. Even while suffering loss, she remained as determined as ever. "Mr. Farris asked me to help ferret out some smugglers. Seems there was a shipment running late, and he had his suspicions."

She quirked her head, like an owl listening for the slightest rustle of undergrowth. "After working with young charges the past five years, I've developed a knack for discerning deception. You are not telling me the full truth, I think."

His brow fairly raised the brim of his hat. "Are you really a governess or an interrogator for the Crown sent here to bedevil me?"

"If you are bedeviled," she glanced over her shoulder, "then I suggest it is your own conscience wreaking such turmoil."

His gaze landed on her lips. A slow burn ignited in his gut. How well she molded against his chest. How right the feel of her in his arms. What would her response be if he acted on such rising desire?

Instant remorse punched him hard, for he ought not feel such things toward a grieving woman. Even so, he couldn't purge the huskiness from his voice. "On that account you are entirely wrong."

She turned forward again, and for a while, they rode in silence, the horse's steady plodding sucking up mud.

"I think that before you intended to meet with Mr. Farris," she said at length, "you were warning those smugglers, were you not?"

"Not warning, helping."

She jerked back to face him. "You promised you were done with thievery!"

The look of admiration in her eyes vanished, replaced by cold shadows, and the loss cut deep and bloody. He shook his head. "I have not broken that promise. A few of the men were in trouble, caught beneath a rockslide at Blackpool Cove. I went to free them—and a good thing I did, or I'd not have seen your horse running loose."

Her shoulders sagged, the rhythm of the mount's gait dipping her head—or was it due to her disappointment in him?

She blinked up at him. "It seems once again I am in your debt."

Her words taught him to hope. The scent of the sea clung to her, every bit as pungent as the loamy smell of the wet earth his horse trod upon. A lock of dark hair drooped on her cheek, as wild as on that first ride they'd shared. He reached for it and tucked the strand behind her ear, wishing for all the world there weren't a barrier of leather glove between his skin and hers. She shivered, from a chill or from his touch?

Oh, hang it all. He yanked off his glove and swept his fingers over her cheek, cupping her face in his hand. She did not pull back. "You are wrong, you know. It is I who owe you. I am a changed man since your arrival. Your candor has caused me to think about my actions, that the end does not justify the means. For so long I've been bent on revenge, thinking I was right by taking back what Brannigan had taken from me, but I've come to see that none of it was mine in the first place. It's always—only—been God's. You helped me see that."

Her head shook beneath his hand. "Not me."

"You." He bent toward her, resting his brow against hers. "Tell me, Helen, what will you do now that your father is gone?"

She edged back from him, the small space between them gaping like a wound. "Return to Ireland, I suppose. Though I hope you'll help me with arrangements for a proper burial before I leave."

Blast! He could hardly bear the inches between them, let alone the entire North Sea. Loosening the reins, he let the horse walk at will and focused his entire attention—and heart—on the woman in front of him. "Of course I'll help."

Her mouth curved into a half smile. "And a good deed requires a kiss, does it not?"

She remembered? He cocked his head, studying her by the shadow of night. "Who told you that?"

"You did." She poked him in the shoulder. "That first night we met."

A charge shot through him, and he captured her hand, pressing it to his chest. Dare he hope the evening they'd met was as indelibly etched onto her heart as it was on his? "You are not as adept at discerning the truth as you claim, for that night I did not speak the full truth."

"Oh?"

He swallowed. Was he ready for this? Was she? The timing was off, couldn't be worse, in fact. But there was no stopping now.

"A deed of such magnitude requires your hand in marriage." His voice lowered to a rasp, not for want of asking, but for fear of the answer. "Will you give it?"

Chapter Eleven

Everything was overloud. The creak of saddle and jingle of tack as the horse shifted weight. Leftover drips of mist working their way down blades of the sward's scrubby grass. Helen's racing heart. How could she accept a proposal on the night of her father's death?

Isaac stared, waiting, rock still. Everything hinged on her answer—for them both. She'd never known such a kind man, such generosity and compassion, and to think he would offer to spend the rest of his days with her. . . . How could she not accept such a gift? Had not Father himself admonished her to open her heart to love? And she did. She loved this man more than life itself.

Twisting her hand in Isaac's grip, she laced her fingers through his, palm to palm—a perfect fit.

"Yes," she whispered.

A simple answer. Or was it? She tipped her face to his, straining to read Isaac's response. And what she saw stole her breath.

Despite the shadow of his hat brim, his eyes lit with an intense fire, with her the sole focus of a love so pure, it shimmied across her shoulders. Her lips parted, dumbstruck. How did one respond to such unbridled passion? She swallowed, fearing she might never be worthy of such adoration.

And then his mouth was on hers.

One taste, and she knew it would never be enough. She'd endured a stolen kiss before, but nothing like this. She leaned into him, clinging to his shirt, pulling him closer. He smelled of the sea, of wind and waves and distant horizons. Warmth spread through her body, driving off the pain of loss and hurt. By the time he pulled back, she nearly slipped from the horse.

"Whoa, now." He chuckled, bracing her up with his strong arms. "I know it is wrong of me to be so happy on the day of your bereavement, but you have made me so." Cupping her face in his hands, he pressed a kiss to her brow. "I love you, more than life and air."

"Oh Isaac—" Her voice broke, and she licked her lips, the leftover taste of him still there. "I love you infinitely more."

She could live here, in this moment, his breath warming her skin. But despite the heat of the man and the fervor of the moment, the chill of her wet gown crept beneath her skin, and she shivered.

He leaned back, gathering the reins. "Time we get you home."

She turned and nestled against his chest as he drove the horse into a canter. Her thoughts sped as quickly as the passing black landscape, too dizzying to sort through. Eventually, her head sank, and she stared at the woolen sleeve of the man—her future husband—holding the reins in a loose grip. It was fine fabric, that of a gentleman, but matted with sand and smelling of hard work. He was a contradiction, indeed, but he was her contradiction. How could a single day hold such exquisite pain and joy?

"Nearly there," Isaac's voice rumbled close to her ear.

The road rounded the swell of a hillock. They followed the curve, and once they cleared the mound, Isaac jerked the horse to a stop. Not far ahead, torches lit the night, four of which were gripped in the hands of mounted redcoats and bobbed alongside a wagon.

Helen squinted at the bright offense. "Why would—?"

"Shh," Isaac warned.

Too late.

The two soldiers at the rear charged toward them. "Hands up! Behind yer heads!"

Isaac stiffened. "Do as they say."

Slowly, she lifted her fingers to the back of her neck. The loss of Isaac's arms around her felt like death.

The larger of the two reached for the reins and led their horse. Were Isaac's strong thighs and his back not a steadying rock, she'd surely have slipped from the saddle. What kind of trouble was this?

A horse tethered to the back of the wagon pawed the ground when they passed. As they moved on, a low groan rumbled in Isaac's chest. In the wagon bed, two men sat upright, torchlight doing crazy things to the whites of their eyes. Another man lay next to them, bloodied and still.

Gooseflesh lifted along Helen's arms. Were these the smugglers Isaac had come to help?

Mr. Farris turned on the driver's seat, a pistol lying beside him. A torch mounted on the wagon's side tinted his face with devilish light. "What's this?"

"You're the one who wanted me out here, and so you find me." Isaac's voice thundered at her back. "Now call down your men. You're frightening Miss Fletcher."

"No, that one fears nothing." Farris's dark eyes landed on her. "Tell me, Miss Fletcher, what are you doing out here on such a wicked night?"

"I—I—" The words stuck in her throat, trapped beneath the stare of the soldiers. Sucking in a breath, she tried again. "I was looking for Mr. Seaton when my horse threw me. My ankle turned, and he found me."

Mr. Farris narrowed his eyes. "A very pretty story, lady—yet I believe not a word of it. Dismount."

Behind her, Isaac shifted, and Mr. Farris snatched up the gun at his side, aiming it at them. "Ah-ah-ah, not you, Seaton."

"For the love of all that's right, man, she's hurt!" Isaac's shout hung on the air, savage in intensity. "She'll not be able to stand."

Farris cocked the hammer, the click of it as sharp as a bullet's report. "That's exactly what I intend to find out."

She lowered her hands, careful, like a piece of glass. One wrong move and the crack of gunfire might shatter bones and lives. Holding tightly to the saddle's edge, she eased earthward. If she landed on her good foot, she could surely stand, for she'd played many a game of hopscotch with her charges.

But at the last moment, the horse shied. She teetered. Hundreds of knives stabbed her foot and ankle. A fiery scream burned out her throat, and she crumpled.

Before muddy gravel bit into her cheek, sturdy arms scooped her up.

And the barrels of four more guns swung their way.

Isaac clenched his jaw so hard, it crackled in his ears. How dare this upstart treat them like criminals? He hadn't even done anything wrong this time! Helen gasped in his arms, from pain or fear, hard to say. Either way, Farris was to blame. Despite the brilliance of the flaming torches, rage painted the whole scene purple.

"Tell your men to stand down!" Isaac's voice shook like a peal of thunder. Good. May they all cower at his fury. "You can see the woman's not playacting. Allow me to put her back on my horse."

"No." Farris lifted his chin and stared down the length of his nose. "Put her up here with me."

Was the man mad? He'd as soon sit her next to the jaws of hell. "I will do nothing of the sort!"

Farris's head lowered like a bull about to charge. The soldiers closed in, eyes bright with the promise of a fight. Farris cocked the hammer of his gun to full open. If that thing went off, Helen would bear the brunt.

Isaac pivoted back a step, shielding her by exposing his own side. "I swear to God, if you so much as—"

"Stop it!" Helen squirmed in his arms, shifting to face Farris.

Isaac widened his stance.

Farris widened his eyes.

"Mr. Farris, there can be no hope for you and I." Helen spoke as to a schoolboy, her tone confident yet instructive. And in that moment, Isaac couldn't have been more proud. Any other woman would have swooned by now.

"This very night I have committed my hand to Mr. Seaton,"

she continued. "I am certain, however, that with your capture of these ruffians, you will be lauded a hero. Better women than I will vie for your attention."

What? Was she seriously complimenting the buffoon? Isaac cocked his head. So did Farris.

"Why would you say. . ." The words died on Isaac's lips as an interesting transformation took place up on the wagon seat.

Farris's chest expanded a full two inches, and his shoulders stood at attention. A toad couldn't have puffed up to a greater swell. "No doubt you are correct," he sneered. Even so, he tripped the hammer closed on his gun. "Stand down, men. These two are not involved with the smugglers. Go ahead, Seaton. Hoist her up."

Isaac heaved a sigh and breathed out, "Well done," into Helen's ear, then he lifted her so that she could reach the saddle and released her when she sat secure.

Turning from the horse, he caught a glimpse of Hawker and Rook, fettered in the wagon's back. A sickening taste soured his mouth. He knew that wild-eyed look. He'd seen it the instant before he'd had to put down one of his best geldings. The comparison punched him in the gut, but what was he to do? Outmanned and outgunned, words and timing were his only allies.

God, please. A little help, here.

He faced Farris. "I would have a word with you. Alone."

Farris snorted. "I don't trust you that far, Seaton. Whatever you have to say may be said here, in front of witnesses."

"Fine." He shrugged. "Though sensitive information is usually heard by the commanding—"

"*Sensitive,*" Farris drawled out the word. "Information?"

Isaac strode the few steps to the wagon seat, acutely aware of the redcoats' gazes stabbing him from all angles. "Besides my rescuing of Miss Fletcher, why do you think it took me so long to get out here? I gave my word to help you, and I have information to do just that."

Farris eyed him. Would he bite the bait? Isaac drew in a breath and held it.

"Very well. Men, keep guard." Farris jumped down from the wagon, his boots slogging hard into the mud as he landed. He kept his gun, but at least he tucked the barrel into his trousers.

Isaac led him to the side of the road, making a show of taking the fool into his confidence—while stalling to come up with something to say.

Farris folded his arms. "Well?"

Exactly. Well what? He scrubbed his jaw, hoping to work loose a magical concoction of words—when a perfectly wonderful idea took root. And grew.

Thank You, Lord.

"These men you have"—he hitched his thumb over his shoulder—"while a fine catch, they are not the real villains."

Farris's brow crumpled. "What do you mean?"

"Look at that wagon. Do you really think those few crates are the sum of what was taken from that cargo? No." He shook his head. "That ship of yours was first waylaid and picked over farther up the coast, four miles from here. The true smugglers are led by a man named Grimlox. Jack Grimlox. If you hurry, you can catch them in the act, with a far better haul than this sorry lot."

Farris stared at him, his gaze unreadable so far from the torches. Would this work?

"So help me, Seaton," Farris rumbled as he unfolded his arms. "If you are lying. . ."

The threat twisted on the air like a rope from a gibbet.

Isaac advanced, towering at least a hand span above the man and using that intimidation to the fullest. "This is the thanks I get for giving you intelligence? You offend me?"

Farris retreated a step, uncertainty rippling across his large lips. "I—I—no, I never meant to offend. My apologies."

Isaac held the stance a breath longer, then backed off, allowing a slow smile to spread. "Well, don't just stand here, man." He swept out a hand. "Go get those lawbreakers!"

"But I'll need my men if I'm to capture an entire gang." His head shook from side to side. "I cannot free the scoundrels I've already caught."

"Not to worry." Isaac cuffed him on the back, the restraint of keeping the swat playful burning his muscles. "As local magistrate, I will see to these men."

"Single-handedly?"

"You've already subdued them." Playing to the man's pride nearly choked him. He scrubbed the back of his neck to keep from tugging at his collar. "I'll lock them up until the circuit judge arrives in Truro, then transport them with the help of a few tenants of mine. Naturally, I shall give you all the credit, for it was you who bagged them."

Farris's eyes narrowed. "Why so accommodating?"

He placed his hand on his heart. "I take my duty to God and country very seriously."

Farris gaped. "I fear I have misjudged you, Mr. Seaton. You are a true loyalist, sir, and I salute you." He clacked his heels together and snapped his fingers to his brow.

Isaac bowed, hiding a smile. "Godspeed, Mr. Farris. May your return to London be victorious."

"Oh, that it shall be. I vow it." Shoving his hand into his greatcoat, he pulled out a key and handed it over, then he pivoted and sprinted away, shouting out orders and untethering his horse from the back of the wagon.

Isaac watched the man go, certain that he was the real victor in this. . .or rather God was.

Chapter Twelve

Mr. Farris and the soldiers thundered off, but despite the danger disappearing into the dark, Helen's heart still beat an irregular tattoo, for Isaac strode toward her. Determined of gait and singularly focused on her, she nearly shrank from the force of his gaze.

He grasped the horse's headstall and shushed away the skittishness of her mount, all while searching her from head to toe with a fearsome eye. "Are you all right?"

"I am." The words were weak. Her smile weaker. But after the events of the day, it was a wonder she functioned at all.

She lifted a hand toward the retreating men. "How on earth did you manage that?"

His teeth shone white in the dark, the only torch remaining on the wagon seat. "Some things aren't black and white, but one thing is for certain—the arrogance in Mr. Farris. I simply used his pride to my advantage."

She couldn't help but return Isaac's grin. "You, sir, are a rogue."

"Is that a step up or down from a smuggler?" He winked, then wheeled about and swung himself up into the back of the wagon.

He worked with sure yet gentle movements while caring for the wounded men. What a husband he would be. What a father.

Father.

Her shoulders sagged. No, her whole body did. Her own father yet lay cold in the cottage, alone but not forgotten. A fresh wave of tears blurred the world, and she forced herself to the present, anchoring her gaze on Isaac's broad back as he moved from man to man.

He squeezed the arm of one. "Bear up, Rook. We'll soon get you to a doctor." Then he crouched in front of another and pulled out a key.

"So, yer a miracle worker now, eh?" The man, all sharp angles and shadows, lifted his face toward Isaac. "Don't know how ye did it, but I thank ye."

"Save your thanks, for your other wagon is lost to the tide, and it was your information I gave to Farris. Now hold out your hands."

The fellow complied but not without complaint. "Flit! What ye goin' on about?"

The sound of shackles clacked onto the wagon bed. Isaac and only one of the other men stood.

Isaac clapped the fellow on the shoulder. "I let it slip that Grimlox and his gang were the true culprits. If Farris is able to haul them in, Brannigan will be implicated. Maybe not a killing blow, but a blow nonetheless."

"Fitting end to 'em both, I say."

Isaac released the man. "Drive this rig onward, Hawker. See that Tegwyn and Rook get care and fast. I've a lady to attend to."

"And a right fine one at that." The dark eyes of the thin man met her across the gap between wagon and horse. "Ma'am." He tugged the brim of his hat.

Helen dipped her head in greeting. "Mister. . . ?"

Isaac hoisted himself up behind her, snugging her back against him. "That's Billy Hawker. Hawker, meet the soon-to-be Mrs. Isaac Seaton."

The pile of bones crawled onto the wagon seat and faced them. "Ho-ho! Welcome to the ranks, m'lady." With a nod of his head, he reached for the reins and nudged the horses into action.

Helen turned to Isaac. She shouldn't be surprised if she awoke from this scene to find it was all a dream. Lifting her hand, she ran her fingers along the cheek of the man who would be her husband, the rasp of unshaved whiskers very real beneath her touch.

"You know, as impoverished as I was, I never thought I'd marry such a fine gentleman as you, so I used to pretend I was a grand lady," she murmured, afraid that if she spoke too loudly, this moment would dissolve. "But you have made it so."

He shook his head. "Once again, you have it wrong, my love. You. . ." He bent, and his lips brushed against her cheek. "Always have. . ." His mouth moved to the hollow near her temple. "And always will be. . ." Heat traced a line down her jaw. "A lady."

He kissed her soundly then turned her from him, enfolding his strong arms around her. She smiled shamelessly as they rode off into the night. Weeks ago he'd been a smuggler—and now she was his lady. Despite the heartache of the day, the irony of it all released a small laugh.

Isaac leaned over her shoulder, nuzzling her cheek. "What delights you so?"

She reached and caressed the side of his face, getting lost in the feel of his skin against her fingertips. "Life. It's a glorious thing."

The Doctor's Woman

Dedication

As always and forever, to the Lover of my soul.

Acknowledgments

Mark Griep: for putting up with me for thirty-two years

Ane Mulligan & Elizabeth Ludwig: for your sweet slash-and-burn skills

Shannon McNear: for sharing your horse expertise and encouragement

Annie Tipton: for believing in me and my writing

Joe Whitson & Matthew Cassady: for your wealth of historical information

Chapter One

Mendota, Minnesota
1862

Emmy Nelson had lived with death for as long as she could remember. She'd watched it happen. Witnessed the devastating effects. Wept with and embraced those howling in grief. Even lost her betrothed—a man she respected, maybe even loved.

But she'd never tasted the true bitterness of it until now—and the acrid flavor drove her to her knees. Early-November leaves crackled like broken bones beneath her weight, but alone at last, she gave in.

"Oh Papa."

Did that ragged voice really belong to her?

Her tears washed onto his grave like a benediction. How long she lay there, crying, she couldn't say; long enough, though, to warrant Aunt Rosamund's manservant, Jubal Warren, to put an end to it.

"Miss Emmaline." Jubal's footsteps padded across the backyard of the home she'd shared with her father, stopping well behind her. "Time we leave, child."

Swallowing back anguish, she forced sorrow deep and waited until it lodged behind her heart. She'd pull it out later, when there were no eyes to watch her grieve.

She flattened her palm on the freshly dug earth and whispered, "Neither of us wanted to say goodbye, did we, Papa?"

Overhead, tree branches groaned in the wind. Fitting, really. The death of a dream and a loved one ought to be blessed with a dirge.

"Miss Emmaline?" Jubal insisted.

This was it, then. Slowly, she rose, wiping the dirt from her hands and the pain from her soul. For now, anyway. She'd put off moving to Aunt Rosamund's in Minneapolis far too long. But walking away from a lifelong hope of settling in Mendota took more than courage.

It took time.

"Doc Nelson? Doctor!" Men's shouts carried from the front of the house. Clearly the news of her father's death hadn't spread as far as she'd imagined.

With a last sniffle, Emmy turned her back on her past and walked away, Jubal at her heels.

In front of the cottage, two lathered horses snorted on the road, distressing her own mare, hitched to a packed cart in front of them. Their riders—dressed in military blue—pounded on the office door. "Doc, open up! There's been an accident."

"I'm sorry, gentlemen, but you'll find no help here."

They pivoted at her voice. Sweat dotted the brow of the shorter man, confusion the other. "Excuse us, miss, but. . ." The taller of the two squinted. "Hey, yer the doc's daughter. Sorry to bother you, Miss Nelson, but where's he at? We need him."

"The doctor. . .my father. . ." She glanced at Jubal for help. How to explain when her chest cinched so tightly, she could hardly breathe?

Jubal stepped forward. "Doc Nelson passed away, going on

two weeks ago, now."

One fellow slapped his hat against his leg with a curse. A curious reaction, one that pasted a scowl on Jubal's weathered face.

"What of the fort's doctor?" she asked. "Why didn't you seek him?"

"Doc Brandley left for the front at Antietam back in September. We been expectin' a replacement ever since, but he hasn't arrived yet."

The tall soldier stalked forward, jaw tight, shoulders stiff, torment clearly trapped inside his skin. He stopped in front of her, his Adam's apple bobbing. Whatever had happened at the fort couldn't be good.

"We need a doctor. Now. It's Sarge's leg. We tied it off as best we could, but the blood was still comin' when we left. It's beyond what any of us can fix. Next to your father—God rest him—yer the best we got." He peered at her, his voice frayed at the edges. "Will you come?"

Jubal stepped in front of her. "Miss Nelson is expected in Minneapolis."

Shoving his cap back onto his head, the shorter man darted around Jubal. "It'll take us too long to get help from the city, miss. Our sergeant could be dead by then." He stepped closer, smelling of horses and desperation. "Surely your father taught you some about healing."

Her throat closed. There was no way the soldier could know how his words brought her papa back to life. . . .

"You have a healing gift, Daughter. It's not for man to chide what God's given. Never be ashamed of what you are."

She nibbled her lip, turning over the memories and

examining them in the weak November sunlight. Should she go? Papa would not only understand her wanting to help, he'd ordain it. Aunt Rosamund, however, would have the vapors.

"Please, miss. It was my bullet what tore him up. I never shoulda—"The tall man's voice cracked, and he wheeled about, head hanging like a whipped hound.

How could she refuse that?

"Very well." She tightened her bonnet strings as she walked to the back of the cart. Jubal protested her every step. Ignoring him, she snatched her father's worn leather bag then faced the men. "If one of you wouldn't mind riding along with Jubal here, I believe it will be faster if I take one of your mounts."

The tall man's eyebrows dove for cover beneath the brim of his cap. The shorter just strapped her bag to the side of his bay. Jubal prophesied the wrath of God and Aunt Rosamund.

And all gasped when she hauled herself astride and snapped the horse into motion.

It was a hard ride, dirt and rocks flying behind her and the soldier. The path to the fort wasn't well used from this direction, making it a challenge to stay in the saddle. By the time they charged through the wooden gates of Fort Snelling, her thighs ached from holding on and her fingers from gripping the reins. The soldier halted in front of the dispensary and hopped down. She followed suit, her feet barely touching the ground before he unstrapped the leather bag and shoved it into her hands. Had her father felt this unprepared, clutching his tools, dashing through a door into moaning and mortality?

Inside, a soldier lay on a table, soaked in blood and sweat. A woman hovered over him, wiping his head with a cloth.

Emmy darted into action with a "pardon me" to the woman

and a visual assessment of the man's leg. Ruined flesh gaped below the poor cloth tourniquet, but at least the fabric held.

Straightening, she unbuttoned her coat and hung it on a peg then grabbed a stained apron off another, all the while spouting orders. "I'll need a bite stick for his mouth, plenty of brandy or whatever alcohol is on hand, and a poultice of milkweed and comfrey. Oh, and two strong men to hold him down."

"Are you mad?" A deep voice boomed behind her. "What you need is a bone saw and a tenaculum!"

She whirled.

Framed in the doorway, a broad-shouldered man shrugged out of a coat—a well-tailored blue woolen. His green eyes assessed her as though deciding which part of a cadaver to cut up first.

She stiffened. Who did this arrogant newcomer think he was? She flashed her own perturbed gaze at the soldier and the woman who had yet to carry out her orders. "I thought you said you required my help?"

The soldier shrugged. "Seems the new doc just arrived, Miss Nelson."

"That's Dr. Clark, if you don't mind." The man stalked past the soldier to a washbasin, rolling up his sleeves to the elbows. Dipping his hands in, he cast her a dark look over his shoulder. "And for God's sake, wash your hands. You look as if you've just ridden in from the backcountry."

Resisting the urge to hide her fingernails, she lifted her chin like a shield before battle. "*Doctor* Clark, if amputation is what you're about, you might as well sign the man's death warrant, for he'll have no livelihood out here with one leg."

"If that leg remains attached, I assure you I will be signing the man's death certificate, and you'll be the one to blame. Do you really want that on your head?" His voice lowered. "Now are you going to assist me or not, Nurse?"

She sucked in a breath. Should she back down? Or worse ...humiliate herself and admit she wasn't a trained nurse at all?

❦

James Clark hid his admiration for the feisty woman beneath a scowl. She was a confident one, he'd give her that, though a field nurse likely had to be strong to survive in these backwoods. Intelligence lived behind those blue eyes, flashing like a lightning strike. Strength pulled a jaunty line to her lips. Sweet heavens! Would that they'd met under different circumstances, for very likely, this was a woman who'd not be swayed by convention. A refreshing change from the ladies out East. Grabbing the brush at the side of the basin, he attempted to scrub away such a thought along with the travel grime from beneath his nails.

Miss Nelson's shoes clacked across the wooden floor, clipped and brisk. Water splashed into the porcelain bowl next to his. "I know it doesn't sound like much, Doctor"—she shot him a sideways glance—"but with a steady administration of laudanum to keep the patient still, I've seen milkweed and comfrey work miracles."

Bah! He snatched the towel off a hook, rattling the washstand with the force of it. This was just the sort of backward medicine he expected to encounter and furthermore. . . furthermore. . .

His shoulders sank. Furthermore, this was the entire reason Dr. Stafford had sent him out here. If he didn't make it past this hurdle, he'd never get that fellowship at Harvard Medical School—the one his father had spent his life on pushing him toward.

Gritting his teeth, James crossed to the patient's side and examined the leg. The flesh beneath the knee was mangled, a hotbed for incubation should gangrene decide to grow. What to do? Dare he try the folkish cure suggested by the snip of a woman?

The fellow writhed, pumping out a fresh wave of blood—and making up James's mind. "Heat an iron, and I'll need those instruments. Now!"

Miss Nelson darted over from the basin. "But Dr. Clark—"

His gaze locked onto hers. "Either we are a team, Miss Nelson, or you can walk out that door." He angled his head toward the entrance. "What's it to be?"

Crimson bloomed up her neck and onto her cheeks. The sergeant groaned, and with a whirl of her skirts, she mumbled, "Fine."

It was a quick surgery. Miss Nelson's fingers were nimble, her instincts keen as she handed him tools before he even asked. She only bristled once, when he set saw to bone, but to her credit, she remained silent. The soldier who'd opted to stay, however, emptied his stomach into a nearby bedpan, and the other woman fled out the door. Just as well. The cold air it ushered in cooled the perspiration on his brow. Despite what Miss Nelson may think of him, removing a body part never came easy.

"There we have it." He tied a final suture, and she snipped the silk thread. Apparently when Miss Nelson committed to something, she did so wholeheartedly.

"While you didn't approve of my methods, your help was impeccable." He waited for her to set aside the tray of used instruments and meet his gaze. "Thank you."

She pressed her lips together for a moment then answered. "You're welcome."

They both washed their hands. Each removed their surgical aprons, their movements in unison. The woman may harbor archaic medical knowledge, but God and country, she acted with precision.

Retrieving her overcoat from a peg, she slipped it on. "Goodbye, Dr. Clark. I wish you the best."

He frowned. Oughtn't a nurse continue tending a patient post-op? "You're leaving?"

"Yes. I am expected in Minneapolis." She fumbled with her bonnet strings. "You see, I'm not—"

A woman's scream leached through the door, and Miss Nelson yanked it open. Worse sounds blasted in on a gust of wind. Children crying. Men cursing. Soldiers, horses, and guns. What in the world?

In four long strides, he drew up alongside Miss Nelson and blinked at the bloody chaos being prodded into the compound.

"Good Lord," he breathed. "What is this?"

Chapter Two

Alarm. Fear. Dread. Emotions riffled through Emmy so quickly, her stomach clenched. She stared, horrified, as a wretched group of Sioux spread over the parade ground like an open sore, mostly women and children, many elders, and several warriors—all sporting bruises. This close, face-to-face with the people responsible for her betrothed's death, she expected to feel some morsel of rage. Yet as she watched a soldier raise a horsewhip against a cringing woman, only one feeling pounded stronger with each heartbeat.

Compassion.

"No!" She jumped down the single stair and sprinted toward the man. "Stop!"

The private swung her way with a vow. "Back away, miss. This ain't no place for a lady. These savages—"

"The only savage I see, sir, is the one with a whip in his hand." She snipped out each word, sharp and pointed.

A scowl slashed across his face. "Oh? Injun lover, are you?" He hefted the whip once more. "Maybe you ought to join them, then."

"And maybe you ought to give me your name and rank, soldier." Dr. Clark shoved between them, his shoulders blocking her view of the man, his voice a steel edge. Though she couldn't see the soldier, she had no doubt the fellow probably froze slack jawed. She'd read once that the growl of a tiger could paralyze its prey. Such was the bass tone of the doctor's command. A tremor shivered through her. She'd hate to be on the receiving end of Dr. Clark's anger.

A tug on her sleeve turned her around. Purple spread like a stain from the woman's left eye, and it had swollen nearly shut. Her split lower lip was crusted over with a scab, but even so, she offered a small smile. "Thank you, lady. You are kind."

Emmy blinked, astonished. "You speak English. . .and quite well."

A black-headed boy with eyes the color of a summer sky grabbed on to the woman's buckskin skirt, crying. She lifted the lad, letting him rest his head against her shoulder before she answered. "My husband is a white man. An agent. He will see you are rewarded when he comes for me."

"No need. I'm sure you would've done the same." The words flew from her tongue before she thought, leaving a bitter aftertaste. She sucked in a breath, stunned. How could she say such a thing to someone who may have supported killing innocents?

The woman's gaze stared straight into her soul. "Yes, I would have done the same."

Emmy breathed out, long and low, then startled when fingers gripped her elbow.

"Miss Nelson, shall we?" Dr. Clark tugged her away from the soldiers and their captives. "I've spoken with a lieutenant. These are the 'friendlies,' as he put it. Those not involved in some sort of uprising. Apparently these people are to winter here, down on the flats and, well, you can see for yourself they're mostly women and children, many sick, some beaten. Would you reconsider your stance on leaving? I. . ."

His jaw clenched, and a muscle corded on his neck. Though she'd known him for hardly two hours, she'd wager whatever he was about to say would cost him a dear price.

"I need you." He bent toward her, a rogue grin flashing across his face. "Though I won't admit to saying that in a court of law."

Over his shoulder, she searched the wreck of humanity. There must be more than a thousand souls to tend in this bunch. He'd need more than her help. He'd need a miracle.

And so would she. If she agreed to this, Aunt wouldn't simply have the vapors—she'd suffer an apoplexy. If Papa were here. . .her heart beat faster. She knew exactly what Papa would say.

Squaring her shoulders, she faced the doctor. "I suppose we'll have to clear this with the colonel."

He cocked his head. "Why?"

"I see by the cut of your clothing that you're not military. Nor am I."

His brow crumpled. "I have a six-month commission waiting for me once I walk through the colonel's door, but you? I thought—"

"I'll explain along the way." She set off with a confident step, fighting a sneeze from the dirt kicked up by her own shoes and those of the soldiers and Indians. Her father had brought her here a few times over the past years, and now the knowledge served her well. She waited until the doctor joined her side before she spoke again. "You might as well know I am no nurse, not officially, anyway."

Dr. Clark cut her a sideways glance. "I don't understand. Your work back there was—" He dodged a soldier who parted them like a rock in a stream. "Let's just say I've worked with many assistants, none as intuitive as you."

For the first time since her father's death, genuine warmth wrapped around her heart, as comforting as an embrace and far more effective than the weak afternoon sun. "I may not have a formal education, but I grew up at my father's side, shadowing his every case."

"He was an accomplished physician?"

"Quite." Despite the pain and misery mere paces to her left, a half smile curved her lips. "Some say the best west of the Mississippi."

"Really? What is your father's name? Perhaps I may have heard of him."

"Dr. Edrith Nelson." Her smile soured. Speaking his name was bittersweet.

Dr. Clark's step hitched, as if her wave of anguish moved him as well. "Did you say *Edrith* Nelson?"

"You've heard of him?"

He snorted. "I don't know if you know this, Miss Nelson, but your father's methods are published in many a forum in the East and are a major factor why my sponsor sent me here. I look forward to meeting him."

"I am sorry that won't be possible." She trudged up the few steps to the colonel's front door and paused on the stoop. Clearing her throat, she fought to summon words she didn't want to say while battling an onslaught of tears. If she let one go, the floodgates would open. "My father passed on a fortnight ago."

Clenching her hands into fists, she braced against the sympathy that was sure to follow, for such would be her undoing.

But a gleam brightened the doctor's green gaze. "You are quite the enigma, Miss Nelson." He pushed open the door. "After you."

For a moment, she stood, mouth agape. Was everything about the man unpredictable?

Inside, a makeshift office transformed the foyer. The doctor stepped up to a soldier perched on a stool behind a desk. "Dr. James Clark and Miss Nelson to see Colonel Crooks."

The man didn't so much as look up from a stack of papers. "Can't you see the colonel's got a mess of murderers out there to deal with?"

"Do you think he'd rather deal with the dysentery and typhoid that are even now infecting every soldier in this fort?" The doctor's words fired out like a round of grapeshot.

Emmy lifted her hand to her mouth, hiding a smile.

The soldier jerked to attention. "Who'd you say you are?"

"Private!" A muttonchopped man wearing colonel stripes at his shoulder leaned out an open door down the hall. "Just send them in."

Emmy clenched her skirts. This was it. Meeting with the commanding officer would change the course of her life—and not in a direction Aunt would approve of.

Should she go through with this? Could she? How did one agree to care for a people who'd stolen Daniel from her so long ago?

❧

James strode through the colonel's door, directly behind Miss Nelson's swishing skirts. The colonel stood near a hearth, lifting the flaps of his dress coat so the heat warmed his back-side. He eyed them upon entrance, yet said nothing, the pull of his sideburns accenting a glower. Except for a gilt-framed painting of the crossing at the Potomac, a clock ticking away on a facing wall, and a mirror opposite a window, the walls were as barren as the man's manners, for he had yet to acknowledge them personally. James expected a certain lack of etiquette out here in the wild, but was this what military life would be like?

Stretching himself to full height, James executed a salute he'd practiced to perfection back at Cambridge. "Dr. James Clark, reporting for service, sir."

The colonel dropped his flaps, his boots tapping out a cadence on the wooden floor as he crossed to the window. With one finger, he swept aside a curtain and studied the commotion on the grounds.

And still, the man said nothing.

Miss Nelson exchanged a glance with James, her brows lifting. Clearly she desired him to break the standoff, yet what more should he say? Dr. Stafford had prepared him for many things on this adventure that were "*for his own good*," but a taciturn officer wasn't one of them.

"I've been expecting you these past four weeks." The colonel's voice ricocheted off the glass. He and Miss Nelson flinched, but the colonel didn't seem to notice, for he continued, "Though I suppose the route here was a bit. . .disturbed."

That put it mildly. A steamship with an unsalvageable boiler. The coach with a broken axel. Dead oxen. Cholera at a wayside. Indeed. Fighting the urge to scratch the stubble on his jaw, he maintained his ramrod stance. "It was a piecemeal journey at that, sir."

The colonel allowed the curtain to fall then pivoted. His gaze slid from Miss Nelson to him. The clock ticked overloud. Angry voices pelted the building from outside. Yet the colonel held the deadlock of stares. What in the world went on behind those gunmetal eyes? If he intended a dressing-down, then why not have at it?

"I can see more information will not be forthcoming until you are released, so at ease. The both of you." The colonel swept his arm toward a few empty chairs as he moved behind his desk. "I expect doctors to be boorish at times, but oughtn't you introduce your wife instead of relegating her to anonymity?"

James choked, glad for the sturdy wooden ladder-back beneath him. Miss Nelson blanched to a fine shade of parchment.

"I am sorry for the misunderstanding, sir." He shifted in his seat. "But this woman is not my wife."

Across from him, the colonel's face darkened. "Then you are worse than boorish. We may be on the edge of civilization, Doctor, but we are neither lawless nor immoral."

In the chair next to him, Miss Nelson strangled a small cry.

"No! Nothing like that." Heat crept up his back, his neck, his ears. Sweet mercy, but it was hot in here. "Allow me to explain."

The colonel sat back in his chair, lacing his fingers behind his head. "Fire away."

James tugged on his collar, coercing words past the embarrassment tightening his throat. He could only imagine the discomfort Miss Nelson felt—for he refused to look at her. "When I arrived just a few hours past, I came upon Miss Nelson caring for a sergeant's wounded leg." The colonel pierced the woman with a gaze as sharp as a bayonet. "What the devil?"

Miss Nelson leaned forward. "Two of your soldiers retrieved me from Mendota, sir. I am Dr. Edrith Nelson's daughter. He's recently passed on, so I came in his stead, being your doctor had not yet arrived."

"I see." The colonel sucked in a breath so large, his chest expanded to the point that he might burst. At last, he stood and rounded the desk, offering his hand to the lady and helping her to her feet. "In that case, I thank you. Your willingness to rally to our aid is appreciated, especially at times such as these."

James rose, unwilling to have a lady stand while he sat. Whatever the manners might be out here, his would not falter.

Miss Nelson dipped her head. "I am happy to serve anyone in need, Colonel."

"You are a credit to your father, Miss Nelson. I shall have a lieutenant see you home."

James snapped to attention. "Sir, I request that Miss Nelson remain, and she's agreed."

Dropping the lady's hand, the colonel swooped over to him like a great bird of prey. "What's this?"

"I cannot tend both the military and native occupants of this fort single-handedly." He worked his jaw, for it galled him to have to repeat his earlier words. He'd been beholden to a lady once before. Never again. Still. . . He set his jaw. "I need Miss Nelson's help. She's proven to be a valuable assistant."

The colonel shook his head. "That may be true, but as I said, this is not a lawless garrison. Only married women or slaves may reside inside these walls."

Miss Nelson lifted a hand toward the window. "Yet you're

allowing an entire population of females to stay the winter, many of which are neither married nor slave."

James clenched his teeth, biting back a smirk. Intelligent and plucky? What other qualities did she hide behind those long lashes?

The colonel narrowed his eyes. "They are captives, Miss Nelson. They do not fall into the aforementioned categories."

James grasped the opening that might be the colonel's undoing—though insubordination might very well earn him a night's stay in the brig. "My understanding, sir, is those natives had nothing to do with an uprising and, in many cases, aided the settlers in escaping. You pride yourself on maintaining a lawful camp, yet I ask you, is justice served by locking up those that are as innocent as the victims of the massacre?"

"They will not be locked up, Doctor. They are free to come and go, though it is for their benefit to remain inside the encampment down on the flats."

"And it is to the fort's benefit if Miss Nelson remains as well."

The colonel's nostrils flared. A bullish snort followed. "It is for the safety of the lady that she be escorted to her home."

"Upon my word, Colonel, I will vouch for the lady's safety the entire time she's here." Immediately he stiffened. That had either been the most noble vow he'd ever given—or the most foolish.

"This is highly irregular!" The commander's voice bounced from wall to wall.

Yet Miss Nelson gazed quietly out the window. "So is that." She indicated with the tip of her head.

"My dear." Once again the colonel reached for her hand,

patting it between his. "Life is hard here, and with winter coming on, it will only get worse."

She lifted her chin, and James couldn't help but marvel.

"I understand, sir, but is it not true that God doesn't always call us to the comfortable places?"

With a long sigh, the colonel released her and turned to James. "Keep your eye on this one, Doctor, for she knows her own mind, and quite possibly the mind of God as well. I will hold you fully accountable for her as long as she's here. Is that clear?"

He nodded, stiff and curt, unsure if he should shout a victory cry or hang his head in defeat. After the death of his parents, he'd been responsible for his hellion of a younger sister, and been glad of it when he finally handed her off to a husband.

Hopefully Miss Nelson would be easier to keep track of.

Chapter Three

A rap on the door startled Emmy awake. Rising, she rubbed a kink in her neck from a fitful first night at the fort then lit the lantern on the nightstand. Guilt had nipped her for displacing the dispensary's steward, but after sleeping on a mattress that hadn't been re-ticked in at least a year, she understood his eagerness to leave these quarters and move in with the smithy.

"Five minutes, Miss Nelson." Dr. Clark's deep voice seeped through the door. "I'll await you by the front gate."

Shivering, she dashed the few steps to her trunk, grudgingly left behind by Jubal. Good thing she'd fallen into bed exhausted last night, for if she'd taken the time to undress, she'd surely be frozen by now. The small hearth had given up its ghost of warmth hours ago. She donned a few more layers then, with a quick snuff of the light, dashed off to meet the doctor.

Outside, a few resolute stars lingered in the predawn sky. The first brittle notes of "Reveille" marched across the compound from a bugle boy atop one of the lookout towers. Emmy drew alongside the doctor where he stood next to the massive fort gates. He snapped shut a pocket watch and tucked it away.

"I hope you won't make tardiness a practice, Miss Nelson."

His green eyes bore into hers, but there was a smile at the edges. Picking up his kit, he offered his free hand and aided her through a smaller opening cut into the wooden ingress.

The sentry's gaze followed their movement, and he shut the door behind them.

Her steps, two to the doctor's one, crunched on the frozen weeds, flattened by yesterday's procession. Grey light colored the world and her mood. The closer they drew to the encampment, the slower her pace. Forgiveness was one thing. Forgetting, quite another. It wasn't this tribe that had taken Daniel's life, but she still felt somewhat a traitor for tending to the "enemy."

Shoving down the feeling, she hurried ahead, surprised at how much ground the doctor had gained. "When you said you wanted an early start in the morning, you might've told me what time to expect. It will be a wonder if anyone's even stirring in the camp yet."

"Which is the best time to make our rounds unhindered, and after making diagnoses, we'll use the rest of the day to administer treatments."

The trail skirted the fort's rock walls, just like her mind circled the doctor's words, trying to make sense of them. Ahh. Of course. Understanding dawned as bright as the orange band rising on the eastern horizon. She peeked up at him. "I gather you're accustomed to a hospital setting."

"I am." He paused at the apex of a sudden sharp descent in the trail and once again offered her his hand. "It's a bit treacherous here. Hold on."

His fingers wrapped around hers, and as they picked their way down to the river flats, he righted her when a rock gave way or her shoe caught in a dip. Each time, the strength in his grasp warmed through her gloves and burned up her arm. A base reaction, surely. His attention couldn't mean anything, for had he not sworn to the colonel to see to her safety? Even so, she liked the way their fingers entwined so perfectly, the way his arm bumped against hers now and again, solid and reassuring.

La! She sucked in a lungful of frigid air, feeling a traitor to Daniel's memory twice over. Better to put her mind on other things than the feel of this man's grip.

"Why are you here, Dr. Clark?" she asked. "You don't seem the sort of man to—"

She clamped her mouth shut. What had gotten into her to speak so freely?

He glanced down at her. "What sort is that, I wonder?"

The first rays of sun stretched across his clean-shaven jaw. His hat rode neatly atop brown hair, brushed back and trimmed since yesterday. Morning light rode his shoulders like a mantle of power. His step was confident, his manners impeccable. She leaned a bit closer and sniffed. Mixing with the acrid scent of early-morning fires rising from the camp, the spicy fragrance of sandalwood tickled her nose, just as she'd expected.

She smiled up at him. "I should think you are better suited to ballrooms and dinner parties than to a rugged outpost in Minnesota."

He chuckled. "Indeed. You are perceptive, Miss Nelson, and very correct. My time here is a temporary yet necessary step if I'm to be considered for a fellowship at Harvard. Competition for the position is fierce. Most applicants have only book knowledge. I hope to gain an advantage by field experience."

The trail evened out, and he released her hand. Cold crept up her arm, and she shivered.

Dr. Clark stepped up to one of the armed guards blocking a crude log gate. Withdrawing a signed pass from the colonel, he handed it over.

The soldier leaned aside and spit then gave the paper back. "Don't know why you want to tend these animals. Ain't worth the time, you ask me."

"I didn't." The doctor's tone lowered. "So open the gate and save your commentary."

The soldier glowered, his skin pocked and ruddy at the cheeks. Red hair, far too long for regulation, shot out from beneath his cap. For a moment she wondered if he'd comply, but with a snap of his head, the other men set about removing the log.

The doctor turned to her with a boyish jaunt to his step. "And so the experience begins, hmm?"

She bit the inside of her cheek. He could have no idea of the apprehension churning in her stomach. Papa would want her to help; Daniel and Aunt Rosamund wouldn't.

Still, she'd given her word.

As she looked over the slipshod village of buffalo-hide tepees, her gaze followed the rise of smoke curling out the tops like pleading prayers—and she added one of her own.

Oh Lord, please use this experience to benefit Dr. Clark and bring healing to the Indians—and to my heart.

<hr />

All the pleasantness of walking with Miss Nelson vanished the moment James stepped into the internment camp. Death was in the air, as tangible as the misty vapor snorted out from the horses they passed. Moaning, coughing, retching...the sounds of suffering nearly drove him to his knees.

Clusters of tepees formed a circle on the patch of cleared ground, bordered on two sides by the confluence of the Mississippi and Minnesota Rivers. Good for fresh water, bad for flooding.

Sharp groans from the tent on his right severed his speculations. He met the eyes of Miss Nelson. "You ready?"

She nodded.

For a moment, he paused at the flap of a door. How exactly did one enter such a shelter? There was no knocker or even something solid to rap against. Ought he call a greeting or—

Another cry of pain and he yanked the flap open and dove in.

The stench inside twisted his gut. Good thing he'd not eaten breakfast. A tiny fire burned at the center, adding fumes to the noxious stink of dysentery. Beside him, Miss Nelson pressed a hand to her stomach, yet did not gag. Two women and three small children huddled on woolen blankets on one side of the tent. A disheveled elder curled into a ball opposite them, releasing another wail.

Reaching into his greatcoat pocket, he retrieved a small pad of paper and a pencil.

Miss Nelson edged closer to him, lowering her voice to a whisper. "Is that all you're going to do, scratch a few notes? Will you not examine her first?"

"No need. The odor in here and the way she's clutching her abdomen says it all. The woman has dysentery. I'll order clean bedding and plenty of fresh water."

"You might want to add castor oil and ginger to that water."

He stifled a huff, anything to keep from breathing more than necessary. "Unconventional, but not dangerous. I suppose it's worth a try."

Though doubtful they understood, he mumbled a thank-you to the tent's inhabitants; then he and Miss Nelson retreated outside to the mercy of fresh air. By now, the sun cleared the horizon, washing the encampment in hope—but not for long. The pathetic bawl of a baby pulled Miss Nelson from his side and into the next tent.

He dashed after her and grabbed her sleeve, holding her back. "Stay next to me. Touch nothing." He didn't need to tell her to cover her nose, for she pressed her palm against her face.

The stench of death hung low and heavy, thick as the smoke suspended over the fire at the center. On one blanket, two skeletal girls clung to each other, locked forever in a perverse embrace. Sometime during the night, both had passed on. Across from them, a woman lay, staring up at their entrance, a baby crying in her arms. Both wore the first bloom of a spreading rash. Once again he drew out his notebook.

Miss Nelson wrenched from his grasp and darted ahead, grabbing a dipper of water on her way toward the babe.

His heart skipped a beat. "Miss Nelson! If that woman has smallpox, you've just exposed yourself."

She didn't so much as acknowledge him, just lifted the water to the woman's lips while she cooed to settle the baby. He watched, horrified and helpless.

"Look closer, Doctor," she called over her shoulder. "It's measles."

A growl rumbled in his chest. "Then you've exposed yourself to—"

"Nothing. I've already had it."

Ought he rejoice or admonish? He settled for a sigh. "I'll have an attendant remove these bodies. There's no more we can do for the woman and her babe but let time heal and set up a quarantine around this tent."

Miss Nelson rose, skirting the small fire. "Clearly this woman can't care for the babe. Maybe I ought stay and—"

"While your concern does you justice, truly, you will be of more help by coming with me." He pocketed his notes and held the flap aside. "After you."

She hesitated, her brow creasing a disagreement. After the space of a few breaths, she swept past him. He ducked out after her, expecting a fight.

Instead, she huddled next to his side, pale faced and silent. What the devil?

In front of them, one of the few native men strode by, neither addressing nor even looking at them. Why would a passing captive cause her skirts to quiver so?

He guided her aside, into the harbor between two tent walls. "Is there something I should know, Miss Nelson?"

She averted her gaze, focusing on tugging her coat sleeves well past her wrists. "It's nothing. I'm fine, Doctor."

He frowned. "Yet you tremble."

"It's cold."

"It's more than that." Setting down his bag, he lifted her chin with a finger, forcing her to quit fussing with her sleeves. "Tell me."

A sigh deflated her. Around them, the sounds of fires being stoked and waking children increased.

Lifting an eyebrow, he cocked his head, an effect that

ofttimes worked like a charm. "Either you tell me now, or I suspect we'll have an audience very soon."

Her eyes flashed. "Very well. If you must know, I was betrothed once. Daniel was a surveyor, the best, really. Which is why the government sought him out. He was on a project west of here. Pawnee country."

Her words slowed like the winding down of a clock, the last coming out on a ragged whisper. "He never came back."

Pain twisted her face, the kind of agony he witnessed when imparting the news of a loved one's death. But this time, a distinct urge settled deep in his bones to gather her in his arms and hold her until the pain went away. He clenched his hands, once again feeling helpless—and dug his nails into his palms.

"Perhaps he will come back." He regretted the platitude as soon as it left his lips.

Her pain disappeared, replaced with a dark scowl. "You do not understand the Pawnee, Doctor."

Morning sun angled between the tents, lighting the complex woman in front of him. No wonder she took the suffering of others to heart, for it was a familiar companion.

He reached for her then lowered his hand, suddenly ashamed. "I am discovering, Miss Nelson, there is much I do not understand."

Chapter Four

Emmy paced at the front gate, working a rut into the dirt. Overhead, the late-November sun was lethargic, the entire world washed of autumn's brilliance. It was the brown time, the dead. . .as if color packed up its bags and fled before winter arrived.

Glancing over her shoulder, she squinted along the parade ground toward the colonel's quarters, past soldiers scrambling for inspection. The door that'd swallowed Dr. Clark an hour ago remained shut. She lifted her eyes higher, over the roof, where a cloud of smoke rose from the river flats below. She'd dallied too long already.

Despite the doctor's instructions to wait for him, she turned to the sentry. "Could you let Dr. Clark know I've gone ahead?"

Morning light caught the fuzz on his chin. The man-boy could hardly be more than sixteen. "Sure, miss. Not like him to be late, eh?"

Her lips quirked. "Over the past three weeks, I daresay we've both learned he's punctual to a fault."

"Truth is"—the sentry's gaze shifted side to side, then he stepped closer, lowering his voice for her ears only—"I'd rather take a whoopin' than live through another one of Dr. Clark's tongue-lashings. But don't tell him I said so."

"Your secret is safe with me." She mimicked his conspiratorial stance. "For I quite agree."

She strolled through the gate—already open for the day—accompanied by the soldier's laughter.

The trail didn't seem as long anymore. She might even wager on her ability to trek it in the dark. This was the first time, though, that no strong arm steadied her on the descent. She missed that. And, surprisingly, she also missed the doctor's banter, stimulating as the black coffee served for breakfast. A frown tugged her mouth as she sniffed. Neither was the air quite as sweet without the hint of his sandalwood shaving tonic. Yes, though this be the same path, this time, everything was different.

Her balance teetered on some loosened sandstone, as unsettling as her rogue thoughts. She threw out her hands, her father's bag nearly flying from her grasp. Pausing, she negotiated her next step and the curious attachment she felt to the doctor. Working long days, side by side, it was only natural to grow accustomed to a person's ways. Surely that's why she missed Dr. Clark's presence this morn.

That settled, she picked her way down the embankment, praying all the way that Private Grainger wouldn't be on sentry duty today, especially without the doctor at her side. The newly built walls of the encampment towered in front of her, and she smirked at the irony of the timbers. The very people group who attacked whites now needed to be protected from them.

She scurried ahead, her heart sinking to her stomach when she saw the shock of red hair shooting out from beneath a private's cap. A feral smile lit his face, one that would surely visit her nightmares. She held out her pass as a buffer.

Ignoring her paperwork, Grainger looked past her. "Where's Doc?"

"I'm sure he'll be along shortly. And I'm also sure you ought to address him as Doctor Clark, whether he's present or not."

"That so?" His gaze returned to her, touching her in places that ought not be touched. "Why don't you wait here? Not safe for a lone white woman in there."

Hah! As if remaining with the private was any safer. She bit the inside of her cheek, reminding herself to be charitable. "I've tended these people the past three weeks, Private Grainger. I know my way around by now."

"Snakes, the lot of 'em. Just waitin' for a chance to strike." Tobacco juice shot from his mouth and hit the ground. Swiping a hand across his mouth, he winked at her. "And yer mighty fine quarry."

She stiffened, taking courage in rigid posture. "Open the gate, or I shall report you."

"Your word against mine."

Heat crept up her neck. He'd never speak this way if the doctor were with her, and she couldn't decide what irked her more—that the presence of another man would stave off his remarks, or the way his tongue ran over his lips.

She gripped her father's bag so tightly, the strain might rip a seam in her gloves. "Who do you think the colonel will believe, Private? A lecherous good-for-nothing hiding behind a uniform, or a lady?"

His face darkened, and he lunged.

But she refused to budge. If he touched her, a court-martial would get him out of here faster than a scream.

A breath away, he pulled up short, a vulgar laugh rumbling in his chest. "Just playin' with ya, missy. Soldier's gotta have a little fun, don't he?"

He raised a fist and pounded on the gate. "Open up!"

She darted inside as soon as it opened far enough for her to pass through sideways.

Makawee's tent—the woman she'd saved from a whipping that first day—was the second on the right. The sound of retching broke Emmy's heart. She never should have waited so long to come.

Emmy tossed up the flap and stepped inside. This late in the morning, the rest of the tent's occupants were on their way to line up for roll. In front of her, a woman bent over a bucket, emptying her stomach.

"Oh Makawee, I'm so sorry I didn't get here sooner." Emmy opened her father's bag and produced a small pouch, the scent of lemon balm and peppermint a welcome fragrance.

Makawee straightened, a weak smile belying the strain on her face. "It will pass, Miss Emmy. It is the way of nature."

"Even so, I've brought you some different herbs to try instead of ginger." She held out the pouch. "It's best for you and the babe if you can keep down food."

Across the tent, a little boy crawled out from a buffalo hide and launched himself at her.

Emmy grinned and swung the lad up in her arms. "Good morning, little Jack. How is this fine fellow today?"

"Growing as strong as his father." Makawee's eyes rested on her son; then she lifted her face to Emmy, pain tightening her jaw. "Have you any news?"

"Not yet. I'm sure your husband is doing all he can to get here."

Makawee's chest heaved, and then the moment passed like a fall tempest, her brown eyes clear and unblinking. "You speak truth, and I thank you."

Emmy reached out her free arm and rested it on the woman's shoulder. "I admire your strength, my friend."

She stifled a gasp. Had that sentiment really come from her lips? What was happening to her emotions? First missing a man she'd hardly known three weeks, and now such respect for a Sioux woman?

Makawee averted her gaze. "It is God's grace. Nothing other."

Emmy's admiration grew, for the woman had not only left behind tradition by marrying an Irishman but her religion as well, turning to the "White Christ," as she called it. Both actions required strength.

Setting down the boy, Emmy patted his head. "I should check on Old Betts, poor thing. I'll stop in tomorrow to see how the new herbs work for you."

"Thank you, Miss Emmy. God smile on you."

"And you."

Outside, natives filtered back to their shelters, clogging the small roads between tents. Apparently roll was finished. She'd have to let the lieutenant know Makawee and her little boy were fine, but first, she ought to get laudanum to Old Betts.

Veering left, she squeezed onto the tight trail sometimes used by the doctor. The dirt path ran along the wall, skirting the tepees.

She raced ahead but then slowed when a warrior stepped

into her path, arms folded, face hardened to flint. There'd be no easy way to pass him. Maybe this shortcut wasn't the best route after all. She turned.

And one tent down, another native blocked her route.

The first ember of fear flared to life in her chest. Surely they didn't mean to trap her. Perhaps they'd simply had a pre-arranged meeting here, that's all—one best not hindered.

Darting ahead, she veered left, onto the path between two tepees—and nearly collided with the chest of another man.

Panic burned the back of her throat. Even so, she lifted her chin. "Let me pass."

He advanced, forcing her back, until the wall clipped into her shoulder blades. A hare couldn't have been more cornered.

Stony faces searched hers. The man to her left pushed back her bonnet and reached for her hair. A flash of morning sun glinted off a knife at his side. *These are friendlies*, she reminded herself. Still. . .how had he gotten a knife in the first place? Worse—her mouth dried to ashes—had that blade taken any scalps?

A tear slid down her cheek. She never should have come here alone. And what would a scream accomplish? Private Grainger would only join in the game.

"Please." She trembled, and the tear dripped off her chin. "Let me go."

"You let her go—alone?" James grabbed Grainger by the throat and shoved him against the timber wall, the smack of the private's head satisfying. "You were issued the same warning as I!"

The private's lips moved like a fish out of water. Just a little more pressure, and the esophagus would collapse, taking the trachea with it. James closed his eyes, praying for his anger to pass. Was this weasel of a man even worth this much passion? Stifling a growl, he threw Grainger to the ground and pounded on the gate. "Open up! Dr. Clark here!"

Grainger coughed and choked.

In the eternity it took for the gate to swing open, James flexed and released his fists, several times over, trying to calm the rage churning in his gut. Blast the colonel for wasting his time on a simple case of food poisoning. Double-blast sentries foolish enough to let a woman walk headlong into danger. And—*God, help her*—blast Miss Emmaline Nelson for her independent streak. Confidence would surely be the woman's undoing.

Clearing the gate, he sprinted to Makawee's tent first, dodging elders and children. She and Miss Nelson had developed quite a friendship, and hopefully the women yet chattered or played with little Jack.

He ducked through the tent flap. "Miss Nelson?"

Inside, the boy played with two sticks and some beads on a nearby fur. Makawee looked up from a pot she stirred over a small fire at the center. But no blond-haired, blue-eyed vixen—or anyone else—was inside.

Makawee stopped her stirring. "Miss Emmy is gone to Old Betts. Is there a problem, Doctor?"

"There'd better not be." He shot back outside, trying to erase the colonel's warning of unrest in the camp, that recent attacks against native women by imbecile soldiers like Grainger had angered the men.

That rumblings of revenge ran hot and thick.

With roll finished and nowhere else to go, women and

children filled the camp roads—and Old Betts resided on the opposite side. It would take twice as long to navigate the main route, so he wove his way through tepees and dodged into the thin space between tents and wall.

Ahead, a few native men blocked the way, but that was the least of his worries. He dashed forward, sure that his heartbeat wouldn't resume a normal cadence until he found Miss Nelson. But as he drew closer, blond hair flashed at the center of the trio. His heart missed a beat. Emmaline stood ramrod straight, tears dripping off her jaw, her father's bag spilled open on the ground. To her left, a man held a handful of her hair to his nose. On her right, a tall warrior bent, burying his face against her neck. And in front, a shirtless brave reached out and trailed his fingers along her collarbone.

James dropped his bag and pulled out a gun.

"Touch her again, and you're dead where you stand." He fingered the trigger.

Three pairs of dark eyes locked onto his.

Only one spoke. "This woman yours?"

"She is." The words sank low in his gut. How dare he claim such a thing? Promising the colonel he'd look out for her was one thing, but this? The flare of the warriors' nostrils, the flash of white in their eyes, told him he'd just announced something far more.

Yet it accomplished his purpose. They filed away, one by one, disappearing between the tents.

Emmaline neither turned his way nor collapsed to the ground. She stood, face washed in tears, staring straight ahead.

Everything in him wanted to race to her side, cradle her close and never let go. But he forced one foot in front of the other, slowly, fluidly, until he stood a few breaths in front of her. "Miss Nelson?"

She didn't move. She hovered somewhere beyond his reach, trapped in the terror of the experience. He'd seen patients succumb to shock, and it was never pretty.

"Emmaline!"

Her chest fluttered with a shallow breath—then heaved. Great sobs poured out her mouth, and James wrapped his arms around her, praying God would use his embrace to bring peace.

"Shh. It's all over. I'm here. I've got you." He rubbed circles on her back, waiting for her weeping to subside. He'd let her go then.

But as her tears soaked through his shirt and warmed his skin, he realized that was a lie. He might release her, but he'd never let her go.

And God help the man who tried to take her from him.

Chapter Five

Wind lashed like a bullwhip through the few inches of open window, slicing into Emmy's back. Setting down her pestle, she pivoted and crossed the few steps of the dispensary to wrench the glass closed. Despite the barrier, she shivered. The morning had dawned sunny and carefree, but now pewter clouds hung low, smothering the fort with a threat. They'd been fortunate thus far with no snow, but with December half-spent, that blessing was stretched tight and ready to snap.

Behind her, the front door blew open, smacking into the wall with a crack. She couldn't help but jump, for since the awful encounter at the encampment, her nerves balanced on a fine wire.

She whirled, and her jaw dropped. A woman entered, her dark eyes burning like embers. Her face twisted by fear.

"Makawee?" Emmy ran to her. How strange it was to see the woman inside wooden walls instead of buffalo hide. "What are you doing here? How did you—"

"Little Jack is missing." Her voice was as raw as the chapped skin on her cheeks.

Emmy stiffened. "What do you mean, missing? How could

he possibly get out of camp?"

"With snow coming, the soldiers led a group to collect wood. I brought Jack. When we were to leave, he was gone. The men would not search, nor let me. I slipped away but could not find him. Please." Makawee's fingers dug into Emmy's sleeve. "Will you and Dr. Clark come?"

Images of the blue-eyed rascal, alone in the woods, maybe crying—maybe hurt—horrified her. Emmy's hand shot to her chest. A two-year-old wouldn't survive long out there.

"I'll find the doctor." She dashed to the sick ward's door. It was doubtful he'd be there, though, for only one private occupied a bed, having imbibed too much and fallen down some stairs. Served him right to break a leg. The man slept open-mouthed on his cot, his snores filling the empty room.

Emmy darted past Makawee, who stood wringing her hands where she'd left her. Opposite the sick ward was a supply room, but that led to a door kept shut, one she beat with her fist. "Dr. Clark?"

She listened, willing herself to hear his strong steps on the other side. Nothing but panes of glass chattering like teeth answered her.

"Doctor!" She tried again.

Nothing.

Resting her fingers on the latch, she hesitated. Dare she? What would Aunt think of her entering a man's chambers?

She sucked in a breath and pushed open the door. "Dr. Clark, please. . ." Her words fell to the floor. No doctor sat at the tidy desk against the wall, or closed his eyes on the made bed, or sat lacing his shoes on the chair in the corner. The orderliness didn't surprise her. That he'd left the building without a word of his whereabouts did.

Retracing her steps, she grabbed her coat off the hook, ignoring Makawee's haunted look. "Maybe the doctor was called by the colonel. Wait here."

She flew out the door. If she couldn't find him, then what? No way would she venture out alone, not after what happened last time. She set her jaw. He had to be there, that's all.

A few soldiers scurried across the parade ground, all eager for the warmth of a fire instead of the wicked air. No one paid her any mind. Since word of the doctor's rage last month when he'd come to her aid, most men left her alone.

As she ascended the steps to the colonel's office, a soldier strode out the front door.

"Excuse me, but is Dr. Clark about?" She craned her neck, hoping to glimpse the doctor beyond his shoulder. "He is needed."

"No, ma'am. Haven't seen him."

The fellow whisked past her, and for a moment, she tried not to give in to panic. Where in the world had he gone? Ought she take a horse and try to find Jack on her own? The question hit her like a boulder fallen into still waters, jarring, disturbing, sending out ripples of fear and trepidation. Her throat closed. No. That was not an option.

The next gust of wind slapped her cheek with icy pellets, and she raced back to the dispensary, where Makawee greeted her with hopeful eyes.

Emmy shook her head. "It appears Dr. Clark is missing as well."

Makawee reached for the door. "Then you and I will go."

"No, Makawee." She tugged the woman back. "It's no more

safe for you to be outside the camp walls than it is for me to be inside. Not to mention that you are with child."

Makawee spun, an angry slant on her lips. "I will not sit here—"

"But that's exactly what we must do. As soon as Dr. Clark returns, he will help. I am sure of it."

"No!" The woman flung out her hands, her voice rising like a fever. "My husband is gone; I will not lose my son too. I will go. I will find him."

"Listen!" Emmy grabbed her friend's shoulders and shook, praying the action would jolt her to her senses. "Either God is in control or He is not. What do you believe?"

The question slammed into her own heart. If she really believed God was in control, would she not sacrifice her safety for the rescue of one of His little ones?

"You are right," Makawee finally breathed out. "The Creator governs all."

"Then let us hope and trust in Him with full confidence, hmm?" She spoke loudly, boldly, forcing the words to fill the frightened cracks in her soul.

Makawee's mouth wavered, not into a smile, not when her son was somewhere out in a land as cruel as the wind beating against the door. But Emmy took it as a smile, anyway.

"You are a gift, Miss Emmy."

She frowned and tightened her bonnet strings. "I doubt Dr. Clark will think so when he discovers I've gone ahead without him."

⁂

Twice! Twice in the space of a month. James kicked his horse into a gallop, following the flattened path of grass that led to a stand of woods. Fool-headed, strong-willed woman. He'd excused the first time she'd ventured out alone, chalking it up to naivete, but after his stern warning to never leave the dispensary without him?

Sleet stung his face, as goading as Miss Nelson's disregard for his rule. This time he ought to take her over his knee when he found her. A cold worry lodged behind his heart as the sleet changed to snow. *If* he found her.

He reined the horse to a walk and entered the trees, leaning forward to study the ground. He should've thought to ask a scout to accompany him. What did he know of tracking anything other than the course of a disease? Already snow gathered in a thin but growing layer, covering leaves that might've been kicked up by hooves. And here in the wood, the last of day's light faded to a color as dark as his hope. Which way would she have gone?

Dismounting, he scanned the area for a better clue. Wind rattled the branches overhead, mocking his rash decision to search for her alone—and then it hit him. He lifted his face to the iron sky.

"I am as culpable as Miss Nelson, eh, Lord? Letting emotion get the better of me, running ahead of You time and again, wanting to help others but not waiting for Your lead. Oh God"— he drew in a ragged breath—"forgive me, even as I forgive her."

The next gust of wind did more than shake tree limbs—it waved a small snatch of cloth tied to the end of a low-hanging branch. His breath eased. He knew that bit of calico, for he'd often admired the way it followed Miss Nelson's curves.

Launching himself into the saddle, he trotted the horse

over to it then squinted in the whiteness to catch another glimpse of bright fabric. There. Not far off. He fought a rogue smile, wondering just how much of her skirt might be missing when he caught up to her.

He didn't wonder long. Ahead, a dark shape walked, a bedraggled swath of blond hair hanging down at the back.

"Emmaline!" He dug in his heels.

"Doctor?" She turned. "Thank God!"

He slid from the horse before it stopped and ran to her. The way she cradled her left arm, the sag of her shoulders, the stream-clear eyes now clouded to muddy waters—all of it screamed agony, and not just from want of a missing boy.

"You're hurt." He reached for her.

"I'm fine." She shrugged away, but not before he caught the slight groan she couldn't disguise.

"I know an injury when I see one. Now are you going to let me examine that arm, or are we going to stand here and waste time?"

Snow collected on her long lashes as she stared at him. It would do no good to prod her further. *Wait for it. Wait.* And there, the pursing of her lips, a standard signal she was about to give in.

She offered up her arm, her nose wrinkling with a poorly concealed wince.

He stepped closer, using one hand to brace her arm, the other to peel back layers of sleeves. "What happened?"

"A falling branch spooked my horse, and he threw me. I landed wrong, and—ah!" She grimaced.

Her pain sliced into his soul as he did what he must— probe for fractures or breaks. "Sorry. Won't be a moment more. You were saying?"

"By the time I stood, my mount was gone. Ow!" She gasped once more then scowled up at him. "That hurt."

"No doubt." Examination finished, he released her. "That's quite a sprain. It's not broken, though it will take some time to heal."

"Good." She sidestepped him and strode to his horse. "Then let's continue."

"Hold on." He pulled her back, taking care not to jostle her injury overmuch. "That arm needs to be wrapped first, and—"

"No, I'll ride with you and keep it as immobile as possible. Little Jack is still out here. His life is on the line, now more than ever." Fat, white flakes collected on her bonnet, adding emphasis to her words.

A sigh—or mayhap defeat—emptied his lungs of air. "Fine."

He hoisted her into the saddle then swung up behind her. She never cried out, but her muffled grunts belied her brave front.

She used her good arm to point. "That way."

He narrowed his eyes, trying to make sense of her confidence in the growing whirl of whiteness. "What makes you so sure?"

"My father was often called to tend settlers here, and—Oh!"

The horse lurched sideways and she slipped. Shifting the reins to one hand, he wrapped his other arm around her, settling her against his chest.

She peeked up at him, an accusing arch to her brow.

He winked. "In situations such as this, Miss Nelson, propriety be hanged."

She nestled back, allowing his hold. As much as he wanted to find the boy and get them all to safety, he gave in to the sweet feel of the woman snuggled against his coat.

"There's a ravine not far from here with a maze of fallen trunks," she continued. "A haven for a young boy in search of adventure."

"How do you know little Jack is in this wood?"

"It's near to where Makawee gathered kindling earlier this afternoon. That and, before the snow started falling, I followed a trail in the dirt from a dragged stick. Wild animals don't play with sticks, but little boys do."

"Except for when it comes to your own safety, Miss Nelson"—he bent his head so she'd hear not only the words but the admiration in his voice—"you are a very wise woman."

She stilled in his arms, and slowly her face lifted to his—but then she leaned forward, pointing, a cry of pain accompanying the movement. "There!"

"Wait here." He missed her warmth the moment he dismounted. Picking his way down the ravine, he alternated between calling for Jack and straining to listen.

Halfway down, he stopped. Then turned.

"Jack?"

Beneath a fallen trunk, in a world of white and cold, a dark little head peeked out, wailing for his mama.

"Thank You, God," James whispered as he scooped up the lad and hefted him to his shoulder. The boy's tears burned onto his neck.

No. Wait.

Holding the boy in one arm, he yanked his glove off the other with his teeth then pressed the back of his hand to the lad's forehead.

Fire met his touch. And as he looked in the boy's throat, a

blaze raged there as well.

He worked his way back to Miss Nelson, thanking God for her injured arm. There was no way she could hold the boy, exposing her to—no. He wouldn't think it. He couldn't be sure of the lad's diagnosis yet, but even so, he would buffer Emmaline by putting the boy in front of him and her behind. She may have survived measles, but he was pretty sure she'd not yet experienced the reason why he'd been absent from the fort in the first place.

Setting up quarantine for those with smallpox.

Chapter Six

Emmy retrieved the last cloth from a bucket of cold water and wrung it out as well as she could with a tender wrist. How many times had she done this the past week? She frowned at the cracked, red skin on her hands. Clearly, too many.

Coughs and a few moans followed her across the sick ward. Winter winds raged against the windows, but the blankets she'd nailed up blockaded drafts from attacking those too helpless to parry. No sense adding more misery to the men suffering from the spate of severe measles.

Major Clem occupied the bed nearest the door. When she bent to lay the cloth on his brow, his eyes popped open, glassy and shot through with red.

His lips worked a moment before any sound came out. "Thirsty."

"Good, I've just the thing for you." She smiled, taking care to mimic the soothing tone her father used to employ. Papa always said healing was more than medicine. *Oh Papa.*

She straightened, once again shoving grief to a cellar in her heart. "I'll be back in a trice with some licorice-root tea, Major."

Crossing to the dispensary door, she eased it open, glad she'd stood her ground for the extra bear grease. The men slept fitfully enough without ill-mannered hinges scraping against their ears.

Sweet tanginess rode the crest of the smoky scent in the room, and she inhaled deeply as she drew nearer the hearth. Some said licorice smelled of wildness, the untamed spoor kicked up by one's feet when tromping through loamy earth, but not her. Why, she'd pour herself a large mug just for the sheer enjoyment of it if they weren't so low on stock.

"Afternoon, Miss Nelson." Dr. Clark's voice entered on an icy gust from the front door. "How goes it?"

She felt the touch of his eyes upon her, and irrationally wished she'd chosen her green serge instead of her drab grey. La! What a thought. She was worse than a moonstruck schoolgirl. Even so, after she returned the kettle to the grate, she smoothed her skirts before she faced him.

The doctor shrugged out of his coat, waistcoat fabric taut across the muscles of his back as he reached to hang it on a peg. Ahh, but she could look at that fine sight all day and never tire of the long lines, of the suggestion of strength and protection. And when her thoughts strayed to what lay beneath that fabric, heat flared up her neck.

"Quite dashing," she murmured.

"Sorry?" He pivoted, head cocked.

She grabbed handfuls of her apron to keep from slapping a hand over her mouth, for surely that would be even more indicting. "Oh, er, the day is quite dashing away from me, I'm afraid. How goes it down at the camp?" She rushed on. "How is little Jack faring?"

One of his brows quirked as he crossed to the counter and set down a package. "Makawee won't let me near him. Swears by the 'old medicine,' as she calls it."

"Good. It is enough you tend the smallpox victims on your own. You needn't add another disease to your repertoire."

A muscle jumped in his jaw. "I am no novice, Miss Nelson. I assure you, I take every precaution."

"Of course." She bit her lip as warmth bloomed over her cheeks. Sweet heavens! What was wrong with her tongue today? Or any day, for that matter. Whenever the man entered the room, her words flew out before she could think. "I am sorry. I never meant to imply such."

Little crinkles highlighted the sides of his mouth as he grinned. "Apology accepted. And you'll be glad to know Jack's rash has stopped spreading."

"Then he's on the mend, unlike a few of the men in there." She nodded toward the ward, though she needn't have—wretched coughing crept from under the closed door. "Truthfully, I fear for Major Clem, which reminds me..." She reached for the mug of tea.

But the doctor stayed her arm with a light touch. "Then I've come just in time. I've brought something."

There was almost a bounce to his step as he retrieved the package from the counter and ripped it open, revealing a small wooden box. He held it out to her like a crown of jewels to be admired. "A new shipment of fresh leeches, which was quite the feat in this weather."

She suppressed a groan but couldn't stop the censure in the shake of her head. "You know my feelings on the matter."

He drew back his box, taking the warmth in his voice with

it. "The siphoning out of bad blood is proven science, Miss Nelson."

"Maybe so, yet my experience proves it weakens the patient. My father said—"

His hand shot up, and what was left of his grin faded into a straight line. "Not another lecture. If your methods are not working with the major, then it's time you use scholarship."

The implication smacked her. Hard. *Scholarship?* As if what she'd been using was nothing but folderol and superstition? For a moment, she clenched her teeth so tightly, crackling sounded in her ears. Perhaps she should give in to Aunt's entreaties, go where she was wanted, find an orphanage in the city and tend to their needs instead.

She met his stare dead-on, not wanting to leave, but not wanting to stay either. "Maybe, Doctor, it's time I leave. You barely consider my medical advice, nor do you use me at the encampment anymore. Give me one reason why I should stay."

❦

Because your beautiful smile will no longer brighten this barracks.
Because you are life and breath and air.

James staggered, pushed back by a rush of emotions and the real reason lodging low in his gut.

Because I fear my heart will stop beating without you.

He raked his fingers through his hair, a desperate attempt to push back the wild thoughts and fatigue that ailed him. This couldn't be. When had this snip of a wilderness woman worked her way so deeply into his soul? A relationship with her would change his plans, his future. . .his everything. Everything he'd worked so hard to gain. Years of study. Of jockeying for position on Harvard's wobbly ladder of success. His goal to achieve all his father had dreamed for him. He should just stride to the door, hold it open, and thank the lady for her service.

And while he was at it, he might just as well grab a knife and stab it into his chest.

For a moment, he searched her eyes, desperately trying to judge if leaving was what she really wanted. Did she?

Sweet mercy! The woman ought to be a card shark the way she hid every emotion behind those long lashes. There was no reading her desire—and there was no discounting his.

He forced words past an ache in his throat. "You should stay because I ask it of you."

"But why do you ask?"

The question gaped like the sharp jaws of a bear trap. If he answered too personally, he'd frighten her away. Too detached, and she'd not feel needed. Either would set her and her bags on the next possible wagon out of the fort.

He caught both her hands in his, hoping the added touch might sway her. "Despite our differences on manner of care, the fact is, Miss Nelson, that you do care. I would be hard-pressed to replace you and, in fact, could not. Truth is, I am in over my head at the encampment with this foul weather. I cannot possibly tend to both the men here and the people down below. Would you force me to choose, knowing what the colonel would have me do?"

A sigh deflated her shoulders. "No. Of course not. I will stay, leastwise until you can manage both."

"Thank you." He squeezed her fingers then released his hold. "If it's any consolation, the colonel is holding a Christmas dinner day after tomorrow. Would you do me the honor of attending with me?"

A small smile lifted her lips. "I suppose it would please my aunt to know I am owning some measure of society out here."

"Good." He returned her grin. Though the festivity might pacify her relative, it would please him even more to have her at his side.

Chapter Seven

Emmy scowled into the small looking glass nailed to her chamber wall, her lips a flawless shade of red, her brows arched to perfection—and a rogue curl dangling front and center on her forehead. Stifling a growl, she eased out one more hairpin from the chignon at the back, praying the silly thing wouldn't fall down her neck, then skewered the curl and stabbed it into the puff of hair on top. Oh, to be a princess and command a lady's maid.

"Miss Nelson?" Knuckles rapped on her door. "Are you ready?"

With a final tap on the pin and a whispered, "Behave!" she whirled from the mirror. "Coming."

She lifted the latch, and her heart skipped a beat. Lamplight brushed over Dr. Clark in a golden glow. Did she not know him to be a man, she'd wonder at his supernatural appearance. His hair was slicked back. His jaw, clean shaven. An indigo frock coat contrasted richly with his white shirt, all tailored to ride the long lines of his body. Her glance slid to lighter blue trousers and Hessians that shone with a polish. She tried to catch her breath, but it eluded her, like a milkweed pod blown open, scattering seeds into a thousand directions.

"I fear I shall have my hands full tonight," his deep voice murmured.

She angled her face to his, looking for a clue. Full of what? Had her hair fallen again? His shiny eyes gave no hint.

"Whatever do you mean, sir?"

"Once we walk out that door, I may have to stave off an entire battalion to defend your honor, for I guarantee"—he winked—"you will turn the head of every officer."

"La, sir!" She swatted his arm. He was a charmer, she'd give him that. "How you exaggerate."

He laughed and retreated a step.

Then, shaking his head, his smile faded. His gaze smoldered. "You have no idea how beautiful you are, do you?"

Heat burned a trail to her belly. She swallowed, trying hard to remember Daniel's face, but all she could see were the green eyes of the man in front of her, the strong cut of his forehead, his cheeks. Oh, she'd loved Daniel, but that was long ago, and truthfully. . .she searched memories, shaking them out like a laundered sheet. No, she'd never felt the kind of sweet ache that gripped her when the doctor's gaze wrapped around her and held her in place.

She swallowed, coaxing out a voice that wouldn't crack. "We ought be going. I've made us late enough as is."

But he didn't move. He stood there, fumbling his hand inside his dress coat. "Wait. I've brought you something."

He held out a small box, nested atop his palm. A young lad offering flowers to his girl couldn't have been more proud.

Emmy bit her lip. Why had she not thought to get him something? "I. . .I have no gift for you."

He pressed the box toward her, so that she had no choice

but to take it. "Ah, ah, ah. Doctor's orders."

It was a poor jest, nevertheless a dear one. She lifted the lid and gasped. "Oh!"

Inside, a silk flower brooch, no larger than her thumb, lay on white satin bedding. She pulled it out and examined the tiny rose, one way then another, letting the light set fire to the deep red.

"How lovely." She peered up at him with a smile. "Thank you."

"May I pin it on for you?"

She handed it over, and his fingers brushed against hers, gentle as a fairy's kiss. He stepped closer, so near she inhaled his scent of sandalwood and masculinity. For a moment, she wobbled on her feet, dizzy from the heat of his body.

"There. All done." But his stance contradicted his words, for he didn't step back, nor did his hand lower. His fingers trailed upward from her collar, slowly, as if asking for permission, then slid across her cheek and rested just behind her ear. His eyes flashed with questions, promises. . .desire.

"James?" she whispered.

He dipped his head, and his lips skimmed over hers like a summer breeze. Closing her eyes, she leaned into his embrace, his arms as strong as a beam that could carry her world. Her heart pounded hard in her ears. This—*this*—was where she wanted to be, wanted to live.

For always.

"Emmy." He breathed her name against her mouth, her jaw, her neck.

She shivered—and pressed closer.

With a gasp, the doctor stumbled back a step. The world stopped. Air and life and hope hovered somewhere overhead, beyond reach. Only the rattle of the night air against her window anchored her to the real world.

He drew his hand across his mouth, and it shook—as did his voice. "I am so sorry."

"Are you?" Despite what Aunt would have to say, a wicked half smile tingled on the very lips that had just been so finely kissed, and Emmy lifted her chin. "I am not so sure I am."

∽◦∾

Miss Emmaline Nelson would be the death of him. Carve it on his gravestone, killed by a woman—a beautiful bit of a woman, all fire and passion. And that is exactly what he loved most about her, the unreserved way she gave herself to that which she cared about.

Beads of perspiration lined up like little soldiers at the nape of his neck. One broke rank and trickled down his spine as he stared at her, her eyes full of the knowledge of what lay in his heart. One fingertip ran across her lower lip. Was she remembering?

Or lamenting?

Ah, yes, but such a kiss. One he wouldn't mind repeating—and one that never should've happened in the first place. Working with her from now on would be awkward at best.

He exhaled a shaky breath. "You are right, Miss Nelson."

Her brows shot up, and a delightful curl fell down to meet them. "I am?"

"Yes." He pivoted and held out his arm, eager for a face full of cold night air. "We ought to be going."

The short walk to the colonel's quarters cooled his feverish skin, so much that he shook beneath his greatcoat.

She shot him a sideways glance. "You tremble as if you

have the chills. Are you well?"

He kicked at some snow with the tip of his boot. "Need I remind you I am born and bred a Boston man? I am not used to such a severe climate."

"Well, I think it suits you."

He frowned. "Why?"

She blinked up at him. "Is your temperament not as extreme?"

The pixie! He grinned in full as he led her up the stairs to the colonel's door. "I fear you're coming to know me too well."

The colonel's wife rushed over to them as they entered the foyer. "There you are! And about time too. We are just going in to dinner."

Beyond her, the last blue tail of an officer's jacket disappeared through a door.

"My apologies, Mrs. Crooks." He spoke as he helped Emmy—Miss Nelson, out of her coat. Giving himself a mental thrashing for his lapse, he removed his coat as well, handing both off to the servant standing nearby. It would not do to think of Emmy too intimately, or her Christian name would fall unguarded from his lips.

Miss Nelson stepped nearer the colonel's wife, mischief in the tap of her shoes. "The doctor was working overtime."

The woman's hands fluttered to her chest. "Nothing serious, I hope."

"Very serious, I'm afraid." Laughter danced a jig in Emmy's gaze as she looked at him.

Blast the woman, and hang the effort of ever thinking of her as anything other than Emmy—*his* Emmy. He tugged at his collar. Gads, but it was hot in here.

"Oh dear! It's going to be a very long winter, I suppose." Mrs. Crooks ushered them to the dining-room door.

Besides the empty chair reserved for the colonel's wife at the foot of the table, only two other seats remained. A servant held out Emmy's seat. James sat opposite, a lieutenant's wife at his right—one very large with child—and a major to his left—one with a sizable interest in Emmy, judging by the way his gaze traveled over her.

The man leaned forward, ogling her as if she were the appetizer now being served. "Major Darnwood at your service, madam. I've only recently arrived. And you are?"

Emmy answered with a small smile—one that did not reach her eyes. "Miss Nelson, Dr. Clark's assistant."

"Oh, *miss*, is it?" He leaned back, elbowing James. "Your assistant, eh? Wonder if I could get her to assist me."

Anger curled his hand into a fist, yet he flexed it and rested his palm on the man's shoulder. "Did you know, Major, that if I apply a little pressure to your carotid artery, which is just a twitch away from my index finger, you'll land in your soup before the next spoonful reaches your mouth?"

The man glowered and shifted in his seat, putting as much space between them as politely possible.

A smirk lifted James's lips, but the victory didn't last long. The lieutenant next to Emmy closed in on her, serving her a slice of roast goose and a whisper, his shoulder brushing flush against hers. Her jaw tightened, and scarlet spread across her cheeks.

James bristled. Enough was quite enough.

He pushed back his chair and stood. Throbbing pounded in his temples. The world tipped. He reached out a hand to grasp the table's edge. Why were there suddenly two colonels sitting where there should be only one?

"My apologies, sir, for interrupting this festivity." His voice rasped, and the duo-colonels melded into one.

No, this could not be happening. Not to him.

He quickly slugged back some wine from his goblet before continuing. "Miss Nelson and I must return to the ward."

"Such a sorry business, Doctor." Mrs. Crooks shook her head. "But your commitment to the men is admirable."

"Indeed. Well then, you are excused." The colonel and all the men stood as Emmy rose. "Happy Christmas to you both."

Emmy's steps clipped next to his, but she held her tongue until they cleared the foyer. "I was enjoying that dinner, despite the few rogues in attendance. You're taking this guardianship thing too far. What is wrong with you?"

Shoring his shoulder against the wall, he shuddered. Heat poured off him in waves.

And his next words barely made it past the raw flesh in his throat. "I am ill."

Chapter Eight

Emmy shoved aside her plate of cold beans on the dispensary counter, having managed only a few more bites of leftover dinner. Her appetite was gone, taking with it the remnants of her optimism. How much longer could James hold on?

The front door opened on a whoosh of cold air. Major Clem entered with a tug at his hat, a dusting of snow stark against his blue overcoat. "Afternoon, Miss Nelson. On my way to file a report with the colonel and thought I'd check in on the doctor. How's he doing?"

The question slapped her hard. She'd been trying all day not to answer it, to ignore the symptoms, the way his life was packing its bags for a long, long journey—one from which he wouldn't return.

"Not good." The words tasted like milk gone bad, sour and rancid.

"Sorry to hear that." He rubbed the back of his neck, sending a sprinkling of white falling from his coat. "But if anyone can pull him through, it'd be you."

She snorted, and though vulgar, it could not be helped. "Your confidence, while appreciated, is misplaced, Major. I fear I've done all I can."

His boots thudded on the wooden planks. He stopped in front of her like a bulwark, immovable and stony. "I don't know much about medicine and such, but here's what I've learned of war. Find out where your enemy is then strike hard as you can, and for God's sake, keep on moving. To stop is to die."

She wanted to grasp on to the strength he offered, but her hope hung as lifeless as her limp hands at her sides. A simple "Thank you" was the best she could manage.

"I trust you're taking great care of the doctor, but give a thought to yourself as well." He nodded at her half-eaten beans before he wheeled about and strode from the dispensary, out into January's brittle arms.

The last light of day colored the room in a lifeless pallor. She shivered and lit the oil lamp. Taking the major's words to heart, she once again hauled out the fat medical book she'd taken from James's shelf. It flopped open from the crease she'd made in the binding, having pored over the same section one too many times.

Rubbing her heavy eyes, she tried to focus on the words. Ink blurred into fuzzy lines. No need though, really, for she could recite the diagnosis and procedures in this chapter without error. The measles had hit James hard, and his body had fought valiantly. But once pneumonia set in, what little strength he'd rallied bled out in rib-breaking coughs that produced nothing other than thick green mucus and weakness.

She slammed the book shut, the noise of it a satisfying *thwack*. This wasn't fair. None of it. She'd tried it all. Papa's treatments. Medical journal advice. Textbook treatises on the proper care of lung inflammations. She'd tended patients like this before, but none of them drained her of every possible cure—or wrenched her heart in quite the same way.

Fatigue pressed in on her, sagging her shoulders. Despite the major's admonition, she considered giving up. Simply march right into James's chambers, lie down by his side, and close her eyes to life along with him.

Wretched hacking hurtled out from his room down the corridor. She jerked up her head, listening with her whole body. This was new. Gurgly. Choking.

Ugly.

She raced from the dispensary and flew into his chamber. "James!"

He writhed on the bed, chest heaving—and a small trickle of blood leaked out the side of his blue lips. Sweat darkened the chest and armpits of his nightshirt. The doctor who'd saved so many lives now fought for his own.

Snatching a cloth from a basin on the stand, she knelt next to him. "Shh. Be at peace, love," she cooed as she wiped his face. "Be at peace."

He stilled.

So did she. Not that she hadn't known the truth for weeks now, but speaking the words aloud made it real. She loved him—the man who at any moment might stop breathing altogether.

Tears burned down her cheeks and hit her lips, tasting like loss. She brushed back his hair, wishing, praying his green eyes would open, that he'd berate her manner of healing. . .and tell her what to do.

"Don't leave me. Do not!" Her cry circled the room, but James neither woke nor stirred.

Defeated, she rested her cheek against his chest, now fluttering with quick breaths. At least the thrashing had stopped. "Oh God." Her voice soaked into his nightshirt along with her tears. "Please don't take him, not yet. Not now. Show me what to do."

All the anguish of the past three weeks closed her eyes. How long she lay there, she couldn't say, long enough, though, that when she lifted her head, darkness crept into the room from every corner.

James's breaths still wheezed on the inhale, rattled around, and gurgled back out. Nothing had changed. Nothing.

Or had it?

She shot to her feet, listening beyond his labored breathing. In the distance, a steady beat pounded on the night air. Drums.

Of course! Why had she not thought of this before?

Darting from the room, she raced to her chamber and grabbed her woolen cloak then snatched the lantern off the counter. She flung open the dispensary door as easily as she flung aside any care for her own safety or caution. What did it matter anymore?

She took off at a run toward the gate, already shut for the night. She might have exhausted every resource known to white man, but Makawee was a master of the "old medicine."

⚭

Scorching heat. Frigid cold. James swam from one extreme to the other, all the while gasping for breath beneath the dark waters of pain. He'd give anything to emerge from this ocean of hurt—even his own life.

Occasionally blessed relief allowed him to float. . .a gentle touch on his brow or water pressed against his lips. But those were not enough to pull him out of the deeps.

And so he sank.

Until the whisper came. No, something stronger. He strained to listen. A mourning dove cooed. The haunting sound reached out like a rope, tethering him to a faraway edge of land.

"Be at peace, love. Be at peace."

He clung to those words, holding fast when his chest burned and his ribs crashed and air was nearly a memory.

Peace.

Love.

His eyes shot open. Maybe not. Hard to tell. So he stared, waiting for shapes to form out of the darkness. Was God's face the next thing he would see?

He blinked. Slowly, his gaze traced silhouettes. Color, though muted, seeped in and spread. Smoky sweetness wafted overhead, altogether foreign and pleasing.

"James?" Fabric swished. Troubled blue eyes bent near to his. "James!"

Ahh, dear one. His heart beat loud in his ears. Could Emmy hear it too?

He struggled to lift his hand, wipe the single tear marring her sweet cheek, erase the fear shadowing the hollows beneath her eyes.

But it took all he had in him to simply open his mouth. "Emmy."

The effort cost more than he could spare. Blackness covered him like a blanket pulled over his head.

When his eyes opened again, morning light streamed in,

kissing the top of Emmy's blond hair. She sat in a chair next to his bed, her face bowed over the pages of a book.

"Em—" he croaked. Clearing his throat, he tried again. "Emmy?"

The book hit the floor.

"James?" She slid from the chair and knelt, face-to-face. "Stay with me this time."

"I'd. . .like. . .to." He inhaled strength, or was it her trembling smile that bolstered him so? "Water? So thirsty."

She retrieved a mug from the nightstand then propped him up with her arm behind his shoulders. More liquid than not trickled down his chin, but it was enough to simply have her embrace sustain him—so satisfying that he drifted away once again.

Next time he woke, the room was empty, save for the ticking of the New Haven clock he'd brought with him from Cambridge. The last light of day peeked into his chamber window—but which day? How long had he lain on this bed?

He pushed himself up, propping the pillow behind his back. The room spun, but his lungs didn't burn, nor did he feel the need to hack until his ribs fractured.

"Well!" Emmy swished into the room with a smile that would shame a summer day. "Good to see you are on the mend, Dr. Clark."

"Oh? It's back to that now?" His voice, while raspy, at least worked this time. "I rather liked it when you called me James."

Fire blazed across her cheeks. She turned from him and poured liquid into a mug. "Yes, well, I tried anything and everything to pull you through."

"Whatever you did apparently worked."

She held the cup to his mouth, and as water dampened his lips, his thirst roared. He grabbed the mug from her and—though she warned against it—drained it. His stomach revolted, and he pressed the back of his hand to his lips.

"When will you listen to me?" She removed the mug then settled the chair so that she faced him.

Slowly, the nausea passed, and he lowered his hand. "I did listen—especially when you called me James."

She smirked. "I see your wit is quite recovered as well. Tell me"—she leaned closer, her worried gaze searching his—"how are you feeling?"

He studied her for a moment. Her cheekbones stood out. Her dress hung loose at the shoulders—and the brooch he'd given her for Christmas was pinned at the top of her bodice. Dare he hope she entertained a place in her heart for him? And if she did, then what? How could a wife fit into his life at a time when he needed to focus on scholarship?

He sank into the pillow. The questions exhausted him. He'd think on them later. For now, better to get her to do the talking. "I might ask the same of you. How do you fare?"

She nibbled her lower lip, one of her stalling tactics. Her chest rose and fell with a deep breath. "I am better, now that I know you are well. You gave me quite a scare, you know. I thought I'd lost you. I tried everything, but nothing worked."

He scrubbed a hand over his chin, where whiskers scratched. He could only imagine the days—weeks maybe—of hard work she'd endured for him. She should be attending dinners and dances, not slogging away in a sick man's chamber. How many other women would willingly suffer through such?

"Yet I live, thanks be to you." His words came out more

husky than he intended.

She laughed. "More like thanks be to God and to Makawee."

"What do you mean?"

"I employed every manner of care I knew for pneumonia. I read through all your books and applied those treatments also. But I believe it was Makawee's methods, the rabbit tobacco, the pleurisy root, that helped you turn the corner."

Roots? Tobacco? How could he even begin to understand that? He frowned. "Preposterous."

"Yet as you've said, you live." She leaned toward him. "Think on that."

He sank farther into the pillow. Had he been wrong? Was there more to healing than the sterile procedures of academia? Maybe knowledge and all he held most dear were not to be found in the East, but rather here, in the middle of a wilderness he'd scorned not long ago.

He fastened on her clear blue gaze a moment more before closing his eyes. "I believe there is much I should think on."

Chapter Nine

With a last shudder, winter turned its back on March and shuffled off, taking along with it the icy chill and the worst of the measles and smallpox outbreaks. By April, spring ran wild with flowers and green and promise, reviving the dead, and spurring Emmy into a sprint down the path from the encampment.

"Hold up," James called from behind.

She waited, content to simply watch him as he strode toward her, his long legs eating up the ground. After having witnessed him near death, she'd never tire of seeing the flush of health on his cheeks or the bounce in his step. The past few months had flown by, working at his side, living for his smile, but mostly drinking in his companionship like cool water from a stream.

"I've got something for you. Hold still." He produced a spray of tiny flowers, each petal brushed with a faint swath of violet. His strong fingers could crush them without trying, but he used his surgeon's skill to work them into her hair like a crown. She'd wished to be a princess once—and now she was.

It took every bit of willpower she owned not to wrap her

arms around him and nestle her head against his shirt. Though they never spoke of it, that kiss on a wintry evening had changed everything.

He crooked his finger and lifted her chin. "Beautiful flowers for a beautiful lady."

Her lips ached, her whole body yearned to rise up on her tiptoes, lean a little closer, and—what was she thinking?

Judging by the gleam in his eye and the way he bent just a breath away, he thought the same.

She smiled up into his face. "Do you like nature, James?"

"I do."

She ran her hands up his arms and lightly rested them on his chest. His heart beat strong against her fingers.

"Would you like to be closer to it?" she whispered.

"I would." He leaned in.

Laughing, she shoved him backward, so that he stumbled into a tangle of sumac.

"Pixie!" he roared.

She giggled and fled down the path toward the road—then pulled up short before running headlong into an oncoming carriage.

"Whoa!" A familiar voice, wooly and gruff, rumbled from the driver's seat.

"Jubal? Aunt Rosamund?" Skirting the prancing horses, Emmy strode to the window of Aunt's lacquered carriage.

"Emmaline?" A gunmetal-grey head peeked out the window, a single peacock feather wagging from her sateen bonnet.

Emmy choked back a sob. The Nelson family high cheekbones and long nose reminded her of her father. "Oh Aunt!

How lovely to see you."

"This is exactly what I feared." Aunt's lips pinched, as did her tone. "Look at you! Running about in the wild. What would your father have to say?"

Emmy bowed her head, feeling as small as the time her aunt had caught her splashing in a puddle as a young girl.

"I think he'd say, 'Job well done.'" James caught up to her side, his presence as solid and strong as the poplars taking leaf around them. "Thanks to Miss Nelson," he said, "there are two new souls in the camp, for she just delivered twins, and breech at that."

Aunt peered at him then rummaged for a moment and produced a set of spectacles, eyeing him as if he were an insect to be dissected. "And you are?"

Emmy stepped forward, filling the gap between the doctor and the carriage. "Aunt Rosamund, allow me to introduce Dr. Clark. Doctor, my aunt, Miss Rosamund Nelson."

"Pleased to meet you, Miss Nelson." He dipped his head in a bow, ever the charmer. "I've heard so many good things about you."

"Have you?" She lowered her glasses and speared Emmy with a frown. "I wonder."

Hooves pounded up the road, heading straight toward them. Jubal's arms strained to keep the carriage horses under control.

A corporal on a bay reined in next to them. "Colonel's looking for you, Dr. Clark. Says you're to come at once."

"Oh? Is someone hurt?"

"Nah. Nothing like that." The corporal's horse pawed the ground, scraping up gravel. "First mail of the season arrived upriver, and along with it, the new doc."

James's brows rose.

Emmy's heart sank. She knew he'd be leaving sometime this spring, but were these halcyon days to end so soon?

James nodded then turned back to her and Aunt. "Forgive me, but I need bid you ladies adieu. Pleased to meet you, ma'am."

He swung up behind the corporal, leaving Emmy to face her aunt alone. Her throat tightened, fearing the purpose for Rosamund's visit. She swept an arm toward the fort's front gate. "Will you come in for tea, Aunt?"

"I didn't come for tea, child." Grooves carved into the sides of Aunt's mouth, forged by a magnificent scowl. "I came to take you home. Get in the carriage."

∽∾∾∾

James slid off the horse with a "thanks" to the corporal, feeling a little uneasy for leaving Emmy alone with her aunt. The woman could intimidate a battalion of dragoons. No wonder Emmy had learned to fend for herself.

A makeshift post office—nothing more than a table with a bag of letters dumped onto it—sat in front of the colonel's quarters. For the first mail of the season, the usual protocol—and discipline—stretched as thin as the cook's gruel. A swarm of soldiers buzzed around, some with stony faces as they read of bad news from home, others letting out whoops of happiness. The worst, though, were those walking away with a drag to their step from receiving no letters at all.

Bypassing the ruckus, James climbed the front stairs then halted when he heard his name called.

"Letter for you, Doctor. Looks all official-like." A private who might better serve as a scarecrow held out a thick-papered document.

"Thanks, Private." Grasping the letter, he retired to a corner of the front porch and leaned against the wall.

His name was scrawled across the front in black ink. Burgundy wax bled into a circle on the back, a single word embossed in the center—*veritas*. He sucked in a breath. Truth, indeed. He didn't need to read the signature inside to know that Dr. Stafford was either opening the door for his advancement or slamming it shut in his face. . .but which did he really want?

He swallowed then broke the seal.

Greetings James,

Word of your stellar performance this past winter season at Fort Snelling has reached my ear. I trust by now that from your experience, you've learned there is more to medicine than textbooks. I know you weren't happy about this arrangement initially, but I hope you've come to see the benefit and necessity. The position for director of surgical instruction is recently opened up. I can think of no better candidate than yourself. It will be a fight, but one I am sure we can win. Catch the next available steamship back to Boston, where we may begin your campaign strategy.

~ William Stafford, MD, MS

Stunned, James tucked the letter inside his waistcoat then ran both hands through his hair. Director? So soon? Could he really bypass being an instructor first? This was unheard of—but so was attaining the sponsorship of Dr. Stafford, one of the most influential men walking the hallowed halls of Harvard Medical. And if Stafford thought he had a chance, then, well... *veritas*. There was no doubt about it.

"Dr. Clark?" A major held open the front door. "Colonel Crooks is asking for you."

He pushed away from the wall, shoving aside further speculation—for now, anyway.

"Pardon me, but you're the doc?" A tall man, tawny headed and with eyes bluer than cornflowers, stepped into his path.

James angled his head. Something about the fellow was familiar.

"I'm Dr. Clark," he said.

The man reset his cap, likely fresh off the steamship and eager for some movement. "I just came from a meeting with the colonel. He said you'd know the layout of the encampment, having tended the inhabitants all winter, particularly who lived in what tent."

"Ahh." He nodded. "So you're looking for someone."

"I am." His hand dropped, and a starved look haunted his blue gaze. "My wife and son."

James took a step closer, studying the man. Like the combining of symptoms to diagnose an ailment, he added up the information and what his own eyes told him. "Let me guess... Makawee and little Jack?"

The fellow's mouth dropped. "How did you know?"

James grinned. "Because except for the hair color, your son is a miniature of you."

"How are they?" The fellow leaned toward him, as if by sheer proximity he might learn the answer.

"They are well, and you will find them very conveniently in the second tent to the right as you enter the camp."

The fellow reached out and pumped his hand. "Thank you."

Then he flew down the steps and sprinted across the parade ground before James could answer.

With a chuckle, he headed for the colonel's office, imagining what a homecoming that would be.

The colonel stood near his desk, nodding at his entrance. "High time you show up, Doctor. I've other matters to attend." He motioned James into the room. "Dr. Griffin, meet Dr. Clark. And Clark, meet Dr. Griffin."

At the mention of his name, a short man pushed himself up from a chair and crossed the room. A few memories of hair tufted near his ears. His handshake matched with a wispy grip.

"Pleased to meet you, Doctor." The man pumped his hand, or tried to, anyway. "Colonel Crooks has been telling me of the hardships you've endured this past winter."

He schooled his face, trying hard not to smirk. This slight fellow wouldn't last the summer. "What doesn't kill us makes us stronger, eh? I'm sure you'll have an easier go of it, though."

The colonel skirted his desk. "Dr. Clark, would you see that Dr. Griffin is familiar with the dispensary and ward before you leave? Oh, and there's a bit of paperwork I'd like to have you take care of as well."

Leave? His breath hitched at the colonel's words. It was so final. So jarring. Like the slamming of a door in an empty house, the implications reverberated in his chest. His work here was done. Finished. It was time to leave the natives he'd come to admire—and the woman he'd come to love.

"Dr. Clark?"

"Hmm? Oh, yes. Of course." He turned to Dr. Griffin and swept a hand toward the door. "Shall we?"

Griffin exited. He followed but stopped at the threshold at the colonel's command.

"Oh, one more thing, Dr. Clark."

"Sir?"

Crooks tapped a letter against one palm. "I've received word the Sioux are to be shipped out West, away from those with long memories and longer arms of vengeance. They'll be under the management of Fort Randall—a garrison without a doctor. You've done a fine job here. Lives were saved because of you. On my word, the position is yours, if you want it."

Him? The one who barely survived a Minnesota winter? He let out a breath, long and low. "I shall think on it, Colonel."

"I couldn't ask for more. Dismissed."

James strode out into the sunlight. How dare the day be so bright when dark and heavy decisions weighed on his shoulders? What to do? Hop a steamship east to his former dream of power and prestige—one that would eclipse any thought of love or family? Or mount up and ride farther west, to a land more rugged than the one he now claimed?

His steps stalled. So did his heart. How could Emmy possibly fit into any of this, especially with an aunt determined to drag her into society?

Well, Lord?

He stood waiting a long time, praying, ignoring the soldiers around him. Waiting for what? A lightning bolt to write an answer in the sky? *Show me, God. Clearly.*

And. . .nothing.

With a sigh, he lowered his gaze—then jerked his face back overhead. Two sparrows, flying in tandem, swooped gracefully toward the west.

Moving as one.

He smiled. It was a small answer, but answer enough. *Thank You, God.*

Setting his hat tight, he set off at a run, straight toward the dispensary.

Chapter Ten

Emmy sat on the edge of her bed, her trunk by her chamber door ready for Jubal to fetch. Her father's medical bag lay in her lap. She ran a finger along the top, smearing tears into the worn leather. Once she moved to Aunt Rosamund's fine Minneapolis home, this bag would be relegated to the attic. Aunt would never allow her to degrade herself by caring for the sick. No more tending to births or coughs or fevers. No more sweet friendship with Makawee and little Jack.

And no more working long days next to James, shadowing his every move, inhaling his scent of sandalwood and strength. She pressed her fingers to her mouth, stifling a sob.

She might as well box up her heart and store that in the rafters too.

"What's this?" James skirted the trunk as he entered the room, the pull of him drawing her to her feet.

Oh, how she'd love to run into his arms, rest her head against his chest, and forget about Aunt and the new life she didn't want. Yet she stood there, as straight as one of the soldiers at attention.

His gaze slid from the empty nightstand, to the bare pegs

on the wall, and finally rested on her. He cocked a brow. "Are you leaving?"

She shrugged, stalling for the right words. How to tell him that in mere minutes she'd be walking out that door forever? Her throat closed, and it took several swallows before she could manage a simple, "I am."

"Oh? What a coincidence." He grinned. "So am I."

She grabbed handfuls of her skirt to keep from slapping the silly smile off his face. Did the man not care their friendship would be ending? That he'd never see her again? Had she been wrong about his feelings?

She drew in a sharp breath. "Evidently your meeting with the colonel went well."

"Better than that." He rocked onto his toes, the movement stoking her anger. "My dream is nearly within reach."

Coldhearted, selfish man! She knotted the fabric tighter, choking the life from her skirt. Had the past six months meant nothing to him that he could ball up all their tender moments and cast them aside like a wadded bit of paper?

So be it. If he could let her go that easily, neither would she hold on. She splayed her fingers, letting her skirt drop.

"Well, then, Dr. Clark, I am happy for you. It's good to know some of us get what we desire. You will no doubt rise quickly to the top at Harvard Medical." She hurled the words like a porcelain teacup against a wall, wishing the impact would break his heart into as many pieces as hers. How could she have been so wrong?

"But I—"

"Goodbye." She swished past him. She didn't need justifications or explanations. Her eyes filled, turning the room into a watery mess.

"Emmy!"

A tug on her shoulder pulled her back.

His breath came out in a huff. "You jump to conclusions faster than a raging bout of chicken pox, woman. Hear me out."

She scowled at his hand on her arm, then up into his face. "What more is there to say? Aunt is waiting for me. I'm bound for Minneapolis, and you're headed east."

"What?" His brows shot skyward. "I never said I was going east. Quite the opposite, actually. I'm traveling west."

His declaration rattled around like rocks in a can, making noise but no sense whatsoever. She stared into his eyes, yet no hint of meaning surfaced in those green pools.

She shook her head. "I don't understand."

"Clearly." He drew closer, entwining his fingers with hers. "Colonel Crooks received orders that the encampment is to be struck and moved to Dakota Territory. The fort there is in need of a doctor, and he's offered me the position."

"But. . .but that's even more wild than here, and it's a far cry from teaching at a medical institution. That's not your dream."

"You're right. Not quite. But this is." He slid to one knee. Slowly, he lifted one of her hands to his lips, pressing a kiss from one knuckle to the next then repeated the action with the other.

Her knees weakened. His warm breath caressed all the way up her arm. What on earth was he doing?

He lowered her hands and lifted his face. His eyes glowed— no, his whole face, from the cut of his square jaw up to his fine, strong brow.

"My dream, Miss Emmaline Nelson"—his voice deepened,

laced with an urgency she'd never before heard—"is that you would not only be my assistant but my wife."

The world stopped. Sound receded. All she could hear was her breath rushing in, rushing out. It took all her concentration to keep her lungs pumping. Had she heard correctly, or was she imagining things? Was this real?

He squeezed her hands. "What do you say?"

◆◇◆

James stood on a cliff's edge, holding his breath. One word from the woman in front of him and he'd fall into her arms—or plummet to his death. She blinked at him, yet said nothing. Not even a murmur. Oughtn't a woman in love say something?

An ember of doubt flared in his gut. As a lad, on the cusp of adolescence, he'd mustered his courage to ask a girl to dance once. He'd often wished she'd snubbed him with a loud rejection, but she'd simply turned her back and walked away, leaving him standing alone, abandoned like an old shoe, pity shining in the eyes of the dancing master—and snickers assaulting him from the other boys attending the lessons. It was mortifying, humiliating.

And that same feeling seized his heart now.

Would Emmy do the same?

Slowly, he rose, his legs as weak as if the winter sickness revisited him. Emmy's eyes did not follow the movement. Her gaze remained fixed on the hands he'd so recently kissed.

"Emmy?" He cupped her face, lifting it to his. This might be it, the last time he held her. The thought lodged bitter at the back of his throat.

He gulped for air, prayed for wisdom, but mostly memorized every freckle and curve on her face. If she declined. . .his heart skipped a beat. *God, help me.*

"I love you, Emmy, with everything that's in me." He choked then cleared his throat and tried again. "I know you dreamed of a home in Mendota, the one you shared with your father, but dreams can change, can't they? Is it possible, in some small way, that I could be your new dream?"

Her eyes filled, shiny and luminous. A tremble quivered across her lower lip. Beneath his fingers, her skin warmed, flushing her cheeks like the first blush on a spring rose.

"Yes," she whispered, barely discernable.

But it was enough.

Sweet mercy! It was enough.

He pulled her against him, and when her mouth touched his, a tremor shook him. Hard. She breathed out his name, again and again. Ahh, but he'd never tire of hearing her say it.

"Yes, yes, yes!" She emphasized each word with a kiss, running her fingers up his back and twisting them into the hair at the nape of his neck. She leaned into him, hungry, searching—

"Emmaline Abigail Nelson!" Thunder boomed from the open door. "Get in the carriage. Now!"

He froze.

Emmy whirled. "Aunt! This isn't what you think—"

"What I think is that it was a mistake to have allowed you to stay here in the first place." Rosamund Nelson eyed him like a buck to be shot through the heart then gutted, leaving his innards to dry in the sun. "And you, sir, are responsible."

With a light touch, he drew Emmy to his side, facing the dragon. In spite of the situation, he grinned. How could he not, when the woman he loved had just agreed to share her life with him? "You are 100 percent correct, Miss Nelson. I have been—and will continue to be—responsible for this woman, for she is soon to become Mrs. James Clark."

Aunt Rosamund threw her hands wide, chasing after words as if she gathered an overturned crate of mice. "Well. . . I. . .Emmaline? Is this what you want? You would give up dinners, dances, society for the hard life of a doctor's wife?"

She turned to him, and this time, there was no hesitation, just a brilliant smile. "Yes, Aunt. There is nothing I want more than to be the doctor's wife. This doctor."

"Well!" Aunt Rosamund sputtered. "I never!"

Tucking Emmy under his arm, James smiled over the top of her head at the woman. "Then I pray that God will bring to you a special someone. As long as you're still breathing, there's always hope."

Hope, indeed. With Emmy nestled against him, it was time to start planning a new hope, a new direction, and together, a new dream.

A dream that would last a lifetime.

A House of
Secrets

Dedication

To the One who knows the secrets of my soul.

Acknowledgments

Thank you to those who polish my stories to a fine sheen:

Elizabeth Ludwig, Ane Mulligan, Julie Klassen, MaryLu Tyndall, Shannon McNear & Chawna Schroeder.

And a huge shout-out to you, readers, who make this all worthwhile.

Chapter One

He's late. Are you worried?"

The question floated across the sitting room like an unmoored specter, haunting Amanda Carston about the constancy of her fiancé. A smile quirked her lips. Good thing she didn't believe in ghosts.

"Come away from the window, Mags. Watching for Joseph won't make him appear any sooner." She rose from the settee, smoothing wrinkles from her gown. "He'll be here."

Maggie turned from the glass, letting the sheer fall back into place. "But it's your engagement dinner. And the *Pioneer Press* photographer will be there. How can you possibly be so calm?" She drew near and pressed her fingers against Amanda's forehead. "Are you feeling ill?"

"Don't be silly." Amanda batted her hand away, frowning. Being late for a dinner party was the least of her concerns this weekend. Coming up with a service project idea by Monday— her first as the new Ladies' Aide Society chairwoman—vexed her more.

Maggie's brow creased. "You *are* worried. Don't pretend."

Slamming the lid on her chairwoman woes, she smiled at her friend. "I am sure Joseph's aunt is used to delaying a meal even with important guests in attendance. A city attorney's schedule is rarely predictable."

"Ahh, but it's not his aunt who alarms me." Light from the gas lamps glistened on the pity filling Maggie's eyes. "What of your father, dearest?"

This time doubt didn't float in. It fell heavy on her spirit like a tempest, and her smile faded. Father would be disappointed at her tardiness. But truly, they all would have been late if he'd had to swing by from the office to pick up her and Mags. Must something always thwart her efforts to please her father?

She whirled and strode from the sitting room. "Let's bundle up so we may leave for Aunt Blake's as soon as Joseph arrives."

Maggie's footsteps echoed into the foyer, and by the time they slipped into their cloaks and secured their hats with a final pinning in front of the big mirror, the knocker pounded against the door.

"No need to trouble yourself, Grayson." Her words halted the butler's trek down the grand staircase. "I'm certain it's Mr. Blake. Don't expect us until late."

Ignoring his scowl and his "highly improper," she swung open the door to the man of her dreams—

And a police officer.

"Joseph?" she murmured.

A smile flashed across his face, brilliant in the dark of the October eve. He reached for her hand and pressed a kiss against the back of her glove, the heat of his mouth warming the fabric. "Don't panic, my love. Just a bit of business left over from the office. Please allow me to introduce Officer Keeley. Officer, my fiancée, Miss Amanda Carston." He leaned in scandalously close, breathing warmth into her ear. "Soon to be Mrs. Joseph Blake."

She arched a brow, unsure if she ought to censure him or wrap her arms around him. Instead, she nodded at Mr. Keeley. "Pleased to meet you, Officer."

He tugged the brim of his hat. "The pleasure is mine, Miss Carston."

Behind her, Maggie cleared her throat.

"My apologies, Miss Turner." A sheepish grin curved Joseph's mouth. "May I introduce you as well? Miss Turner, meet Officer Keeley. Officer Keeley, Miss Turner, my fiancée's confidante and partner in crime."

Amanda stepped closer to Joseph, speaking for his ears alone. "Does your aunt know to set another place?"

He winked down at her. "The officer won't be joining us for dinner. He's along to help me attend to an unfinished matter beforehand. Now shall we?"

He offered his arm, and Amanda wrapped her fingers around his sleeve. Unfinished business? Whatever it was must be important, but tonight of all nights? She puzzled over the mystery until the feel of his muscles riding hard beneath her touch drove her to distraction. Inhaling his familiar fragrance of sandalwood and ink, she was hard-pressed to figure out which made her more weak-kneed— the intimacy of knowing his scent, or his husky voice caressing her ear.

"You look lovely tonight," he whispered.

Her cheeks heated. Good thing Maggie and the officer walked ahead—and what a pair they made. Him tall. Her short.

A canyon of difference between a suit of blue and the golden gown of a railroad tycoon's daughter.

Joseph helped her into the carriage, and she settled next to Maggie, the men on the opposite seat. The driver urged the horses from the circular drive onto Summit Avenue, and just as she opened her mouth to ask Joseph about his unfinished business, the carriage turned left.

Left?

She peered out the window. Indeed, they headed east, not west, rolling past the old Grigg place. Despite being in the company of a strapping fiancé and a lawman, she shuddered at the eerie sight. At the front of the lot, half-burned timbers reached into the night sky, dark on dark, like blackened bones trying to escape from a grave. Beyond the remnants of the gatehouse stood the ruins of a once-grand home, bricks holding in secrets like a jealous lover, guarding rumors of foul play. If the city was going to do nothing about this blight, then maybe...perhaps...

The seed of a glorious idea took root. This just may be the service project she'd been looking for. Indeed, the more she thought on it, the larger the idea grew.

Until the carriage turned left yet again. She squinted into the darkness as they traveled farther from their engagement announcement. "This isn't the way to your aunt's."

"No, it isn't. As I've said, a small bit of business first. Merely a short detour."

Joseph's words pulled her gaze to him. "Where are we going?"

"To Hannah Crow's."

Amanda's jaw dropped. Maggie gasped, her fingers

fluttering to her chest. Officer Keeley took a sudden interest in looking out the window. Clearly he was in on this—whatever *this* was.

"Joseph Blake!" she scolded. "Why on earth are you taking us to a brothel?"

◈◈

Like an arc of lightning, blue tinged and life threatening, the flash in his fiancée's eyes struck Joseph—with humor. The little firebrand. He stifled a grin. He could get used to such passion, but he sure hoped not. Her fiery spirit was what attracted him to her in the first place.

"I thought you might like to see the culmination of a year's worth of work," he said.

"Mr. Blake." Amanda's friend clutched her hands to her chest, eyes wide. "Surely you've never set foot in such a place?"

Amanda studied him a moment more, then leaned sideways, lips twisted into a smirk. "Don't fall for his dramatics, Mags. He's playing us with as much finesse as his violin."

Keeley elbowed him. "You've met your match in that one, sir."

Indeed. Why was God so good to him? He folded his arms and relaxed against the seat, memorizing how the passing streetlights bathed half of Amanda's face in golden light, the other dark. The contrast was a perfect picture of what lay beneath. . .pluck and humility. Softness and steel.

"I suppose she'll suit," he drawled.

She swatted his knee. "You, sir, are a scoundrel."

He caught her hand before she could pull it away and kissed her fingertips. "Ahh, but I am your scoundrel, hmm?"

Color deepened on her cheeks. "Not if we never make it

to our betrothal dinner. Father could always change his mind, you know."

Joseph rapped the carriage wall, urging the driver to up his pace, then faced Miss Turner. "My soon-to-be wife is somewhat used to my unorthodox ways, but I can see you are not. In answer to your question, Miss Turner, while I am well versed in Hannah Crow's business, I have never entered her establishment. My aim is to shut her down, and I've finally found a way. That's why Officer Keeley is with us tonight."

"Wonderful news!" Amanda beamed at him—a smile of which he'd never tire.

Miss Turner frowned, eyeing the policeman. "Are you expecting trouble?"

"Don't fret, miss." Keeley tipped his head at her. "I'm merely a formality, a witness to the delivery of a document."

The grind of cobbles beneath the wheels changed to a gravelly crunch as the carriage eased off Summit and onto Washington Street. Miss Turner balanced a hand against the side of the carriage as they lurched around a corner, or did she clutch it for courage? Amanda's gaze found his, and he searched the blue depths. Was she afraid as well?

Nothing but clear admiration blinked back. "I am so proud of you, even if your timing is a bit off."

Law and order! With regard such as this, he could conquer more than a brothel—he could take on the world. He leapt out of the carriage before it stopped and patted his coat to make sure the injunction still rode inside his pocket. This was it. Finally. A night he wouldn't soon forget.

He and Keeley climbed the stairs to Crow's House of

Hair. Hair products, of all things. The sign, the business, the audacity fooled no one. More went on behind those velvet drapes than the production and distribution of supposed growth elixirs—and everyone knew it. Sorrow punched him hard in the gut for the women trapped inside, chained by desperation and lost hope. He bit back a wince. The thought that Elizabeth had died as such nearly drove him to his knees.

He swallowed against the tightness in his throat and reached to ring the bell, but his finger hovered over the button. Something wasn't right. Lifting his face, he narrowed his eyes above the doorframe. The House of Hair sign was gone.

Keeley nudged him. "What are you waiting for?"

Exactly. So what if the sign was missing? He shook off a foreboding twinge and punched the button.

No answer.

He stabbed his finger on it again.

And. . .nothing.

Keeley shouldered past him and pounded the door so that it rattled in the frame. "Open up! We know yer in there. Don't make me bust down this—"

The door swung open. A glass chandelier rained beams of light onto a woman buttoned tight from toe to neck. Hannah Crow could be anyone's saintly aunt. Prim and proper on the outside—but that grey silk encased wickedness and greed.

Joseph stared at her angular face, refusing to look past her. One glimpse of a young girl tangled in her web would undo him, despite standing on the brink of this victory.

Oh Elizabeth. Would that you'd been able to escape such a fate.

"Mr. Blake." Mrs. Crow dipped her head, a nod toward

respectability—the closest she'd ever get. Then her dark gaze glittered, little lines spidering out at the creases of her eyes. "Bit late for you to be calling. Is this business or pleasure?"

"Entirely my pleasure." He handed over the injunction.

Hannah's eyes scanned back and forth, top to bottom, and in case she didn't understand all the legal jargon, Joseph added, "According to a recent addition to ordinance 245.1, your conditional use variance is null and void. In essence and practicality, madam, this is the end of your business."

"Well, well. . ." She lifted the paper high and released the document to the October breeze.

Keeley growled. "Even if that paper blows to kingdom come, Mrs. Crow, I seen you take it. I seen you read it. I'll swear to that in court."

She smiled at him as she might a mark with no money, her chipped eyetooth reminding Joseph of a sharpened fang. "No need, Officer. There will be no hearing. That ordinance means nothing to me. My home is no longer a business, just a humble abode."

A genuine smile tugged at Joseph's lips. "Nice try, Mrs. Crow, but that won't help you. This property is zoned for business, so either way, you're finished."

Her hand disappeared inside a pocket, and she pulled out a folded document, offering it to him with a feline stretch.

What sorcery was this? He yanked the paper open. Snippets of phrases pummeled him back a step. Emergency city council meeting. Dated the previous day. Zoning changed to residential. Signed by Willard Craven.

A slow burn ignited, from stomach to throat. Craven! He should've known.

Wheeling about, he stalked toward the carriage and called over his shoulder, "We'll see about this."

And he'd have to—or he'd be out of a job by month's end, his sister's death still unavenged.

Chapter Two

Most of the shameless maples had already disrobed for their coming marriage to winter, but a few discreet maidens refused to shed their orange and red leaves. Amanda lifted her face and relished the spot of colorful brilliance in front of the ruined Grigg house. Surely if God created such beauty in the midst of ashes, He could do anything. . .like help her—for it would take heavenly assistance to accomplish the plan she was about to undertake.

A small flame of guilt kindled in her heart, and she closed her eyes. *Forgive me, Lord.* For indeed, He already had helped her at dinner last Friday night. Not a miracle of Red Sea proportions—for Father had been snappish over her tardiness. But at least he'd not made too big of a scene, especially when Joseph took full responsibility for their lack of punctuality.

Behind her, carriage wheels rolled to a stop, and her eyes popped open, pulling her back to the present. Was she ready for this?

"This is an interesting venue for our Ladies' Aide Society meeting." Maggie's voice turned her around.

Her friend's glance drifted to the burnt gatehouse. She

crossed the boulevard and stopped on the drive next to Amanda. "What are you up to?"

Direct as always—which is what she loved most about Mags. No guile. No secrets. Amanda smiled. "I had a wonderful idea."

Maggie's lips pulled into a pout. "If it involves the Grigg house, then it might be your last idea as chairwoman. The place is positively haunted."

A parade of lacquered carriages rolled up the street, one by one stopping to let out an array of colorful gowns. One in particular was more stunning than the rest.

Maggie shook her head. "I'm surprised Lillian agreed to meet here."

"She didn't. . .exactly."

Maggie pulled her gaze from the women swarming their way. "How did you manage that?"

She shrugged. "I sent a note to her driver, along with a little incentive."

Maggie's brows drew together. "I hope you know what you're doing, dearest."

Her breath caught in her throat. So did she.

Lillian Warnbrough, one part peacock, the other lioness, led the remaining nine members of the Ladies' Aide Society to a standstill in front of Amanda. Without so much as a "Good afternoon" she started right in. "I demand to know why we are meeting outdoors like common laborers."

This was it. *Lord, give me strength.* Amanda stiffened her shoulders—and her resolve—then flashed a smile. "Ladies, I have a surprise for you."

Lillian faced Amanda with a thundercloud of a scowl. "Do

not tell me you're thinking of holding the fall festival here."

"No, of course not." It was a struggle, but she held on to her smile, albeit tightly. "I've found our next project, the Grigg home."

Lillian sniffed, the closest she ever came to an outright snort. "I hardly think removing a blight in our neighborhood would be looked kindly upon by the"—she waved her hand toward downtown—"less fortunate."

Her smile slipped. The only type of aid Lillian liked to supply was that which benefited her. Amanda bit the inside of her cheek lest unkind words slide out with her proposition.

Counting to ten, she smoothed her skirts before she spoke. "I suggest we renovate, not remove. While it's true we've helped the poverty stricken with their housing, I feel there is more work to be done. And aid is what our society is all about, is it not?"

Some ladies huddled closer, clearly interested. The rest looked to Lillian for her response.

But Amanda charged ahead before anyone could object. "We shall remake the old Grigg house into a school for the downtrodden."

Lillian's head shook before Amanda even finished. "Ridiculous. There are already schools. Many, in fact. This is a waste of time." She turned away.

"You're right on that account, but children of the poor do not attend those schools. Did you know there is an ordinance excusing the absences of those unable to dress properly?"

Lillian whirled back, a gleam of victory shining in her eyes. "Opening another school will not change that."

Amanda sucked in a breath. If she could pull this off,

not only would the poor of St. Paul receive an education, but her father might finally see that she—a woman—could do something of value. She clasped both hands at her waist and stood taller. "True, yet we will not only provide the institution, but the uniforms as well. It's a victory for us in that there will no longer be a decrepit piece of property driving down costs of the adjoining lots, and an even bigger triumph for the poor children who will receive an education. And in the grand scheme of things, you must agree, Lillian, this would be a huge conquest against ignorance and destitution."

A few birds chirped. What leaves remained rustled in the breeze. But no one said a word. Not even Lillian.

Amanda lifted a helpless gaze to Maggie.

She smiled back. "I think it's a wonderful idea."

Lillian huffed. "I suppose it has its merits." She stepped so close, the sparks in her eyes burnt holes in Amanda's confidence. "But know this: I will not have your little scheme interfering with our fall festival. It's tradition, something you seem to have a hard time grasping." She retreated a step to stare down her elegant nose. "There is no possible way we can arrange a respectable dinner and ball by mid-November if we do not begin plans by the first. So, I counter your proposal. If, as chairwoman of the society, you produce the deed to the Grigg house, then we parcel out the renovation to the lowest bidders."

For the first time since the meeting began, the tension pounding in Amanda's temples began to slip away. Success was at hand.

Lillian narrowed her eyes. "If you cannot secure the deed

by the end of October, however, this little endeavor is over. In the meantime, the rest of us will begin working on the festival."

What? She threw out her hands. "How am I to purchase a lot on my own in less than one month? How am I to even find the owner?"

Lillian quirked a perfectly arched brow. "You concede, then. Good." She spun, her hat ribbons hitting Amanda on the cheek. "Come along, ladies. We have a festival to plan."

"No!"

Lillian spun back. "What did you say?"

For a second, her knees trembled. She glanced over her shoulder, picturing the many lives that would be changed from this renovation. This *had* to work.

She lifted her chin. "I shall have the deed in my hands by the thirty-first."

A wicked grin pulled up the sides of Lillian's pouty little mouth. "A fitting deadline to purchase a haunted house, is it not?"

◦◦◦

Striding through the front door of the Minnesota Club, Joseph swept off his hat. He gave a brief tip of his head at the coat check as he draped his topcoat over his arm. He wouldn't be here long enough for that. Hopefully.

"Mr. Blake! What a pleasure." The maître d', Pierre François, rushed from his podium. He greeted Joseph with a firm handshake and an accent that was no more French than Joseph was a Shetland pony.

"I suppose it has been awhile, eh, François?" He patted the man on the back. "How goes it?"

"Ahh, you know. A little intrigue, a lot of tips." He waggled his eyebrows. "And good thing you've kept hold of your top-coat. *Ze* club is a little brisk tonight, despite the hearth fires."

"Don't tell me you still haven't replaced the boilerman?"

"Oh-ho-ho. . . '*zen* I will not." François chuckled. "Though I hear tell a new one is soon to be hired. Let us hope he is not *très incompetent,* or it will be a long winter. Now then, how can I be of service to you tonight, monsieur?"

Joseph peered past François's shoulder, into the lounge area of the gentlemen's club. From this angle it was impossible to see much. He cut his gaze back to François. "I'm looking for Mr. Craven. Is he here?"

"He is." François nodded. "Shall I direct you?"

He held up a hand. "No need, thank you."

As he slipped past the maître d', he pressed a coin into the fellow's hand. He strode through the grand pillars standing tall on either side of the entrance and entered the ornate receiving room of the Minnesota Club, the haunt of movers and shakers. The room reeked of bourbon, smoke, and far too much power. A chill snaked up his pants leg. François wasn't kidding about the sorry state of warmth in here. It would be a *very* long winter if they didn't get that boiler going.

Ahead, a few senators huddled at a table, playing a game of five-card draw. Near the hearth, a tycoon and a judge warmed their backsides while engaging in an even hotter debate. How many deals were struck in this room? How many underhanded schemes?

Across the room, near the servants' door, Willard Craven sat ensconced at a table between two gas lamps. The brilliance illuminated splotches of red on his fat cheeks, a skin problem he'd acquired from too much malt liquor. In fact, everything about the man was too much. The white satin bow tie and winged collar. The jeweled rings flashing on his fingers. His ego. He watched Joseph approach, the cigar in his mouth flaring to a hellish color as he puffed away.

Joseph stopped two paces from him. "A word, if you please, Craven."

"Well, well. . ." Willard punctuated the air with his cigar, pulling bureaucrat wannabes into his orbit. "Witness, my dear fellows, a rare sighting of the *attornicus maximus*, a creature who generally hides in a cloister of righteousness and justice and who seldom partakes of company carrying the faintest whiff of debauchery. Tell me, Blake"—he rolled the cigar between forefinger and thumb as he spoke—"have you finally stepped down from your pedestal to rub shoulders with us wretches?" With his free hand, he snapped his fingers. "Porter! Another chair, please."

Joseph halted the porter with a shake of his head. "No need. This won't take long."

"So, you've not come to drink or game?" Craven took a drag on his cigar and blew out a puff of smoke. "I thought not."

Such dramatics. It was a struggle to keep his eyes from rolling. "You know why I'm here, Craven."

The big man shrugged, the shoulders of his tuxedo rolling with the movement. "Can't imagine."

"Your little meeting of the zoning commission doesn't fool me. There's a rat at city hall, a pack of them, and you're the leader."

"Pish! It's always a conspiracy with you." Craven chuckled then tamped out his cigar in a crystal ashtray. "There was nothing more devious about that meeting than astute revenue generation. Profits were down on business, and residential property taxes are on the rise. Changing the zoning will be a boon to the city."

Of all the bald-faced lies. Joseph clenched his hands into fists, fighting to keep them at his side. "Hours before I was to sign and deliver an injunction? You expect me to believe that?"

"Come, come, Blake. Why don't you trade your sour grapes for a glass of Bordeaux?" He lifted his hand to once again snap his fingers. "Porter—"

Joseph grabbed Craven's wrist, squeezing until the bones ground beneath his grip. "I don't know how you discovered what my next move was going to be, but I'll save you the trouble of wondering what I shall do next. I'm coming for you, Craven. Mark my words, I *will* uncover the real reason you protect Hannah Crow."

Wincing, Craven jerked his hand away and shot to his feet. Red crept up his neck, matching the splotches on his face. "Back off, Blake, or I'll see your name linked to the brothel in a way you won't like. I wonder what your pretty fiancée will have to say about that."

The threat cut deep, exposing a raw nerve he did his best to always keep hidden. If Amanda or—God help him—her father knew of his family's history with brothels, his aunt's dire prediction would come true: "*No respectable woman will have you if the truth is known.*"

He sucked in a breath, nearly choking on Craven's leftover

cigar smoke. Any show of weakness would be blood in the water. His lips pulled into a sneer. "She'll never believe your lies."

"Why, my dear fellow, I'll be so convincing that even you will doubt yourself. And a scandal attached to the great city attorney will not bode well for the mayor's re-election now, will it?"

Joseph gritted his teeth, hating the way Craven's words burrowed under his skin.

Craven leaned forward, the stink of tobacco and whiskey fouling the air. "The loss of your job, the loss of your love... Tell me, is shutting down one house of ill repute worth so much?"

Chapter Three

Grabbing her hat with one hand, Amanda leaned over the side of Joseph's phaeton, closing her eyes against the thrill of speed. A completely brazen act, the breeze teasing out bits of her hair, but so irresistible. How could one pass up facing a glorious Sunday afternoon when winter would soon squeeze the life out of everything?

She glanced back, expecting a raised-eyebrow reprimand from Maggie. But her friend was a small dot, blocks behind, riding in Mr. Rafferty's lumbering coach.

"Chicken *and* an apple pie?" A low whistle traveled on the wind.

She snapped her attention back to Joseph and caught him in the act of lifting the lid on the picnic basket at their feet. She batted his arm with a fake scowl. "No peeking, sir."

A mischievous grin stretched across his face, highlighting a single dimple on his cheek. "Be thankful that's all I've peeked at." He aimed a finger at the hem of her gown.

Her gaze followed to where he pointed and—great heavens! She bent and snatched the fabric from where it had snagged up near the railing, exposing the lace of her petticoat and far too much of her stockinged leg.

Tucking the fabric between her calves and carriage, she straightened out her gown and her dignity—then promptly changed the subject. "I met with the Ladies' Aide Society on Monday."

"Oh? And how does it involve me?" He winked—and a thrill charged through her.

Even so, she pursed her lips into a sulk. "You make me sound like a criminal."

His eyes twinkled, the lift of his brow altogether too handsome. "And you are skirting the question."

"I was merely conversing. Any fiancé would take interest in the matters of his betrothed."

"Ahh, but you forget I am used to divining truth from felons. So judging by the contents of that basket"—he leaned close and nuzzled her neck—"the smell of wild rose perfume, your gown of blue, all of which are my favorites, you are about to ask me for a favor. You needn't go to so much trouble though, love. I would grant you anything." He swept out his free hand as they rumbled down the hill, into the innermost part of the city. "Even up to half my kingdom."

"Well. . ." She nibbled her lower lip. Maybe now was as good a time as any. "It's not exactly a kingdom that I want."

"But you do want something, hmm?"

"Yes." She flashed him a grin. "And you're the man to help me get it."

She darted a glance from road to sidewalk, building to building, and when satisfied no pedestrians looked their way, she stretched up on her seat and kissed his cheek.

"Well now." His gaze smoldered down at her. "How can I

refuse that? What is it you want?"

"The title to the Grigg house."

The gleam in his eyes faded, and he faced the road. "Why would you want that?"

She frowned. Would he need as much convincing as Lillian? "I've had the most wonderful idea. What if the decrepit Grigg house was made into a school for the poor? With uniforms and hot lunches and the chance to leave poverty behind? Think of the possibility."

Perhaps he was thinking of it, for a muscle tightened and loosened on his jaw. But he said nothing, just kept a firm hold on the reins as they wove their way through the innards of St. Paul.

She touched his sleeve. "You will help me, won't you?"

"Whoa, now." He spoke to the horse—or did he?

"Joseph?" She stared at him. For the first time in their relationship, an alarm bell rang.

"Look at that." He pulled the horse to a stop and angled his head.

Leaning forward, she followed his gaze. They'd stopped at a crossroads. On the corner nearest them, a young boy, more dirt than skin, held out a torn newspaper, equally as filthy. His cries to sell it competed with a much larger and louder boy on the opposite corner. At the younger lad's feet, a babe in a basket whimpered, lusty enough to be heard in the phaeton. Want and need haunted the caverns of their hollowed cheeks. Their clothes, rags really, hung off their bones like garments pegged to a clothesline.

Amanda's heart broke. These were exactly the kind of children she wanted to help. She turned to Joseph. "Is there not a law you can enforce to keep little ones at home with their mother?"

He shook his head. "It's very likely their mother is off working, as is their father." His tone lowered to a growl. "If there even be a father in the home."

"Surely something can be done."

"I cannot right all the wrongs of the world." He gazed down at her and tapped her on the nose. "But I can right this one."

Tying off the reins, he hopped down from the carriage.

What was he up to?

※

Joseph strode from the carriage, pleased for the diversion. If Amanda knew who really owned the Grigg title, his card house of helping brothel girls would collapse. He squatted in front of the younger boy, who was four, possibly five years old. The purple beginnings of a shiner darkened one of the lad's eyes. The other was swollen from tears, salty tracks yet visible on his dirty cheek.

"Buy a paper, mister?"

Pity welled in his throat, and he swallowed. "Tell me true, lad, did that boy"—he hitched his thumb over his shoulder, denoting the news seller on the opposite corner—"steal your papers?"

Without warning, the lad kicked him in the shin. Pain shot up to his knee. Little urchin! He stifled a grimace and avoided glancing back at Amanda, who surely hid a smile beneath her gloved fingers. Well, so much for donning his gallant-knight armor.

But the battle wasn't over.

He straightened and wheeled about. Dodging a passing omnibus, he stalked over to the lad's competition. A large, freckle-faced boy held out a handful of ripped and dirty newspapers. Calculating eyes weighed and measured him, glinting with far too much knowledge for one not yet a man. No wonder the other lad hadn't ratted on this boy. Were he ten years older, Joseph would think twice about crossing the bully without Officer Keeley at his side.

"Buy a paper, mister?" His tone was gravel, hardened by life on the streets.

"No." Joseph pulled out his wallet. "I'll take them all."

"Caw!" The bully's freckles rode a wave of astonishment. "All right. That'll be fifty cents." He held out his hand, palm up, shirtsleeve riding high enough to reveal a small *s* tattooed on his inner wrist.

The mark confirmed Joseph's suspicions. He pulled out a nickel and flipped it in the air. The coin landed in the dirt.

Though he towered at least two hand spans above the bully, the glower the boy aimed at him punched like a right hook. "I ain't stupid. That ain't a fifty-cent piece." Even so, his foot stomped on the money, trapping it beneath his shoe.

"If I were you, I'd take what's being offered, then run far and fast."

A foul curse belched out of the bully's mouth. "Shove off!"

He widened his stance and impaled the boy with a piercing stare, one he'd perfected when confronting a defendant. "I'm the city attorney. I could have you arrested."

The bully turned aside and spit, then swiped his hand across his mouth. "I ain't doin' nothing wrong. You ain't got nothing on me."

Joseph chuckled. "I don't need a valid reason. Any charge will detain you in jail for a few days."

A smirk smeared across the bully's face. Were he born on top of the hill instead of below, this kid would give Craven a run for his position. "No matter. I'll come back out here, takin' what I want, when I want."

"I think not." Joseph grabbed the boy's wrist and turned it over. "By the look of this mark, you're one of Stinger's boys."

The bully wrenched from his grasp. "So what if I am?"

"Haven't you heard? Stinger is in jail. If he finds you've taken money without giving him a cut—and trust me lad, rumors abound in prison—well, I don't think you'll be back on this corner anymore." He bent, leveling his own scowl at the boy. "Or anywhere else, for that matter."

The bully's face blanched, freckles standing out like warning beacons. Papers landed in a heap on Joseph's shoes. All that remained of the boy was the stink of both an unwashed body and fear as he tore down the street.

Scooping up the papers, Joseph strolled back to the other corner, two sets of eyeballs watching his every move—the lad's and Amanda's. He dropped the newspapers at the boy's feet and took out a fifty-cent piece, pressing it into the boy's grubby hand. "That ought to be enough for you to go on home now, eh?"

The boy stared up at him, mouth agape. He didn't say anything. He didn't have to. Gratitude poured off him in waves.

With a tussle of the boy's hair, Joseph pivoted and rejoined Amanda in the carriage. The same hero-worshipping sparkle lit her gaze. Hopefully this meant she'd forgotten about the Grigg house as well.

"That's exactly what I love about you, Mr. Blake."

He grinned. This little venture had been a victory in more ways than one. "What's that?"

"You always do the right thing."

Chapter Four

Amanda's shoes tapped on the marble floor of city hall's lobby. This early on a Monday, suits in various shades of navy and black darted in and out, the smell of bay rum after-shave and determination thick in the air.

Skirting the large information desk at center, she proceeded up the grand staircase that opened onto a gallery of offices. The heart of the city beat here. She sped past the mayor's door, cringing at the raised voices inside, bypassed the next two doors, and finally stopped in front of the fourth, Joseph's name painted in golden ink on the frosted-glass pane. Twisting the knob, she entered a small reception room. After a fruitless week of trying to find out who held the Grigg title, she couldn't wait any longer to enlist Joseph's help.

"Why, Miss Carston!" Joseph's secretary, Mary Garber, more mouse than woman, twitched her lips into a smile. "Good morning."

"Morning, Mary." She smiled back. "Is Mr. Blake in?"

"He is, but. . ." If the woman had whiskers, they'd be quiv-ering. She ran a slim finger down a column on a sheet of paper. "Your name isn't on the schedule. Is he expecting you?"

"No." She leaned over the desk, cupped a hand to her

mouth, and lowered her voice. "This is a secret ambush."

"Such intrigue. Perfect for a Monday morning." Mary popped up from her chair and scurried to the door leading into Joseph's office, opening it wide for Amanda.

"Mary? What's. . ." Joseph's question stalled as Amanda stepped over the threshold.

For a moment, her breath hitched. She'd never tire of the way he looked at her. More than love simmered in that gaze. More than desire. The warmth of his brown eyes reached out and held her, cherishing her as the most valuable of God's creations. Her. The sole focus of such tenderness. She wished she could package it up and carry it around with her all day.

In four long strides, he wove around his desk and pulled her into his arms. "This is a nice surprise." His lips pressed against her cheek then slid like a whisper across her jaw toward her ear. "Would that I could kiss more than propriety allows."

A tingle settled low in her tummy. If she turned her face, his mouth would be on hers. But if Mary were to walk in and find them so entwined—

She pulled from his embrace. "Soon."

"Not soon enough." He cocked his head to a rakish angle. "You know there'll be no stopping me once you're my wife."

She glanced over her shoulder at the open door leading to the reception room then frowned back at him.

He grinned. "Don't worry. If nothing else, Mary is discreet." He swept out his arm. "Have a seat. I'm pleased you're here, but surely you've not taken a sudden interest in legal briefings?"

She sank onto the leather chair while he leaned back against his desk in front of her.

"No, not briefings," she began, "but I do have a legal matter with which I could use your help."

"Oh?" He folded his arms, one of his professional stances. Good. Hopefully he'd take her seriously.

"I mentioned my interest in the Grigg house yesterday, but then there was the matter with the newsboys, and Mr. Rafferty's incessant chattering." She averted her gaze. Her words would be embarrassing enough. "Nor did you make conversation easy on the drive home with the way you. . ." Her face heated.

"The way I what?" His sultry tone, edged with laughter, challenged her to look at him.

She refused, but it was hard to fight down a small smile. "You know I cannot think when you hold my hand and rub little circles on my wrist."

He said nothing.

She dared a peek. La! What a mistake. The heat in his gaze was enough to singe her modesty—which was likely the exact effect he hoped for. She squared her shoulders. "Regardless, I am here now, making my request today. I need to acquire the title to the old Grigg house by the end of the month, yet I've been shuffled from office to office with no success. I thought you might be able to get it for me."

Unfolding his arms, he retreated to the other side of his desk. For a while, he didn't say anything, just tapped a finger on the mahogany.

"You'll need to go to the deeds office," he finally answered.

"I've been there. No luck." She leaned forward in her seat. "Surely you can hasten the process."

He shook his head, his brown gaze completely unreadable. "I am sorry, Amanda. I cannot help with this project of yours."

"Cannot?" She sank against the cushion. The word made no sense. Without his help to speed along her search for the title, she'd never make Lillian's appointed deadline. Her first project proposal would be a dismal failure—one that wouldn't improve her father's opinion of her, either. No, she simply couldn't accept either outcome.

She straightened, folding her hands in her lap. "I am sure it won't take long."

He sighed. "With the mayor's upcoming election, I don't have the time."

The rejection stung—but only for a heartbeat. She'd learned long ago that determination fed off rejection and grew the larger for it.

She stood. "I understand. I should get busy as well, then. Good day, Joseph."

She strode to the door, but a strong hand on her shoulder turned her back.

"Please, Amanda, don't take this personally." He wrapped his arms around her, drawing her close, the nearness of him melting some of her resolve. "You know I'd do anything for you, but not this. Not now. Save the Grigg project for another time."

She couldn't help but run her hands up and down his back, loving the feel of strength beneath his suit coat. "I do understand, and I should not add to your burdens."

He crooked a finger, lifting her chin with his knuckle. "Then we are agreed?"

"Of course." She quirked her lips into a saucy smirk.

Of course she wouldn't add to his burdens—but that didn't mean she'd give up getting that deed on her own.

Joseph waited until the outer office door closed behind Amanda before letting his smile slide off. Tenacious woman! A trait he admired—but not this time.

He strode to his secretary's desk, flexing out the tension in his fingers. "A telegram, if you please, Mary."

"Yes, sir." She pulled out the form, pencil poised.

"To the Rev. Robert Bond, Chicago, Morse Park, Number Twelve." He paused as her fingers flew. "Urgent, *Stop*. Transfer title, *Stop*. Must be your name, *Stop*. Only yours, *Stop*."

Just as her pencil caught up to his words, the outer door opened once again, followed by a booming voice. "Hey Blake, the mayor wants to see you, and he's in one devilish mood."

Joseph turned. His friend and fellow attorney Henry Wainwright stood on the threshold. Waggling his eyebrows, he mocked, "Devilish. Devilish. Devilish."

A smirk twisted his lips. "Been prodding you with his pitchfork so early in the week, has he?"

Henry opened the lapels of his suit coat, revealing the vest beneath. "Got the holes to prove it."

"I best not keep him waiting, then." He glanced back at Mary as he headed for the corridor. "Send that telegram immediately, please. And thank you."

"Yes, sir." Mary's voice followed him out into the hall.

Henry already was striding off in the opposite direction. "Good luck, Blake."

Blowing out a long breath, Joseph advanced down the corridor. Was this a death march? Not that he hadn't expected it. Still, a man on his way to the gallows couldn't help but have his throat burn.

Both of the mayor's office doors were open, outer and inner. A bad omen. The old lion likely sat on his haunches, ready to strike as soon as Joseph entered his lair. He nodded at the matron manning the secretary desk, a drill sergeant compared to his mousy Mary.

"Good morning, Miss Strafing. Mayor Smith is expecting me?"

Her lips puckered, a perpetual look for her. Either the woman sucked on lemons to keep in practice or the sourness inside her refused to be held in. "He is."

"Thank you." He stalked into the mayor's den and stood at attention. Better to be on the offensive, for weak prey attracted rather than repelled. "Good morning, Mayor Smith."

"Blake. Blake. Blake." The man shoved back in his chair and stood, planting his hands on his desk. A strategic position to launch an attack—one Joseph often employed on the accused.

"Do you know what day it is, Blake?" the mayor asked.

He'd learned long ago never to look directly at the man. To do so jumbled his thoughts. One could not help but stare at the collection of tiny growths dotting the mayor's face. Oh, the fellow tried to hide the things with whiskers, but the sparse white hairs only magnified the darkened moles. Truly, only a mother could love that face, which explained why Mrs. Smith's portrait hung on the wall behind the man's desk—and that's exactly where Joseph pinned his gaze. "Today is October 13th, sir."

"Not the date, man. The day."

He hesitated. What kind of trickery was this? "It is Monday, sir."

"Ah…Monday. Monday. Monday. Yet you told me Hannah

Crow's brothel would be shut down by Friday." The mayor's voice sharpened. "A week ago Friday. I've since heard otherwise. Is that true?"

The turn of conversation and the mayor's annoying quirk of repetition left a nasty taste at the back of Joseph's throat. He swallowed. "True, sir. The zoning commission—"

"Enough!" The mayor's eyes narrowed. "Do I need to remind you the general election is less than a month away?"

So that was to be the man's game, eh? Wielding his future employment as a scythe to his neck. He gritted his teeth then finally ground out, "No, sir."

"What's my slogan?"

Rage burned a trail up from his gut. Pandering to the pompous fellow never came easy—but for now, with only three months until the wedding, he'd have to take it for Amanda's sake. After New Year's, though, all bets were off. He'd find a different position, maybe even open up his own practice.

"I'm waiting, Blake."

" 'A clean city is a strong city,' sir." He clipped out the slogan, direct and sharp.

"Clean. Clean. Clean." The man stepped away from his desk and crossed to the front of it, emphasizing the rest of his words with an index finger on Joseph's chest. "Do you think a brothel in the center of St. Paul upholds the image of cleanliness?"

He stifled the urge to shove the man back a step. "No, sir."

"My re-election hinges on this." His tone lowered to a growl. "So does your job."

The muscles in his legs hardened, the restraint of lunging forward almost unbearable. Bullies came in all sizes, from the ragged, young news seller to this well-dressed power broker.

He forced a calm tone to his voice—barely. "Trust me. I want to see Crow shut down as much, if not more, than you. I assure you I am working on it."

"Working. Working. Working." A chuckle rumbled in the mayor's chest. "See that you are, or you'll be lucky to be working as the city dog catcher. Dismissed!"

He wheeled about and strode from the office—and there sat Willard Craven. Judging by the man's leer, he'd heard everything. Joseph's hands curled into fists. Ah, but he'd love to punch that smug look off Craven's face.

Ignoring the man, he stomped back to his office. What a day. Lifting his gaze to the ceiling, he silently prayed—for truly, what else could he do?

Help me find a way to shut down that brothel, Lord, and thwart Craven. And soon.

Chapter Five

"For the record, I think this is a terrible idea."

Amanda frowned at her friend. "You've said that. Repeatedly. Come on."

Crouching low, Amanda darted from the cover of an overgrown hedge and sprinted across the open expanse of the Grigg backyard. Amazing how fast one could move without skirts. If Joseph or—God forbid—her father saw her racing about in trousers belonging to Maggie's brother, well. . .a wicked smile curved her mouth as she motioned for her friend to follow. She'd just have to make sure no one saw them.

This late in the day, dusk cast a shadow from the remains of a porch roof to the door, large enough to hide in. She charged forward, wrapping herself in darkness as she might a cloak.

Maggie pulled up breathless beside her. "Remind me again . . .why we are doing this?"

Reaching for the doorknob, she shot her friend a sideways glance, then tried not to giggle. Though she likely looked as ridiculous herself, Miss Margaret Turner garbed in britches was a sight to behold. "I already told you, Mags. Father and Joseph are too busy. The registrar at the deeds office refuses to deal with a woman unless a man is present. I've spent the last week since I spoke to Joseph about it trying to find an answer, but there's no way for me to get a look at that deed to find out who owns this place. So here we are. There's got to be a clue, a book left behind with an inscribed name, maybe even an old family Bible. Something. Someone I could contact."

She shoved open the door.

Maggie's hand pulled her back. "No, that's not what I mean. Why are you going to such trouble to find out who owns *this* house in particular? There are other buildings in which to create a school, others easier to renovate. Some that Lillian might not frown upon."

"I know. You're right. It's just that. . ."

That what?

She blew away an errant hair tickling her nose and stared up at the house. A bat swooped out a broken third-story window. The corner of the roof bled tiles, which had long since given up on clinging to the rafters. For years the place had been abandoned. Unloved. Forgotten.

A tangible picture of her life before Joseph Blake.

She pulled her gaze from the house and hiked up her trousers, riding low from the jaunt across the yard. Fitting that Mr. Charles Carston's daughter now wore the pants of the son he'd never had.

And there it was—the truth.

She turned and faced Maggie. "I fear you know me too well, my friend. I suppose this is my last attempt to do something grand in my father's estimation before I leave his home."

"Is it that important to you?"

"It is." Tears stung her eyes, and she blinked them away. "I would have a happy ending to this chapter in my life." Her chin rose. "Now, are we going to do this before it gets too dark?"

"Very well." Maggie stepped forward and linked arms with her. "But I still think it's a terrible idea."

They crept together into a back room. Dirt coated the floors. Empty pegs poked out from a wall, save for one, where a stiff, mildewed canvas hung like a piece of meat on a hook. An upturned bucket lay in one corner. Amanda stared harder. Wait a minute. That was no bucket. The dark shape darted for the open door.

Maggie shrieked, her nails digging into Amanda's arm. Together they sprinted blindly down a corridor and into another room.

Panting, Maggie slapped her hands to her chest. "This. . . is. . .a. . ."

"Terrible idea," Amanda finished. Her own heart beat loud in her ears. That had been a scare, but a raccoon or stray dog or whatever that had been was not going to get the best of her.

She caught her breath and scanned the room, what she could see of it anyway. Hard to tell with the last of day's light hovering near the windows. This might've been a grand room, once. Large. Stately. But now wallpaper blistered on the walls, blackened plaster lay in piles on the floor, where sporadic floorboards yet remained. What a ruin.

Ignoring the rubble, Amanda picked her way over to an old desk tipped sideways, nearly tipping sideways herself as her toe caught in a hole in the floor.

Maggie groaned. "This isn't safe. I'm leaving."

"Hold on, Mags. I feel sure we'll find something." Yanking out drawer after empty drawer, Amanda rummaged faster. "If it makes you feel better, go stand by the front door and wait for me there."

Maggie's footsteps padded off. Then stopped. "Did you hear that?" Her friend's voice squeaked.

Amanda straightened and listened, having turned up nothing but an empty inkwell and broken pen nibs. "What?"

"The floorboards upstairs. They creaked." Maggie's words choked into a whisper. "We are not alone."

"Of course we're not." She flicked her fingers toward the ceiling. "There are probably squirrels racing around up there. Wait outside if you like."

Maggie scooted one way, Amanda the other. In a smaller room across the hall, a few old books lay riffled open on the floor.

She snatched one up, paper crumbling as she paged through it. No names. Just a lot of dust that tickled her nose. Fighting a sneeze, she grabbed the other book and—paused. Plaster bits rained down on her head. Was something heavier than squirrels upstairs?

Straining hard to listen, she held her breath and glanced up. Another poof of ceiling sprinkles dropped. Then another. And another. Paces apart. Traveling in a straight line.

As if a person were walking.

Maybe this *had* been a terrible idea. Her stomach twisted and her mouth dried to bones. She couldn't shriek if she wanted to—nor did she need to.

Maggie's scream ripped the silence.

❦

Autumn evenings generally fell hard and fast. So did the lad who'd sprinted down the Grigg front driveway and sprawled in the gravel. Another boy disappeared through a hole in the side gate. Joseph narrowed his eyes. What mischief was this?

He jerked his gaze to the third-floor window. The drapery was wide open—and the timing couldn't have been worse.

Anger ignited a slow burn in his gut. If those boys had discovered what he'd so carefully kept hidden this past year, the whole operation could grind to a halt. Well, then. . . he'd just have to put the fear of God and man into the remaining lad.

He took off at a dead run and hauled the hoodlum up by his collar. "What are you doing—?"

His words, his rebuke, his very thoughts vanished with the last light of day. Wide blue eyes stared into his. Blond curls escaped a tweed flat cap, framing a cherub face. A fresh scrape bloomed on one cheek, set below a tiny crescent scar. Recognition punched him hard.

"Amanda?" He'd experienced many a surprise in twisted legal cases, but this? His hand fell away, and he retreated a step, shaking his head to clear it. "What are you doing here? And dressed like a boy, no less?"

Tears sprouted at the corners of her eyes, rolling out one after another. "Joseph. . . I—I can explain."

"You'd better." His voice came out harsher than intended. But sweet mercy! She had no idea what she might've seen. The hard work she might've undone. The women's lives she might've ended—

The danger she'd been in.

He clenched his jaw so hard it crackled in his ears. "You could've fallen down a loose stair and broken your neck! What were you thinking?"

She cringed. "I didn't. . .think."

Choppy little breaths strangled whatever explanation she attempted. He'd get nowhere trying to bully an answer out of her.

Sighing, he wrapped his arm around her shoulder and led her to a boulder, away from the drive and far from the street. It wouldn't do for the city attorney to be seen embracing a boy.

"Just breathe." He pressed her down onto the rock and dug into his pocket, retrieving a handkerchief. Dropping to one knee, he dabbed the blood on her cheek and dried her tears. As much as he'd love to throttle this woman, his anger slowly seeped away with each quiver of her lip.

When her chest finally rose and fell with regularity, he started over. "Now then, let's try this again. What are you doing here, dressed like this?"

She sucked in a last, shaky breath. "Trying to find a name."

"A name." Even repeating it, the reason made no sense. "I don't understand."

She blinked as if she were the one perplexed. "I told you I wanted to acquire the deed to this place. I need the name of the owner."

He frowned. "You also told me you'd wait until after the election."

"I never said that."

"What?" Crickets chirped a singsong beat as he revisited their last conversation in his mind. "You stood there, in my office, and agreed to give up this project of yours until later."

She wrinkled her pert little nose. "I agreed I wouldn't burden you, not that I'd give up my quest."

"Of all the absurd, irrational. . ." Stuffing the handkerchief away, he pressed the heel of his palm to the bridge of his nose and the ache spreading there. Would married life be this confusing?

"Joseph, you don't understand. If I fail at my first project, Lillian will never let me live it down. And Father…" She heaved a great sigh, as mournful as the breeze whistling through the barren branches. "All my life I've tried to be the son he never had. I thought that this time, as a chairwoman, he'd see me as a success."

The hurt in her voice sobered him, and he turned to her. "But the only good opinion you need is God's, my love. And that you have. His and mine."

She blinked, eyes once again filling with tears—and the vulnerability he saw there broke his heart.

He skimmed his fingers over her cheeks. "You *are* loved. Trust in that. Believe in that."

Pulling her into his arms, he lowered his mouth to hers. A kiss wouldn't solve everything, not a hurt so deep, but that wouldn't stop him from trying anyway. Slowly, she leaned into him, hopefully surrendering some of the pain she harbored.

By the time he released her, she gazed up with luminous eyes—but this time not from weeping.

"I love you, Joseph Blake."

"I love you too, soon-to-be Mrs. Blake." He tapped her on the nose.

She smiled. Slowly, her brows drew together beneath the rakish boy's cap. "Wait a minute…what are you doing here?"

He glanced up at the darkened house. As much as he yearned to be completely honest with her, he yet owed it to his aunt for the promise she'd wrenched from him years ago. Of course he'd reveal the truth eventually, but now? Breathing in the scent of Amanda's sweet lilac cologne, feeling the warmth of her next to him in the cool of the eve? The thought of her possible rejection punched him in the gut.

No, not yet. Soon, but not yet.

Donning his attorney mask, he gazed back at her. "I decided to walk home from the office tonight and heard a scream. And a good thing I came upon you instead of someone else. Now, shall I walk you home and sneak you in before your father sees your attire? Hey. . .where did you get those clothes anyway?"

"My secret." She grinned.

Leaning close, he kissed her forehead and whispered against her soft skin, "Fine, hold on to your secrets. For now."

He stood and offered his hand—for he would hold on to his, for now, as well.

Chapter Six

Yawning away the last bit of sleep, Amanda stretched her neck one way and another, then entered the dining room. She might need more than one cup of coffee this morning. Was Maggie this weary after last night's intrigue at the Grigg house?

But as soon as her foot crossed the threshold, her step faltered. Ensconced in a chair at the far end of the big table, her father gripped an open newspaper as if it kept him afloat. Which it did. He could no more navigate life without his precious business section than a ship without a rudder. Strange, though. He usually took breakfast hours before her.

"Good morning, Father." She crossed the room and pecked him on the cheek, his whiskers as prickly as his usual disposition.

He mumbled something, more a rumble than a greeting, without pulling his eyes from the newsprint.

She retreated to the sideboard and reached for the silver urn, steam yet curling out the spout. Good. Nice and hot. After pouring coffee into her cup and stirring in some cream, she seated herself opposite her father. "I am surprised to find you at home this late in the morning."

The paper lowered slowly, revealing Charles Carston's face inch by inch, from the white hair crowning his balding head to the frown folding his mouth nearly to his necktie. "Indeed. I should be at the office, but I need to speak with you, Amanda."

His gaze pierced like a flaming arrow. She swallowed a mouthful of coffee for fortification, heedless of the burn. Had he found out about last night? "Sounds ominous."

"It is." He folded his paper, crease after crease, using the methodical movement and the tick-tock of the mantel clock to batter her nerves.

Finally, he laid the *Pioneer Press* beside his plate. "I've heard rumors, Amanda."

She set down her cup, sickeningly awake without having finished it. "Oh? What rumors?"

"A tale of inappropriate behavior. . .by my daughter."

Her stomach twisted, and she shoved her cup away. How had he found out about her escapade of the previous evening? Maggie couldn't have told, for she'd be censured as well. And certainly not Joseph. She pressed her napkin to her mouth, hiding her trembling lips. Who else could've seen her?

She lowered the napkin to her lap, clutching it as tightly as he had the paper. "I don't know what you're talking about, Father."

"Mr. Warnbrough saw you traipsing about city hall the other day, unaccompanied I might add. Do you know what kind of women frequent city hall alone?" His fist slammed the table, rattling the water glasses. "Harlots!"

She stifled a flinch. Barely.

"Betrothed or otherwise, it is not seemly for you to be seen chasing after Joseph Blake in public." His eyes narrowed, pinning her to the chair. "I am ashamed of you."

Her stomach rebelled, queasiness rising up to her throat. Could he never think the best of her? "But I did nothing of the sort."

"You deny an eyewitness?" Red crept up his neck, like a rising thermometer about to explode. "One of my esteemed friends?"

"No. I deny your conjecture." She shoved back her chair. Breakfast now was out of the question. "I was not 'chasing after' Mr. Blake. Honestly, Father, what kind of daughter do you think you raised?"

"Then what were you doing?"

She turned from his awful glower and stared out the window. How dare the sun shine so merrily on this horrible morning? She'd have to tell him about the Grigg project, but it was too soon. Too uncertain. Not yet a conquest she could offer him to gain his regard.

"I asked you a question, Amanda."

He left her no choice. Inhaling until her bodice pinched, she slowly faced him. "As chairwoman of the Ladies' Aide Society, it is my assigned duty to acquire the deed to the old Grigg estate by the end of the month."

"The Grigg house?" His brows met in a single line. "What on earth for?"

"I had an idea to turn it into a school. An institution." The more she spoke, the deeper his scowl—and the stronger her determination to change his disapproval to admiration. "The Grigg home will provide a safe place where children of need can receive an education without wilting beneath the scrutiny of those who deem them unfit to be taught."

He shot to his feet, his chair rearing back from the sudden movement. "Why this obsession with the poor? Surely you know the Warnbroughs and others frown upon such associations. We must play by society's rules. Furthermore..."

His voice droned on while he paced the length of the table. Her eyes followed the movement, and she gave the appearance of listening, but truly there was no need. She'd heard this tirade so often she could stand at a podium and present it with as much gusto as he.

"...Or find ourselves counted among the outcasts. You are a lady of upstanding circumstance. Why can you not be happy with dinners and dances?"

Disgust choked her as much as the aftertaste of her coffee. She stood and tipped her face to frown up into his, despite her being shorter than him by a good six inches. "And why can you not soften your heart toward those less fortunate? Life is more than entertainment, a fact the privileged have a hard time understanding."

"That *privilege*, Daughter, I have worked long and hard to achieve." His words bled out as if from a deep, jagged cut. "Yet you dare undermine all that I've accomplished, knowing from where I've come. I do help the poor, more than you're aware, but I will never—*ever*—live amongst them again."

Her vision swam, and she forced back tears. It was a sharp blow, one that stung. Not only was she not the son he'd always wanted, but she was an ungrateful, spiteful daughter as well. She padded over to him and placed a hand on his sleeve. "I didn't mean that, Father. I know you've worked hard. Please—" Her voice broke, and she swallowed. "Forgive me."

He pulled from her grasp and stalked to the door without so much as a backward glance.

⚬⚬⚬⚬

Swinging down from the carriage in front of city hall, Joseph closed the door behind him. Too bad it wasn't as easy to shut out the ruckus of itinerant merchants, hawking their goods like carnival barkers on State Street. Strange that Craven didn't change the zoning around here, for his office faced the busiest side of the road.

He retrieved a coin and paid off the cab driver just as his friend Henry Wainwright charged toward him.

"The hero of the day!" Henry's meaty hand slapped him on the back. "Congratulations on finally breaking that Hofford case."

Joseph shot him a sideways glance. "A little premature, don't you think?"

"Hah!" He shoved a newspaper into his hands. "Don't play coy with me, Blake."

What the devil? Shaking open the front page, he focused on a bold headline: FINANCIER CHARGED WITH EXTORTION.

Scanning further, he read: "Last night in a swift move by City Attorney Joseph Blake, the underhanded dealings of the Hofford Financial Group were finally brought to an end as Phillip Hofford was taken into custody."

What? The words were like rocks cast into a pond, sending out ripple after ripple. How could that be? He was still waiting on a deposition from his informant, Hofford's brother-in-law. This made no sense, especially since he'd spent the evening secreting Amanda home from the Grigg house, then dining with her.

He continued. "Blake cast a wide net to entrap the unscrupulous Hofford, enlisting the aid of other departments and even that of the city council, chaired by Mr. Willard Craven."

The newspaper drooped in his hand. Craven. He should've known. But why would Willard help him with this when the man did nothing but thwart every effort to shut down the brothel? He scrubbed his jaw with his free hand. Could it possibly be a peace offering?

He rejected the idea immediately. Men like Craven didn't go out of their way to help anyone for such a trivial ideal as peace. Something smelled as rank about this as the fresh pile of horse droppings landing on the cobbles behind him.

"Drink tonight at the club?"

Henry's voice derailed his train of thought. "Sorry. What?"

"I said, meet me at the club for a celebratory drink tonight?"

Club. Craven. Their last meeting barreled back. Craven hadn't linked his name to the brothel, as promised, but instead dished it to the press by tying him to an extortion case. A very public way of sending him a message. Bribery in the open, for all to see. Leave it to a degenerate like Craven to come up with the idea of hush publicity.

"Did you even hear me?" Henry asked.

He shoved past his friend and wove his way through businessmen and legal aides. Darting into the lobby, he took the stairs two at a time. This early in the day, the scent of coffee and aftershave clung to the men he passed, until he neared Craven's office. There cigar smoke tainted the hall like a yellow stain. Joseph shoved the door open. No secretary graced this single room. Craven wasn't important enough, which almost made Joseph smile.

He strode from door to desk and slapped the paper onto the mahogany. "I'm only going to say this once, Craven, so listen up. I cannot be bought."

The man's waistcoat jiggled as he chuckled. "My dear Blake, think of it as one colleague helping another. You were stuck. I merely gave you a push—or rather, I pushed Hofford's brother-in-law. I should think you'd be grateful for the positive publicity."

He clenched every muscle to keep from leaping over the desk and grabbing the man by his collar. "I don't need your help," he choked out. "I need you to get out of my way."

"That shouldn't be a problem." Willard stabbed out his ever-present cigar into an overflowing ashtray, little poofs of grey exploding past the edge. His smile flattened into a straight line. "I'll stay out of your way, as long as you stay out of mine."

"Are you threatening me?" His voice cracked, but it couldn't be helped. Who in their right mind threatened a prosecuting attorney?

Willard tented his fingertips, tapping them together in a systematic rhythm. "I prefer to think of it more like a promise."

"Well I have a promise for you, Craven." The muscles in his hands shook with the force of keeping his fists at his sides. "I will find out what it is you're hiding. There are no secrets that time will not reveal."

Leaning forward, Willard jabbed his fat finger onto the date of the newspaper. October 21st. Just two weeks from the election. "Too bad time isn't on your side."

Chapter Seven

Joseph stormed down the corridor until he hit a brick wall—a man-sized slab of muscle and bone. Henry Wainwright angled his head toward the alcove of a bay window, and Joseph had no choice but to retreat into the recess. Wainwright was possibly the most easygoing man he'd ever known—yet the most dogged in the rare instance an ambition overtook him. Apparently Joseph was that ambition today.

Henry folded his arms. "You can't run off, disappear into Craven's office, then try to breeze past me without a word. What's going on?"

Glancing past Henry's broad shoulders, Joseph scanned the hallway. Empty. Even so, he tempered his voice. "You know that Hofford case? I had nothing to do with it. Craven got the man to talk, not me."

"What?" Joseph's scowl lowered his friend's volume. Henry shuffled closer. "Why would he do that?"

"He wants me to back off from shutting down the brothel." Saying it aloud stoked the fire in his belly. Never. He'd never back off. Craven or not.

Henry slowly nodded. "I think I know why. I was going to tell you at the club tonight, but now's as good a time as any."

"What do you have?"

"It's not hard evidence, mind you, but. . ." This time Henry glanced over his own shoulder, waiting until a delivery man scuttled past with a stack of boxes before he spoke again. "I overheard Tam Nadder—you know, the errand boy—boasting with the other runners about his exploits at Hannah Crow's. How he'd saved all his money for one night of pleasure. . .yet he's sporting new clothes and shoes today."

"So a runner spent all his money and is wearing new clothes." Joseph raked fingers through his hair, a desperate attempt to comb through Henry's information. "Sorry, but what has this to do with Craven?"

"I'm getting to that. Tam said some gent paid him not to mention he'd bumped into him at the brothel. The boy didn't name any names, but he gave a pretty accurate description of your friend Craven, bragging to his friends how he could turn this into a regular payment to stay quiet."

Joseph's lips twisted. How ironic. The exploiter being exploited. God certainly had a sense of humor.

"I knew Craven was involved, but I didn't know it was that personal." He blew out a long breath, mind abuzz. "If I can get Tam to talk, it would expose Craven's corruption. And if I could get him to go back to Hannah's—document she's still in business—it would shut her down." Humor rumbled in his throat. "All this time I've been using my legal bravado to end that brothel, and God laughs at my pride by sending an errand boy."

Henry's big hand landed on his shoulder, fingers squeezing encouragement. "Well, what are you waiting for? Go close that brothel. For Elizabeth."

His heart constricted in response, and he nodded, holding Henry's gaze. "Thank you, my friend."

"Yeah, well it's on you to buy me one at the club." Henry cuffed him on the arm then sauntered away.

"Tonight, Wainwright," Joseph called after him before speeding off to his own office.

He swung through the door with a grin. "Cancel my morning appointments, Mary. I'll be out for a bit."

"Yes, sir." She held up a paper, waving it like a flag. "Want to take this telegram with you?"

He shot forward. Indeed. This was shaping up to be a banner day. Snatching it from her grasp, he read:

DEED TRANSFER IS A GO *Stop* PAPERWORK FILED ON MY END *Stop* ROBERT BOND

Balling up the paper, he dashed into his office with a bounce in his step and yanked out the bottom desk drawer. He removed a stack of files and deposited the pile onto his desk, then pulled out a penknife and pried up the false bottom of the drawer. A single document lay beneath—one more piece in a puzzle finally coming together. He pulled it out as Mary peeked her head in the door.

"The mayor wants to see you. Says it's urgent."

A sigh deflated his chest. Now of all times? He set down the document and faced his secretary. "I'm on it. See that no one enters this office while I'm out."

⧼⧽

Amanda forced dignity into each step as she exited the Ladies' Aide Society meeting, smiling goodbyes and see-you-soons.

But the instant she set foot in the hallway, she fled from the building and hailed a cab, huddling on the seat until Maggie caught up. Tears burned her eyes, but she refused to let them spill. Not even one. Not on account of that she-devil in a dress, Lillian Warnbrough.

The carriage lilted to the side as Maggie climbed up. She gathered one of Amanda's hands in hers and patted it as the cab jerked into motion. "That was horrible. Simply awful. Lillian had no right to question your competency with such scathing remarks. She's jealous that you got elected chair and she didn't." Her patting stalled, and she leaned close, peering at her with a puckered brow. "Are you all right, dearest?"

For a moment, the compassion in Maggie's green gaze almost unstopped her tears. She sucked in a shaky breath. "I admit it has been quite a day. First my father, then Lillian."

"Poor pet. How to make this afternoon better?" Maggie released her hand and leaned back against the cushion. Grinding wheels and street sellers competed for attention, until Maggie shot forward and turned toward her. "I know! How about we stop by Delia's Delights for a pastry? That ought to set you to rights."

Just then the cab lurched around a corner, swaying back and forth. Back and forth. Like the tea in her stomach. Amanda pressed her fingers against her stomach. "Nice try, but I don't think so."

"All right. Then let's drive to Lake Como and feed what geese remain." Maggie nudged her shoulder. "That always makes you smile."

"Not in the mood." She sighed.

"I see. This calls for something drastic." Grasping the edge of the cab door, Maggie craned her neck out the window. "Driver, city hall, please."

"City hall!" Amanda grabbed a handful of her friend's cape and tugged her back. "You know my father doesn't want me seen there."

A Cheshire cat couldn't have grinned with more teeth. "Then we shan't be seen, darling."

"For once, I think you're the one with a terrible idea. Even if we're not seen, Joseph told me in no uncertain terms that he's too busy to help with the Grigg project."

"He told *you* that. He never told me." Lacing her fingers, Maggie perched her chin upon them like a practiced coquette. "With two of us batting our eyelashes, he can't help but spare ten minutes to escort us to the deeds office, hmm? I'm certain this will work."

Despite the awful day, a half smile lifted her lips. "Since when did you get so devious?"

"La!" Maggie rolled her eyes. "Years of being your friend have taught me a trick or two."

The cab pulled up to city hall, and Maggie climbed out first, making sure no one they knew strolled about. Before they attempted a dash to the door, a small group of dignitaries and their wives departed from a line of carriages behind them.

"Here's our chance," Maggie whispered. "I told you this would work."

As the group passed by, they matched pace at the rear, blending in. By the time they cleared the foyer and gained the stairs, Amanda breathed easier. Perhaps this day truly was improving. They swung into Joseph's office as if a guardian angel had ushered them all the way.

Mary looked up from her desk, her little nose twitching. "Good afternoon, Miss Carston, Miss Turner."

"Good afternoon, Mary." Amanda pushed the door shut behind them and advanced. "Is Mr. Blake in?"

"I'm afraid he's not here, though he said he'd be gone only the morning." She glanced at the big clock on the wall. "I expect he'll return shortly, but I can't promise anything."

Outside in the hall, men's voices grew louder. Amanda edged toward Joseph's office door as the footsteps stopped in the corridor. Suit shadows blocked the frosted window, and panic hitched her breath. What if those men came in here? What if one of them knew her—or worse—her father?

"We shall wait in Mr. Blake's office, Mary."

"I'm sorry, miss, but Mr. Blake said no one was to enter his office until he returned."

"Surely I'm not *no one*." She grabbed Maggie's sleeve and fled to the safety of Joseph's sanctuary before Mary objected any further. The smell of him lingered in the room, sandalwood and ink, all masculine and strength, which did much to calm her nerves.

Leaning back against the door, she shot a glance at Maggie. "What if someone comes in and sees us before Joseph arrives?"

Maggie whirled toward the desk, her skirts coiling around her ankles. "Have a little faith, my friend." She grinned. "Is that not what you always tell me? Oh! Look here. How sweet."

Sweeping up a silver frame perched on the corner of Joseph's desk, Maggie handed over a photograph—and all Amanda's angst melted away. How could it not? Joseph, smiling down at her, their fingers entwined. Tenderness in his gaze. Love in hers. Marking them as one though it was but an engagement photo. How sweet that he'd taken the time to frame and keep it where he could see it at all times. The man was positively romantic.

The first genuine smile of the day bloomed on her face, and she crossed the small office to set it back on his desk. Her sleeve riffled the top paper on a pile of documents next to it, and she straightened the stack. She turned to Maggie—then spun back. Surely she hadn't seen. . .Joseph's name would be on lots of documents, of course.

She picked up the top paper, scanning the contents, and the world shifted on its axis.

A deed. Joseph Blake's signature on the owner's line.

For the Grigg house.

Chapter Eight

Joseph raked a hand through his hair as he strode down the corridor, then worked to straighten his necktie. Were mayors of other cities as insecure as this one? Three hours— *three*—of going over the past four years' worth of cases that could be exploited for good press. If he'd known the position of city attorney involved this much hand-holding and politics, he'd have taken up horse training instead. He smirked. Maybe he ought to invest in a good horsewhip anyway to prod along the next inevitable re-election meeting.

He breezed through his office door, counting the days until the election was over. "That took longer than I expected. Clear my schedule for the rest of the day, if you please, Mary."

His secretary glanced up. "I can clear all but one, sir."

He cocked his head, waiting for an explanation.

Mary's lips quirked into a smile. "Your fiancée and Miss Turner are in your office."

His gaze shot to the clock. Half past two. Dinner wasn't until eight. That's all he'd promised her for today. . .wasn't it?

He looked back at his secretary. "Am I forgetting something?"

One of her thin shoulders twitched. "Not that I know of."

"Hmm. Thanks, Mary."

He strode into his office then froze. At his entrance, two sets of eyeballs skewered him through the heart.

Amanda glowered, cheeks aflame. Her friend stood near the window, wringing her hands, then without a word, dashed past him. The door slammed, sharp as a gunshot.

He stared at the paper in Amanda's hand and then at her. Alarm ramped up his heart rate, making a whooshing sound in his ears.

Her lips pinched. No, her whole body did. Like a gigantic, clenched fist. Ready to strike.

"You!" Her voice tightened to a shrill point. "You lied to me!" Her hand shot out, the deed to the Grigg estate quivering in her grasp. Good thing it wasn't a gun.

His heart stopped. His breaths. Time and sound and life itself ground to a halt.

"I—" He swallowed and tried again. "I never lied to you, I swear. I just never told you."

Amanda splayed her fingers, the document fluttering to the floor like a lost dream. "You weren't too busy to help me. You were too deceitful."

He edged closer. Carefully. Walking on glass. One wrong step and they'd both shatter. "Now hold on, love. I can explain."

"Do not think to call me your love!" The temperature in the room plummeted, so cold, so chilling her anger.

"Amanda, please, calm down." He reached for her. If he could but hold her, maybe he could right this wrong.

"No!" She shrugged off his hand, recoiling from his touch. "I cannot calm down. I will not."

Rage sparked in her terrible gaze. Without warning, tears sprouted. Her mouth trembled, and she pressed her fingers to her lips. A sob overflowed. Followed by more. Until shaky little cries and gasps for breath took over.

There wasn't one thing he could do about it.

He was a beast. A cad. What kind of man did this to a woman?

God, what do I do?

Powerless, he snatched a chair and dragged it to her side. "Please, sit. You're overwrought."

She didn't look at the chair. Or at him. She stood there, staring at the floor, shaking her head. Would she ever look at him again?

"How?" Her voice came out ragged. "How could you have let me go on about renovating the Grigg estate if you had no intention of ever letting it happen?"

"It's not like that. I only asked you to wait."

An iron rod couldn't have stiffened any more rigid than her spine, and when she finally did lift her face, he wished she'd still stared at the floor, so dead-eyed was her gaze.

"Why do you own that house, and why didn't you tell me?"

"It's. . ." His shoulders sank. He'd talked his way past hung juries and determined judges, but this? Impossible. The jaws of a trap snapped into his very bones. He couldn't reveal the Grigg home as a safe house, not yet. Not until Hannah Crow's brothel was shut down, for where would the girls go who wanted to escape?

He pinched the bridge of his nose, avoiding her eyes. "It's a secret. For now. But I promise you, all will be made clear to you soon. Very soon. You must trust me on this."

"Trust?" The word pinged around the room like a bullet. "Oh that's a very pretty word coming from your mouth. How is one to trust a deceiver?"

Deceiver? His jaw clenched from the direct hit. He'd been nothing but honest! Guarded, yes, but truthful. He stiffened. "Did you not say that I always do the right thing?"

"The right thing is to transfer over that deed and renovate the place into a school. Immediately."

"I can't. Not yet." Each word cost him. Strength. Faith. Hope. Until he was gutted and empty.

Her blue eyes, shimmery and red-rimmed from weeping, sought his. "Why?"

He swallowed. *Oh God, what is the lesser sin here? Breaking or keeping a promise? Either way I fail a woman I love.*

"I. . ." He pressed his lips tight and shook his head. "I'm sorry, Amanda."

"So am I." Clutching handfuls of her gown, she stormed to the door. "Don't bother calling on me, for I won't see you. Ever again."

❧

Air. She needed air. But even that might not be enough. How was one to breathe with a heart that wouldn't beat? Blood that refused to flow? How could she possibly face the future, her friends, her father?

Amanda fled from the unbearable questions, tearing out of Joseph's office, into the hallway—and crashed headlong into a big chest. And why not? The rest of her life was one big train wreck.

She bounced back a step and bumped into Maggie, who'd caught up from behind, sandwiching her between friend and possible foe. Willard Craven smiled down at her, a toothy grin, yellowed by age and cigars. Did he know her father? Would he tell that he'd seen her exiting Joseph's office?

Did it even matter anymore?

"Someone's in quite a hurry." He leaned closer, searching her face. "Are you all right, Miss Carston?"

"I. . .I. . ." She stammered, but it was not to be helped. Too much anger and far too much hurt choked her.

"We are sorry, Mr. Craven." Maggie advanced to her side. "Forgive our haste. We must be leaving."

"Of course." He tipped his hat toward Maggie but then wrinkled his brow at her. "Why, you're pale as a sheet, Miss Carston. Are you feeling faint? Perhaps you ought to sit until the spell passes. My office is just down the hall." Stepping aside, he swept out his hand.

"No. I am—" She was what? Devastated? Undone? Barely able to stand? She clutched Maggie's arm for support. "We would not trouble you, Mr. Craven. Good afternoon."

She turned.

But coming down the opposite end of the corridor, Lillian's father, Mr. Warnbrough, strode toward them.

She whirled back. "On second thought, I should like to sit."

"Amanda!" Maggie whispered under her breath.

"This way, ladies." He crooked both arms.

Maggie shot her a sideways glance with a small shake of her head.

Footsteps thudded on the tiles at her back, growing more distinct with each passing second.

What to do?

Placing her hand on Mr. Craven's sleeve, she pled with

Maggie via a gaze. Her friend had no choice but to take his other arm. The three of them moved down the hallway as one, leaving behind Mr. Warnbrough, Joseph's office—and Joseph. The betrayer. The master of secrets. . .

Oh Joseph.

Her heart fluttered, and by the time Mr. Craven ushered them into his office and pulled out a chair, she folded into it, fighting sniffles and a fresh flood of tears. Maggie swooped in next to her, patting her back.

"Oh my dear, Miss Carston." Mr. Craven yanked out a handkerchief and handed it over, then pulled the only remaining chair in the cramped office to face hers and Maggie's. "You are distraught. I may not have a daughter of my own, but I hope you will think of me as a father figure. Is there anything I can do to help?"

Dabbing her eyes, she tried to speak past the little squeaks in her throat. "I think not."

"I have learned that sometimes merely unloading the weight on one's soul is enough to get you back on your feet, especially to impartial ears." He reached for her hand and patted it. Gently. Tenderly. Nothing at all like her father had ever done.

He leaned nearer. "You are amongst friends, Miss Carston. Miss Turner and I have strong shoulders, should you like to lessen your burden."

She glanced at Maggie. Worried green eyes stared back. Ought she share everything here and now? Get it over with? Find release? "I don't know what to say."

Mr. Craven gave her hand a little squeeze, comforting, lending strength. "I find it's best to start at the beginning. Tell us everything that's happened."

She sucked in a breath. It would feel good to shed all this emotion. Slowly, she deflated. "Very well."

Chapter Nine

W hat am I going to do, Henry?" Joseph dropped his forehead onto his hands, ignoring the banter filling the Minnesota Club. How dare the world continue in such a merry fashion when all the happiness in his life had been wrung out?

A whining moan drifted out of the heat register, as haunting as Amanda's last words. . . *"I won't see you. Ever again."* Glass scraped across wood, and a bottle slipped into his circle of vision on the table.

"Have a drink, man. You'll feel better."

"No." He shoved the whiskey back at Henry. "I deserve to feel this way. I never should have kept secrets from Amanda in the first place."

Henry chuckled. "Ain't a man alive who don't hold a few cards close to his chest."

A bitter taste filled his mouth. "Yeah? Well, look where that got me."

"She'll come around."

"I don't know. I hurt her pretty bad." The memory of Amanda's tears, the shock, the pain pooling in her eyes was an image forever seared into his heart. He shook his head. "She has every right to hate me."

Henry's grey eyes sought his, probing deep. "You still want her?"

"More than anything." Did that ragged voice belong to him? He swallowed.

Henry reached for the bottle and refilled his glass. "Then go after her."

Joseph spread his hands wide. "How? She said she'd never see me again."

"Find a way." He tipped back his head and the glass in one swift movement. "You'll only have one shot at this, so make it count. Tell her everything. If she's the woman for you, and I think she is"—he slammed the glass onto the tabletop—"like I said, she'll come around. But she needs to be told, despite your aunt's wishes."

Joseph nodded in agreement. His heart, not so much. How could he break a promise he'd made to the woman who'd raised him since a lad?

Drained, he hung his head. Would that Henry's words might come true, but there was no guarantee. "I don't know. Happy endings are for fairy tales, not real life."

Another squeal screeched from the heat register, higher in pitch. Henry snorted and jabbed his thumb toward the register. "You've still got a shot at a happy ending, but if that boiler man keeps this up, he's sunk."

The scent of gin and tobacco hit Joseph's nose an instant before Willard Craven swaggered to a stop alongside his chair. "Join me at my table, Blake."

He scrubbed a hand over his face. Could this day seriously get any worse? "Not tonight."

Craven hitched both thumbs in his waistcoat. A strutting rooster couldn't have posed with more bravado. "I think you'll want to hear what I have to say."

"I'm not in the mood." His voice sharpened to a fine edge, drawing the looks of a few senators sitting nearby.

"You heard the man," Henry added, shooting Craven a scowl.

Craven eyed them both. "Two words: Grigg house."

Exhaling in disgust, Joseph shoved back his chair and followed Craven over to his little piece of the kingdom near the back door.

Craven sat.

Joseph folded his arms, refusing to comply. "Let's have it."

Willard pulled out a cigar from an inside pocket while nodding his head toward the empty chair across from him. "Is there nothing civilized about you?"

"Not when it comes to you." Nearby, brows rose. If he didn't want this turned into a dog and pony show, he'd have to sit.

But it took all his strength to ignore Craven's smirk as he sank into the chair.

Pulling out a pocketknife, Craven flipped it open and carved precise little cuts into his cigar, whittling the end into a V shape. Each slice rubbed Joseph raw.

"I just came from a council meeting. Thought you might be interested in the results." Craven held up the cigar for inspection. Apparently pleased, he slapped shut the knife and tucked it away. "A certain property on Summit Avenue was brought to my attention earlier today. Something had to be done."

"What's your point?"

Retrieving a silver box from his pocket, Willard removed a match and struck it against the rough edge on one side. He waited until the flame caught, then worked to light the outside edge of the cigar, rotating it for an even burn.

Sweet mercy! This was more than a man could take. Joseph ground his teeth and waited.

Finally the man laid the match on the ashtray. "The Grigg house has been condemned and is in the process of being appropriated for public use. Whoever owned that property will take a big loss in more ways than one."

"You got something to tell me, man, now's the time."

Craven wrapped his lips around the cigar, drawing in puffs of air, then exhaled in a single stream—right at Joseph. "Looks like the city attorney may be facing manslaughter charges. Oh... that'd be you, wouldn't it?"

Joseph shot to his feet. If he stayed any longer, he'd be guilty of first-degree murder. He pivoted to return to Henry's table—until Willard's words stopped him cold.

"Apparently you haven't heard about Tam Nadder, then. Poor lad. I sent him on an errand over to the Grigg house this afternoon, right before the committee met."

His hands curled into fists, nails digging into his palms, the sharp sting a welcome sensation.

"The young fellow nearly broke his neck falling down the stairs. Even now he's fighting for his life over at St. Joe's."

Joseph wheeled about, rage as keening as the next squeal from the heat register. "If this is your handiwork, I'll have you locked up so tight, you won't be able to breathe!"

Gaslight painted Willard's face a pasty hue. "Don't blame

me for your negligence. If you'd taken better care of your property, such an accident wouldn't have happened in the first place."

In two strides, he closed the gap between them, towering over Craven's chair. "How did you find out?"

Craven exhaled smoke like a dragon. "Seems you're not only negligent about property, but women as well."

A roar rumbled in his chest. He grabbed the man by the lapels and yanked him to his feet. "Leave Amanda out of this!"

The banter in the room stopped. The swoosh of heads and chairs turning their way circled like autumn leaves caught in an eddy.

Craven clucked his tongue. "Why, the poor little lamb ran straight into my arms for comfort after your betrayal."

The words ripped through him. The thought of Amanda anywhere near Craven punched him in the gut, the sickening feeling spreading like a wound. Amanda would never willingly plot with Craven against him. The blackguard had likely manipulated her.

He rocked onto the balls of his feet, ready to spring forward—

And at the same time an ear-shattering explosion shook the building, throwing him to the floor.

What on earth? Hard to tell with the buzzing inside his head and chaos erupting around him on every side. Tables tipped. Bottles broke. Men and servants scrambled to get out the front door. Joseph staggered to his feet and coughed, an acrid stink thickening the air.

Craven shot up from his chair, their eyes locking as the

back door burst open. Servants poured out. So did super-heated air, smoldering white clouds, and a shout for help from belowstairs.

Willard stared at the smoke-belching door—then bolted. Away from the cry.

Coward!

Ducking, Joseph charged toward the sound and into hell. *God, help me. Help us all.*

The next cry was more faint, yet still audible. He pitched forward on the stairs, catching his hand on an exposed timber to keep from plummeting headfirst. "Where are you?"

"Here." The word traveled on a spate of coughing near the bottom of the stairs.

Joseph pressed on, horrified at what he might find. How had the boilerman even survived the explosion?

The stairs ended, opening onto a hallway, the top half clouded with smoke. To his left, a door hung crooked from one hinge, barely concealing a black maw gaping like an open grave. The smell of dirt and fear added to the stench of fire.

"Hurry!" A ragged voice called from the hole.

Joseph shoved the door aside and dove into what appeared to be a tunnel of some sort, but he didn't go far. A fallen beam pinned the man's leg just inside. The fellow didn't stand a chance of moving it. Still, he struggled to free himself.

Edging past him, Joseph angled for the best position to lift the thing.

The man peered up at him, the whites of his eyes a stark contrast to the darkness. This was no boilerman, not in a ruined suit and tie. "Thank God Craven sent you."

Craven? No time to think on that now. Straddling the fallen end of the beam, he squatted, praying for the strength of Samson. "I won't be able to lift this much, but at the slightest movement, pull away for all you're worth."

He yanked the wood upward, straining every muscle and grunting from the effort. Sweat dripped down his forehead, stinging his eyes.

The man yelled, "Free!"

He dropped the beam, chest heaving.

A bright flash erupted from the hallway, followed by another explosion. They had to get out of here. Now.

"I think my leg's broken." The fellow groaned.

Blast! Joseph grabbed the man beneath the arms and hefted him up, supporting him on the side of his injured leg. He lugged the fellow to the stairway, until a horrific thought stopped him cold. "Are there any others trapped in there?"

"No," the man hacked out. "I left Hannah's alone."

The man's revelation was as dazing as the awful heat licking their backs. He half dragged, half shoved the man up the stairs. No wonder Craven always sat near the back door, gatekeeper to a terrible secret, likely getting a cut of the money. When he got out of here—*if* he got out of here—he would finally have all the evidence he needed to shut down the brothel and go after Craven.

At the top of the stairs, smoke erupted in black swirls, darkening the top half of the club. Crouching, Joseph ignored the man's screams as he forced them toward the front door.

He cleared the pillars, charged into the foyer, freedom and air yards away.

But a few steps later, something hard and dull cracked against his skull—and the world went black.

⚬⚬⚬

The downstairs clock chimed midnight. The last toll struck the final nail into the coffin of the worst day of Amanda's life. Though she was fully dressed, she shivered from the ghostly echo leaching through her bedchamber door. Standing at the window, she stared into a night as black and endless as her thoughts. Outside, wind gusted, rattling tree limbs like bones. A storm would break soon. A tempest. And why not? If nature mimicked her life, then the world ought to be ravaged.

From the recesses of the downstairs foyer, the front door knocker hammered out a loud report. She stiffened. Only tragedy or terror called at such an hour. Dreading both, she snatched her shawl off the end of her bed and cracked open her door. Down the hall, her father did the same, only he held an oil lamp, the circle of light casting macabre shadows against the wallpaper.

"Go to bed, Amanda," he grumbled as he swept past.

She fell into step behind him. "Sleep is out of the question."

The words trailed her down the stairs. Indeed. She may never sleep again, so tormented was her heart. Oh, the silly thing still beat, but merely from habit. Joseph's betrayal had seen to that.

Grayson reached the door before them, and at Father's nod, the butler swung it open.

A dark shape entered, smelling of smoke. When Father

raised his lamp, Henry Wainwright removed his hat, a fine sprinkle of ash falling to the floor. He tipped his head toward them both, his grey eyes devoid of their usual sparkle. "Mr. Carston, Miss Amanda, I come with hard news."

Father's gaze shot to Grayson. "Light the lamps in the sitting room."

Henry shook his head, hair spilling onto his brow from the movement. "There's no time."

Amanda swayed, or maybe the floor did. Whatever Mr. Wainwright had to say couldn't be good. She rushed out of the shadows toward the light and clutched her father's arm. "What's happened?"

"There was a boiler explosion at the club. I escaped, but Joseph. . ." Henry's mouth twisted. "A pillar caught him on the head. The doctors aren't sure if he'll make it."

Aren't sure. The words taunted like demons. Trembling started in her knees and worked its way up her legs, until she gripped Father's arm tighter in a vain attempt to stop it. When she'd told Joseph she'd never see him again, she'd never meant anything this final. Her heart lurched. What if he left this world without peace between them?

Oh God. Not death.

Henry stepped closer, pity etching creases at his eyes. "I'll take you to him, if you like, with your father's permission, of course."

She lifted her face to her father, seeking his approval without words. Her voice wouldn't move past the lump in her throat even if she tried.

Father's jaw worked, harsh lines furrowing the sides of his mouth. Then, surprisingly, the movement stopped. The lines softened. So did his tone. "Go. You have my blessing."

She froze. For the first time, he looked past convention, what others might think, and stared straight into her heart.

"Thank you," she whispered.

Grayson held out her cloak, and she moved from the house to Henry's carriage like swimming through a murky pond. Gloom painted the night sky with a black brush, air cold and damp as a cellar. By the time Henry seated her and clicked his tongue for the horse to walk on, thunder rolled a bass warning.

This late at night, no other carriages traveled on Summit. Just her and Henry and the awful knowledge sitting in her soul that even now Joseph might be dying.

Henry glanced at her. "I, uh, I suppose there's no easy way to say this, but Joseph told me what happened between you and him today."

She stifled a gasp, but truly, should she be so astonished? This man had been friends with Joseph since their days of rock skipping and knickers. "You know?"

Henry nodded. "I think there's something you should know too. That man of yours is faithful to a fault."

Faithful? Neglecting to tell her that he owned the very property she'd been trying to acquire was faithful? She cleared her throat to keep from scoffing.

"Joseph's too pigheaded to tell you, so I will." Henry sighed, as blustery as the next gust of wind. "He was using the Grigg estate as a safe house. You know how big he is on closing down Hannah Crow's brothel, right?"

A safe house? What did that even mean? Her hat lifted, and she righted it with a quick grab, ruefully wishing everything could be as easily set straight. "I fail to understand how the two are connected."

"I'm getting to that." A flash of light and a crack of thunder interrupted him, and he paused to rein in the horse, which shied toward the curb. "When the Grigg house, dilapidated as it was, came on the market, Joseph snatched it up on the sly, allowing and even spreading the rumors that it was haunted. That way no one would go snooping around and possibly discover his operation."

"What operation?"

"Blast it! Joseph should be the one telling you this. Not me." Henry clicked his tongue and snapped the reins. "Pardon the delicacy of the topic, Miss Amanda, but allow me to be blunt. It's near to impossible for a woman to leave behind a tawdry lifestyle on her own. Besides the haunted house rumor, Joseph also let word spread, woman to woman, that if any wanted to escape the brothel, all they had to do was make their way to the Grigg house and hide upstairs. When he saw the drapes opened in the third-floor window, then he knew a woman wanted out. He'd go at night and escort her to the train station, where he'd pay her fare to Chicago. From there, his reverend friend, Robert Bond, helped the woman find a new life."

"Joseph? My Joseph did this?" Though it was hard to believe, everything Henry said rang as true and clear as the next arc of lightning. Perhaps she and Maggie had not been imagining things when they'd heard footsteps, and this would explain why Joseph had been so close at hand when they'd run from the house.

She looked up at Henry, the next strobe of light harsh

on his face—as severe as the single question girding up what remained of her anger. "Why did he not tell me?"

"Because he was hoping to be done with this by now. He kept trying to shut down the brothel, and once that happened, he'd sell the Grigg house. End of story—and not really a story for a proper lady's ears to hear. He was trying to protect you." Henry gazed down at her, grey eyes hard to see in the dark, but the steadiness in his voice was pure and true. "There are things in this world that are ugly. Evil. Things no one should have to know."

Rain broke then, pattering on the roof like tears. A whimper caught in her throat. She'd gotten so caught up in her own schemes to right this world that she'd failed to think others might be doing the same.

The wind shifted. Rain needled her cheek from the open side of the carriage, as stinging as her misguided pride. The closer they drew to the hospital, the more carriages and pandemonium crowded the streets, despite the late hour. Henry wove through undaunted, shouting bold threats to clear the way.

She hated to distract him, but the need to know flew past her lips. "Why did Joseph want to help the brothel girls in the first place?"

He slowed the horse to a halt and tied off the reins. "The rest is for Joseph to say." He hopped from the carriage and rounded the back of it to her side, reaching to help her down.

She grasped his big hand—and didn't let go even when her feet hit the ground. Gas lamps burned on each side of the hospital entrance. A man, leaning heavily on another, staggered out the front door, sorrow etching his face. But at least he was walking. Unlike Joseph. What would she find when she went through those doors?

"I'm afraid, Mr. Wainwright." Her voice shook. So did her legs.

He squeezed her hand. "So am I."

Chapter Ten

Amanda paused in the doorway leading to Joseph's ward, trying hard not to breathe too deeply of disease and despair, a trick she'd learned to master over the past couple of days. Mortality lived here as insidious as the stains on the white walls. Though scrubbed clean, years of blood and toil marred the plaster with a sickly grey.

Dr. Beemish, frocked in a knee-length lab coat, strode down the center aisle toward her. "Good day, Miss Carston. I hope you know what a welcome sight you are. Your care for Mr. Blake and the others is commendable."

"All I have to offer is a listening ear or a hand to hold. Not much for those who were so horribly injured." She shuddered thinking of the disfigured gentlemen she'd comforted, then searched the doctor's face, pleading for a morsel of good news. "How is he?"

The doctor clasped his hands behind his back. "I shall be frank with you, my dear. If Mr. Blake doesn't wake soon, I fear he might not at all."

She stared at him, dry-eyed. She'd cry if she had any tears left. But nothing remained. She was a shell, a husk. Held together by skin alone, for her emotions had checked out that first night she'd seen Joseph lying on white sheets, bloodied bandages swaddled around his skull. Deathly still.

"But take heart in this." Dr. Beemish reached out and gripped her arm, imparting strength. Or maybe courage. Hard to tell, for despite his action, she felt none.

"The rest of Mr. Blake is sound and whole. Body functions are normal. Reflexes without flaw. Should he regain consciousness, recovery will be swift."

"Thank you, Doctor." She used her confident voice, but it was fake. Everything about the last forty-eight hours had been a ruse of backbone and pluck on her part. Lies, all. Though she'd labeled Joseph as such, she was the liar.

Once Dr. Beemish swept past her, she let her shoulders sag. Walking the aisle to Joseph's bed, she trembled from the coldness inside her soul—then froze, jaw dropping.

Two beds over, dark brown eyes stared into hers.

"Joseph!" She darted ahead and sank to his side, afraid to hope. What if this wasn't real? "You're awake?"

"Apparently." Voice raspy, he cleared his throat. "Water?"

She grabbed a pitcher from the bed stand and poured a glass, hands shaking. *Oh God. Oh please. Oh, thank You!* Cradling Joseph's bandaged head, she lifted the water to his mouth. Most dribbled down his chin, darkened by two days' worth of stubble, but even so he offered a weak smile when he finished. "So good."

Replacing the glass, she leaned closer to study him. Purple bruised the skin near one temple. A cut on his chin scabbed over in a jagged line. But he was alert. Aware. And all the more handsome because of it.

"How are you feeling?" she asked.

"Been better." He reached to finger his bandages, and did such a poor job of concealing a wince, she couldn't help but smile.

He reached for her. "You're here."

"I am. I—" Her voice cracked, and the dam broke. Elation, gratitude, sorrow, grief—too many emotions bubbled up and flooded her eyes, running down her cheeks and over his fingers.

"I was so afraid!" she cried.

"Shh." He fumbled his thumb across her cheek, wiping away tears. "Help me sit."

She sucked in a shaky breath. For his sake, she had to pull herself together. Swallowing the lump in her throat, she took his hand in both of hers, lowering it to his side. "You've only just awakened. Do you think it wise?"

"Wise or not"—he grunted as he tried to push up on his elbows—"I must."

Stubborn man. Beautiful, stubborn man whom she could not live without. Fighting a fresh round of tears, she tugged up the pillow behind him and helped him settle upright. Seeing his gaze, soaking in all the love she read in those brown depths, she blurted out everything that'd been bottled up inside.

"Oh Joseph, I'm so sorry I jumped to conclusions. I didn't expect the best out of you, but instead ascribed the worst." She pressed her knuckles against her mouth, stopping a cry.

"All's forgiven, love." Battered and beaten, likely in pain, he used such tenderness that it hurt deep inside her. "You didn't know."

"But neither did I trust! I let self-pity blind me. I couldn't see that you weren't trying to thwart me. You were merely working on a more urgent plan than mine. I treated you abominably, without waiting like you asked—" She froze as a stunning realization hit her. Hard. Her mouth twisted into a rueful pinch. "Just like I do to God."

"God knows I've done the same, yet He's always there to pick up the pieces."

She shook her head. How could such goodness, such kindness be understood? "I don't deserve it. Nor do you deserve how I treated you."

"You may not think so when I tell you everything." He reached for her hand again. "I have much to say."

His face paled.

Was this too much, too soon? "Joseph, please rest. It can wait."

"No, I've waited long enough." He entwined his fingers with hers. "Too long."

❧

The warmth, the intimacy of Amanda's palm pressed against his was as right as finally telling her the full truth—more right than the agreement he'd made with his aunt.

"As you know, I own the Grigg house," he began. "Or did, until the day you discovered the deed."

"You. . .you don't own it anymore?"

He shook his head. Bad idea. The dull throb beat harder, pounding against the inside of his skull. Shifting on the pillow, he pushed up a bit more, easing the ache and allowing him to continue. "I transferred the title to my colleague, Reverend Bond, in Chicago. When you first came to me about the Grigg estate, I knew you'd be successful at sleuthing out who it belonged to, for such are your keen abilities."

A pretty red flushed her cheeks, deep enough to shame a spring rose.

"So I unloaded the deed." Two beds over, a fellow patient moaned—and the sound resonated deep in his gut. How to explain this? "It's all so complicated. I hardly know where to begin."

Amanda patted his hand. "Let me help. Your friend Henry filled me in on most everything, but not all. He told me about your plan to provide a way for women to escape from Hannah Crow's—which, I might add, is quite a reckless and noble thing for a city attorney to do." Sunlight slanted in through the window above his bed, creating a golden halo around her head. Her smile shined even brighter. "But the thing I don't know is why? Why take on such an endeavor in the first place?"

"Elizabeth," he breathed out, then clamped his jaw. Could he do this? Of course he should, despite his aunt. But how to say the words that would blight his sister's memory in the eyes of the woman he loved and tarnish his family's reputation?

Amanda's brow puckered. "Your sister? What has she to do with this?"

He stood on the edge of a riverbank—the wild, raging river of the past. It was either step back now or jump in whole and possibly drown from the truth.

He jumped. "While it's true that Elizabeth died in California, the circumstances are not what my aunt allows everyone to believe. My sister didn't die in childbirth. She died in a brothel. Elizabeth was a woman of ill repute."

He expected the gasp. The look of horror. But when Amanda's face softened and she rested her palm against his cheek, he never predicted such tenderness in her gaze.

"I am so sorry. For you. For her. She must have been desperate, indeed."

"Desperate?" He grimaced, then winced from the pull of scalp against bandage. "That and more."

"What happened?"

"There was a man—Peter Gilford. Elizabeth loved him, yet Father would not grant his blessing. He went so far as to forbid her to ever see the man again. It was an ugly affair. Peter ran off to California. Elizabeth followed, headstrong to a fault." He deflated against the pillow, awful memories weighing heavy, wearing his spirit to the bone. "Father was right about Peter. He was a shiftless fellow, leaving my sister penniless on the streets of San Francisco."

"How awful!"

The clack of heels on tile entered the far end of the ward. Amanda glanced up at an attendant who rolled in a cart on wheels. The smell of some kind of stew spread throughout the room. "Looks like lunch. You must be famished. Finish your story later. I promise I will not leave your side."

Ahh, but that was good to hear. Aunt had said no respectable woman would have him if the truth of their family was known. For the first time ever, he wondered what other false views Aunt had convinced him to adopt, but with the attendant approaching nearer, he'd have to save that line of thought for another time.

"I am nearly finished. Elizabeth wrote, asking for money. Father refused, telling her to find her own way home. She did the only thing she could to earn her fare—and it was the death of her. She was trying to get back here, that's all. She just wanted to come home." Grief and guilt burned his throat, leaving a nasty taste at the back of his mouth. The smell of the stew turned his stomach. "If only I'd known at the time, but I was off at school. I failed her, Amanda. I failed my sister."

"Ahh, love, in your own words, you didn't know." She squeezed his fingers. "And you came up with a way to save others like her. She wouldn't think you a failure. She'd be proud of you, as am I."

The admiration heating her gaze burned straight to his heart, and he squeezed her hand right back. "You were wrong, you know."

Her nose scrunched up. "How's that?"

He lifted her knuckles to his lips. "I am the one who does not deserve you."

Epilogue

Two weeks later

A few stubborn oak leaves let loose and skittered to the road in front of the carriage. Amanda admired the way the horse high-stepped along the cobbles, then turned her face and admired the driver even more. The bruises had faded to a faint shade of yellow around Joseph's eye, hardly distinguishable now, especially in the twilight. The cut on his chin still stood out, though, and would leave a scar, but the mark would ever remind her of how close she'd come to losing him.

"You study me as if I might vanish." Pulling his gaze from the road, he grinned down at her. "Go on. Ask me again. You know you want to."

She flattened her lips. Ought she be annoyed or thrilled that he knew her so well? She peered closer, and concern won out. "Are you certain you're up to this? Maggie will understand if we don't make her house party."

"I'm far better than Tam Nadder. That poor fellow has a long haul of it, learning to walk with crutches for the rest of his life. I've got a banger of a headache still, but that's all." Reaching his arm along the back of the cushion, he tucked her closer to his side. "And besides, we won't stay long. I don't want you turning into a pumpkin, and I promised your father I'd have you home at a decent hour. I'm surprised he allowed me to take you unchaperoned in the first place."

She leaned back, resting her head against his arm. She'd never tire of the feel of him. "I think Father's changing, in a good way. Not that convention isn't still important to him, but I'm starting to think I might be important to him as well."

"Why the change?"

Exactly. Why? She'd turned that question over like a furrowed plot of earth these past two weeks. "While he didn't lose any close friends in that explosion, he did know some of the men who died and many who were injured. I really thought that my position as chairwoman would be the thing to impress him, but turns out my simple act of continuing to visit those men even after your release impressed him more. And in a smaller way, perhaps he realized how empty the house will be without me when we marry."

" 'When we marry.' I like the sound of that."

So did she. She closed her eyes, soaking in the blessing of the man beside her. For a while they drove in the silence of naught but the wheels on the road and the occasional rattle of branches in the wind. Anytime now and she'd hear the crunch of the Turners' drive—but the carriage lurched sideways onto crackling twigs and weeds.

Her eyes flew open. "Hey, this isn't the way to—what are we doing here?"

Joseph flashed her a smile as he guided the horse up the overgrown Grigg drive. "Close your eyes."

She narrowed them. "What are you up to?"

"I've got one last secret to reveal." He tapped her on the

nose. "Now close your eyes."

With a frown, she obeyed. The carriage halted, then canted to the side as Joseph hopped down. His footsteps rounded the back then stopped. A warm hand engulfed her fingers, and he guided her to the ground. What was he up to?

Ten steps later, he stopped. "All right. You may look."

She blinked open her eyes. There, in the fading light, a freshly painted sign hung on the weathered post of the Grigg front porch. Black letters spelled out: Carston Blake Academy.

Her jaw dropped, and she turned to him. "What's this?"

"Here is your building for your new school. There's no need for a safe house anymore, now that Hannah Crow's has been shut down for good. Not that other brothels can't open up, I suppose, but with Craven run out of town by the angry wives of club members, I don't think that will happen for a very long time. And besides"—he flashed her a smile—"I couldn't very well let you go to that Ladies' Aide Society meeting on Monday and take yet another beating from Lillian Warnbrough, could I?"

The tenderness in his voice, the depth of emotion in his brown eyes, and the warmth of his mouth as he pressed a kiss to her brow turned the world watery. Wrapping her arms around his waist, she nuzzled her face into his chest. "You know what I love about you, Joseph Blake?"

His chuckle rumbled against her ear. "That I always do the right thing?"

"No." She shook her head, loving the strong beat of his heart. "Everything."

Michelle Griep's been writing since she first discovered blank wall space and Crayolas. She is the Christy Award-winning author of historical romances: *A Tale of Two Hearts*, *The Captured Bride*, *The Innkeeper's Daughter*, *12 Days at Bleakly Manor*, *The Captive Heart*, *Brentwood's Ward*, *A Heart Deceived*, and *Gallimore*, but also leaped the historical fence into the realm of contemporary with the zany romantic mystery *Out of the Frying Pan*. If you'd like to keep up with her escapades, find her at www.michellegriep.com or stalk her on Facebook, Twitter, and Pinterest.

And guess what? She loves to hear from readers! Feel free to drop her a note at michellegriep@gmail.com.

Check out more books by Michelle Griep!

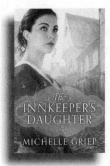

The Innkeeper's Daughter
by Michelle Griep

Officer Alexander Moore goes undercover as a gambling gentleman to expose a plot against the king—and he's a master of disguise, for Johanna Langley believes him to be quite the rogue. . .until she can no longer fight against his unrelenting charm.

Paperback / 978-1-68322-435-8 / $14.99

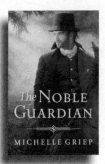

The Noble Guardian (June 2019)
by Michelle Griep

Cynical lawman Samuel Thatcher arrives just in time to save starry-eyed Abigail Gilbert from highwaymen. Against his better judgment, he agrees to escort her to her fiancé in northern England. Each will be indelibly changed if they don't kill one another. . .or fall in love.

Paperback / 978-1-68322-749-6 / $14.99